Mausoleum

Books by Justin Scott

Thrillers

The Shipkiller
The Turning
Normandie Triangle
A Pride of Royals
Rampage
The Nine Dragons
The Empty Eye of the Sea (published in England)
The Auction (published in England)
Treasure Island: A Modern Novel

Mysteries

Many Happy Returns
Treasure for Treasure
The Widow of Desire

Ben Abbott Mysteries

HardScape
StoneDust
FrostLine
McMansion
Mausoleum

With Clive Cussler

The Wrecker
The Spy

As J.S. Blazer

Mysteries
Deal Me Out
Lend a Hand

As Paul Garrison

Thrillers & Sea Stories
Fire And Ice
Red Sky At Morning
Buried At Sea
Sea Hunter
The Ripple Effect

Mausoleum

Justin Scott

Poisoned Pen Press

Library of Congress Catalog Card Number: 2007927878

ISBN: 978-1-59058-971-7 Trade Paperback

Poisoned Pen Press
6962 E. First Ave., Ste. 103
Scottsdale, AZ 85251
www.poisonedpenpress.com
info@poisonedpenpress.com

Printed in the United States of America

To Amber Edwards: Thank you for Words and Music

Chapter One

It was too gorgeous a summer day to kill someone. Rain last night left high pressure in its wake and every leaf and every blade of grass gleamed. Even if you felt too angry, envious, betrayed or thievish to appreciate such weather and shot him in the back, I would have thought that the air was too sweet, the sky too blue, the sun too soft, and the breeze too crisp to roll him over and shoot him twice more in front.

Besides, Newbury's Village Cemetery was already jam-packed with the living.

Half the town was there, led by my Great Aunt Constance Abbott who steadied herself with one gloved hand on her silver-headed cane and the other on my elbow as we walked grave to grave to watch neighbors costumed in period dress portray the ghosts of "Newbury Notables—Gone But Not Forgotten."

Newburians were having a fine time that summer celebrating our Tercentennial by resurrecting the past. A baseball game played by 1879 rules was scheduled next for our 300th birthday party, then a fireworks picnic that the fire marshal swore would burn down the woods. All this commemorating was having the wonderful effect of introducing newcomers to old. And if long-time residents of modest saltboxes were not yet shaking hands with Hummer-house arrivistes, they were at least exchanging smiles.

Aunt Connie and I stopped to listen to Rick Bowland, an IBM commuter who was impersonating Silas Barrett in vest and shirt sleeves. Silas had founded the first general store on Church Hill Road. Rick had moved to Newbury a few years ago and worked hard on volunteer boards, committees, and commissions. A cross-every-t-and-dot-every-i fellow, he had nailed old Silas right down to his merchant's pursed lips as he read aloud from general store account books. We listened for as long as we could.

Moving on, we could hear faintly the voice of my life-long next-door neighbor Scooter McKay—publisher, editor, and ace reporter of the weekly *Newbury Clarion*—sailing uphill from the Abbott plots, "Yo, ho, ho and a…"

I hurried Aunt Connie in the opposite direction.

This change of course stood us face to face with an aggressive addition to the burying ground—a brand new mausoleum purchased for half a million bucks from a website that offered to "Engrave your family name above the door." Tall, wide, and gaudy, sporting mirror-polished granite, a bronze door embossed with acanthus leaves, and a spiked fence to hold back the riffraff, it stuck out like a McMansion in an apple orchard. Frequenters of the Yankee Drover's cellar bar had nicknamed it, "McTomb."

The only other mausoleum in the ancient graveyard was a 19th Century structure erected by the first generation of McKays to mint money publishing the *Clarion*. Call me old-fashioned, call me too old for my years, but it seemed somehow more substantial than the new one. Smooth—not polished—blocks of Vermont granite stood on a firm base of rough-cut stone, and it had fluted pillars and a Greek Cross on its peaked roof. A stained glass window depicted a scantily-clad Pre-Raphaelitic fellow, lither than any McKay I ever met, cranking a printing press.

The cemetery hosted other smaller eruptions of eternal ego scattered here and there: squat monuments, narrow obelisks, fenced family plots. But when I cast my eye up and down the wide, gentle slope I could see that most Connecticut Yankees who died in Newbury deemed a simple headstone marker enough in this world. Even the McKays, always public spirited, opened their spare catacombs to their neighbors as a sort of deep-winter purgatory when the ground was frozen too hard to dig graves.

Connie liked the new one even less than I did. It loomed over the modest headstones of two of her schoolmates, twins who had died of scarlet fever in 1923. "What on earth could possess a young man to erect such an extravagant memorial?"

The "young man" was in his forties.

My great aunt loved the English language and took pleasure in full sentences delivered with a flourish. Knowing she would find no joy in "Afraid of kicking off early?" I answered, "Perhaps he fears an early demise."

"Then he's recklessly immodest, considering the demands of the afterlife. Better to embark steeped in humility. And, Ben—" She fixed me with remarkably clear stone-blue eyes. Her fine features were framed by white hair and a straw picture hat. Beauty lingered. On a good day like this one, she could still pass for eighty.

"Yes, Connie?"

She stared a long moment, then shook her head as if dodging a mosquito. "Sorry. Lost my thought."

Connie—my Aunt Connie—Miss Constance Abbott of Main Street—stood with the help of her cane and my elbow almost as tall as she had learned to at Miss Porter's. Always abstemiously slender, she was getting much too thin. And her memory had begun to lock up, occasionally—unpredictably—terrifyingly. The transient ischemic "mini-strokes" that preyed upon her brain had swept the ground out from under my hope that she was indestructible. But her voice was still as clear and noble as her standards.

"What is that chiseled on the lintel?" she asked, squinting dubiously at the mausoleum and pretending to read:

'Made a pile of money?
Afraid no one will notice when I die?
Now they'll never forget me?'"

Grand-nephew-ic obligations included acting the straight man for a woman who remembered vaudeville: "I think it says, 'Grose.'"

"Well gross he is."

"The English Grose, with an 'e'."

"I *know* who Mr. Grose is. I have heard things that would curl your hair."

Little escaped Connie's attention in Newbury. She cherished the town and nourished it with gifts like our grand Town Hall and a library as comfortable as a Fifth Avenue club.

"What things that would curl my hair?"

"I do not repeat gossip."

Too bad. Gossip was the lifeblood of my dual career: real estate agent and private investigator. Gossip snared me exclusive listings of old estates before my competitors learned they were for sale. Gossip hinted where the bodies were buried.

The gossip I had already heard repeated speculated that Brian Grose had moved to Newbury from California, where he had struck it rich developing shopping centers or condos or some such blight on the land, and now telecommuted part-time to a venture capital group that specialized in real estate. Nothing hair-curling about that: we're close enough to New York City to visit for pleasure, but way too far for a daily commute; and Brian Grose was not the only entrepreneur who had moved to Newbury to enjoy the pleasures of emailing in his bathrobe.

Otherwise, Developer Grose seemed to be in youthful semi-retirement, thank God. All he had developed here was his own mega-mansion atop Mount Pleasant Road, which he slathered with stucco, a building material better suited to drug-lord enclaves of Miami than New England's stony hills. Fortunately for passing drivers, Grose's extravaganza was screened by Newbury Forest Association trees. When Grose tried to cut the trees to extend his view, a famously-rapacious New York negligence lawyer, to whom I had sold an "antique" weekend retreat, had sent a chilling letter on behalf of the Forest Association, of which he was a trustee. Grose wrote a huge check to the Forest Association's open-space fund and everyone calmed down. Briefly.

Soon after the tree battle, Grose had somehow gotten invited to serve on the board of the venerable Newbury Cemetery

Association, and before *that* turned into the current cat fight with lawyers, injunctions, and appeals, he had managed to grace the Village Cemetery with his shiny new mausoleum.

The old timers who had ten or twelve generations under the hillside had gone predictably nuts and wrested control of the Cemetery Association back from the gross insurgents. Someone had gotten mad enough to graffiti-paint in blood red, "Go Back To California And Take This With You" on it. (Congenitally decent as most Newburians, the vandal had applied his or her elegant copperplate script with water-base paint that had washed off without a trace.)

But Grose had allies among the recently-moved-to-town Mega-Mansion horde who were thrilled to discover a hot new one-ups-ing contest that reduced the purchasers of six-hundred-thousand BTU stainless-steel outdoor grills and gold-accented Lexi to piker status. So if the courts settled the imbroglio in Brian Grose's favor, his would be neither the last nor the gaudiest eternal self-storage unit crowding the green slopes.

Scooter McKay's voice echoed like distant thunder. "…and a bottle of rum."

I maneuvered Connie toward Sherry Carter, a world-class exhibitionist, who was jumping around temptingly in a tight, thin leotard playing Madame Irinakov—a dancer friend of Isadora Duncan, who had kept a summer place in Newbury in the 1920s, back when passenger trains still delivered vacationers.

Connie touched a glove to her ear. "Why do I keep hearing Scooter McKay?"

Fortunately, another noise distracted her, a remarkably loud *thump! thump! thump!* interrupted by the eardrum-slitting *skreeeeeeek!* of a buzz-saw.

The Chevalley clan had wheeled a clattering, belching, hissing antique one-cylinder stationary gas engine beside the 1905 headstone of Ezra Peck, who had been the first Newbury farmer to invest in modern technology. Snaggle-toothed Sherman Chevalley, mean and lean as a very tall snake—and larcenous as a packrat—tended the machine which was transmitting power by long belts to a corn sheller, a water pump, and a circular mill saw of the type silent movie villains used to threaten maidens. He wore a period farm-hand costume that looked much like his daily attire, minus the Budweiser cap. Recently paroled, again, Sherman had been persuaded by his mother that community service would look good on his resume' in the event he had occasion to discuss his aspirations with some future parole board.

Sherman had protested that the show was too "Main Street," for a swamp Yankee from Frenchtown. But now that he was drenched head to toe in black grease, bleeding from a monkey-wrench-skinned knuckle, choking on blue exhaust fumes, and deafened by the shrieking buzz saw, Sherman was so happily engaged with his machinery that he would not have noticed being shackled to the front pew of Newbury First Congregational.

"If an object makes a racket," Aunt Connie said, "a Chevalley will buy it."

I suggested the far more likely, "Borrow or steal."

I'm a Chevalley on my mother's side. My father, in the one bold act of his orderly life, scandalized Main Street by marrying a dark-haired beauty of French extraction back when his parents' and grandparents' generations still embraced Yankee prejudices that predated the Indian wars. The Chevalleys, descendants of Anton Chevalier, first resident of the town stockade ("carousing," the charge) live on the cold, wet north slopes of Frenchtown, most in double-wide house trailers. When it became time to build the railroad in 1840 no one had doubted that the tracks should define the border between the two communities.

At the next grave stop, Rick Bowland's lovely, flaky wife Georgia played a 19th Century portraitist who had made a career painting the wives of men who had bought summer estates in Newbury after striking it rich in the Civil War. Nearby, Ted and Sally Barrett, the handsomest couple in town, portrayed an 18th Century minister and his wife who had led breakaway Congregationalists into the Church of England in the days when the town took schisms seriously.

First Selectman Vicky McLachlan—one-time love of my life—and her live-in fellow, my old friend and lawyer Tim Hall, read from the love letters of a couple who had been buried side by side during a small pox epidemic. I got tears in my eyes and a sidelong glance from Vicky that I'm still trying to decipher.

"What is Scooter McKay doing in the Abbott plot?" Connie asked, her tone reminiscent of a banker contemplating a felon in the vault. The way the Notables course was laid out, I had been unable to prevent us from drifting ever closer to the "Yo, ho, ho-ing" in the original section of the cemetery where the head stones were too weathered to read the names.

Connie led the way and there was no stopping her. Leaning hard on her cane she covered a lot of ground for a lady in her nineties.

"Is that a parrot on Scooter's shoulder?"

"I believe Scooter rented one this morning."

The parrot complemented the latex saber scar glued to Scooter's cheek, his black eye patch, his cutlass, the pigtail slung over his shoulder, and the incredibly valuable brace of 18th Century matchlock pistols Scooter was holding for his black-sheep brother, Scupper McKay: a well-known antique dealer whom Federal agents wanted to know better. (I was looking into it for Scooter who was worried. The Feds, it seemed, wondered if Scupper was the missing link in a chain that already entangled a former governor, a politically-connected New Haven developer, a Watergate condo in the name of a wife not wed to the former governor, and a lowball appraisal of an extremely-rare Connecticut highboy, which had mysteriously vanished along with Scupper's arch business rival.)

Scooter's wife, Eleanor, was shooting photographs for the *Clarion*. Their daughters were cowering behind a elm, praying that Constantine's Abbott's grave would swallow Scooter up before their friends came along. And Lorraine Renner, an angular, quite striking brunette who had a small business making wedding DVDs, was video-ing every piratical grimace in hopes,

I presumed, that Scooter would exchange some free advertising space for a record of his performance.

Connie's lips drew tight as piano wire.

She is the sole heiress of the wealthy Abbott line, sired by Constantine who had sensed winter coming several weeks after founding Newbury and skipped out to seek his fortune at sea. Less adventurous Abbott cousins stayed behind to chop down trees, dam the river, plant crops and shovel snow. Twenty years later, when they had carved out the beginnings of a nice little town, Constantine came home from the sea one of the richest men in the Colonies. His progeny got busy investing in clippers to ply the China trade, canals, whale ships, railroads, repeating rifles, brass, clockworks, shipyards, helicopters (a Russian refugee named Sikorsky was tinkering down in Stratford), and land—always land—never touching capital and cautiously diversifying. Or, strictly speaking, "money laundering," as the common name for Constantine's maritime riches was "pirate loot."

In case anybody failed to get the message, Scooter had planted a skull and crossbones on a staff beside old Constantine's headstone, which had not weathered one bit since an 1870 great-great-great grandchild—Connie's grand-father—replaced the original sandstone with expensive granite.

Connie's lips barely moved. "It seems to me that Scooter MacKay could have portrayed some member of his own family—such as the swineherd who founded their newspaper—instead of ours."

Her "ours" was kind, but not entirely accurate. While my full name is Benjamin Constantine Abbott III, the Constantine only reflects an Abbott custom of hanging wealthy relatives' names on kids in the futile hope that those in the more direct line of fortune will open their coffers. My side of the Abbotts, those cousins who stayed behind, kept on being farmers, tradesmen, preachers, horse traders and, starting with my great-grandfather, real estate agents. They often served as selectmen of their nice little town, which was no way to get rich if you were honest, which they were. I was the only one who had ever made a ton of money, but that was during a misspent youth on Wall Street doing yeoman service for bubbly exuberance—and the loot hadn't lasted longer than it deserved to.

"*Scooter McKay!*" Connie raised her cane.

On the verge of blurting, "Aye, Me Hearty!" and unsheathing his cutlass, Scooter lost his nerve and turned pale. There were few men in Newbury under seventy who did not recall delivering the newspaper to Miss Abbott's mansion, or raking the front yard under her watchful eye, and Scooter had lived his whole life directly across the street from her. How he thought he could get away with this act was beyond me.

His daughters crept toward a bigger elm. Eleanor got very busy swapping out her camera's memory card, and Scooter fell back on the manners we learned as day-students at Newbury Prep. He swept his pirate hat off his head and bowed low. "Good afternoon, Miss Abbott."

"You just wait until the next tercentennial, Scooter McKay."

"The *next*—yes, Miss Abbott?"

"I will portray your great-grandmother Emily, the pig farmer. And I will bribe the fattest McKay children I can find to portray piglets."

A sudden blast of organ music drowned out the sound of hefty teenage daughters weeping and saved Scooter from having to come up with a polite, much less bright rejoinder. The music was so loud it seemed to fall from the sky. Bach (his Mass in B-Minor, I learned later), thundered down the hill, echoed to Main Street and, judging by the volume, halfway to Massachusetts. It was both moving and exuberant, but it totally derailed the Notables' Tour.

All eyes focused on the Grose Mausoleum. I had not believed the rumor that Brian Grose had installed surround sound to entertain him through Eternity. Now that rumor sounded stentorianly true.

"Ben," Connie said, "please do something about that."

I hoofed it up the hill to tell him to put on a headset and worked my way through the crowd gathering around Grose's spike fence. Up close Bach shook the ground. I expected to find Grose sitting inside the thing's foyer, mind blown on his own loudness. But the mausoleum was shut tight as a bank vault. I climbed over the front gate, stepped under the portico, and knocked on the thick bronze door, which had the effect of making very little noise, while hurting my knuckles a lot.

I looked down for a rock to bang on it.

Instead of picking up a rock, I stepped back, gingerly. Then I took out my cell phone, and tapped 911.

Chapter Two

"Benjamin Constantine Abbott III" on Resident State Trooper Oliver Moody's caller ID was not a name to put a smile on his grim face or warmth in his truculent voice. We had been butting heads since I was a mutinous teen.

"What do you want, Ben?"

I had to clap a hand on my ear to hear him over Bach. "Come up to the cemetery."

"What part?" The cemetery was enormous, much of it open space—wooded Castle Hill—reserved to bury generations unborn.

"Brian Grose's mausoleum."

"Are you tying up a 911 emergency line to report an act of vandalism?"

"Blood is seeping out of it." I would have thought a mausoleum door would be sealed at the bottom, but I was standing in sticky, half-dried blood and tracking it on the grass.

"Sure it's not red paint?"

"Not this time. Better bring the ambulance—And Ollie?"

"What?"

"Maybe a wrecker to open the door. It's locked tight."

"Ben," Connie called. "Is everything all right?"

She was surrounded by a crowd of kids and parents who were watching anxiously from the fence. They couldn't see the blood, but they knew something was wrong and now they heard sirens in the distance. I called, "Would some of you kids please find Scooter McKay and Ted Barrett and Rick Bowland?"

The guys came running and gently moved people away.

Sirens descended; Ollie's cruiser whooping, the ambulance howling, the wrecker's air horn baying like a pack of pit bulls. Ollie got there first. The volunteer EMTs and Chevalley Enterprises Garage tied for second.

Ollie, six-foot nine-inches from his storm trooper boots to the top of his broad-brimmed Stetson, and wearing a grey uniform so crisp that he might have ironed it out of sheet metal, crouched down for a close look at the blood. He beckoned Betty Butler from the ambulance. "I don't want to mess up a crime site. How fresh is this? Could they still be alive?"

"No way I'll say no," said Betty. "Open the door."

Ollie beckoned Donny Butler, the Cemetery Association's groundskeeper who was hurrying up to see what the excitement was about. Donny was shaggy, craggy, and cadaverous, and every woman in the cemetery brightened at the approach of the handsomest gravedigger in New England.

"You got the key?"

"Nope." Donny did not look unhappy that there was a problem at Grose's mausoleum. Last Spring, with a couple of beers in him, he had used the rusty bumper of his pickup truck to clear the cemetery service road of a "Freakin' Yuppie Audi" which Brian Grose had parked inconsiderately. Harsh words invited a poke in the eye and Grose had pressed charges, calling the beaming owner of a body shop as his first witness and a bored ophthalmologist as his second.

"Open the door," Ollie told Pinkerton Chevalley, a large cousin of mine who was looming beside his wrecker like the Grand Coulee Dam.

Pink issued heavy tools to a pair of our vandalistic cousins he had brought along.

"Open the door."

Dennis and Albert swaggered up to the mausoleum grinning at this amazing turn of luck. I overheard Dennis mutter, "You believe we are getting *paid* to nuke this 'sucker?"

"Right in front of Ollie. And he can't do squat."

They attacked the bronze with crowbars and sledge hammers. They were powerful young men, and they made a wonderful noise almost as loud as Bach, but didn't do much to the door. In fact, all their banging and crashing had no effect at all, except for some gouges and scratches. Pink stepped in, shouting over the din, "The blood's coming under the door. That means there's a crack under the door. Shove your bar in the crack. Morons."

Albert and Dennis did as they were told. Perplexed, they stopped.

"What?" chorused Pink and Ollie, the first time the anti-social Pink and his natural enemy the state trooper ever agreed on anything.

"The bar's stuck."

Pink, known to bench press a Harley Davidson when in a playful mood, yanked it out with one hand and tossed it at Dennis. *"Open the door!"*

Sweating, grunting, Dennis and Albert attacked again.

Betty Butler said, "Somebody could be bleeding to death in there. We really ought to open the door."

Pink, who regarded all women except his mother as inept food and sex delivery systems, turned red from his cap to his black Chevalley Enterprises T-shirt. "What do think we're doing, Betty?"

"I got some dynamite," said Dennis. "It's in the—Oww! Whad you hit me for?" He swung back, punching his brother before he realized that Albert was nodding his Minotaur head in the direction of Trooper Moody who, even before 9/11, had taken a dim view of explosives in the hands of private citizens—especially Chevalleys. "Oh, yeah," said Dennis. "Thanks, Dude."

Aunt Connie said, "Here's Grace Botsford. She'll have a key."

Grace's father, Gerard, who had died last March in a car crash at age ninety-five, had been president of the Newbury Cemetery Association for as long as anyone could remember and had appointed Grace treasurer when she came home from Connecticut College in 1970.

"She was brave to attend the Notables. Gerard so loved this ground."

Grace, who had just turned sixty, had run the family insurance agency with her father and never married. Father and daughter had served on virtually all the town's unpaid commissions at one time or another and they had been a fixture at the old families' lawn parties and garden tours: white-haired Gerard resplendent in seersucker and straw hat; Grace, old-fashioned in silk, tall and straight on his arm.

Grace took a sealed envelope from her purse, tore it open, and handed a key to Trooper Moody.

Next question was, had the Chevalley vandals so damaged the door that the key wouldn't open it. Trooper Moody inserted it, turned it. Even over the roar of the music, I could hear a massive lock like a Fox Lock clank inside. Ollie grunted in triumph and pulled the door open. Softly colored light poured into the foyer from a stained glass ceiling, which if we had thought about it could have been more easily broken open than the Fort Knox door.

Connie's white glove bit into my arm. Grace Botsford pressed her hand to her mouth. Pinkerton Chevalley and Oliver Moody chorused, "What a mess." Albert Chevalley threw up on Dennis Chevalley's boots, and one of Scooter's daughters snapped a photograph too gory to print in the *Clarion*.

Chapter Three

Brian Grose lay on his back on the polished floor. The vast oozing hole in his chest would surely have killed him. But whoever had shot him had finished the job by shooting him twice in the forehead. Two neat holes in front had exited violently in back, and the man's death was, to bowdlerize Pinkerton Chevalley and Trooper Moody, one holy mess.

"Turn off that music," said somebody.

"Don't touch anything," shouted Trooper Moody. "Everyone step back. Back, back, out of the way. Don't touch anything."

I said to Cousin Pink that whoever had turned the music on must have set a timer. Pink said, "No shit, Sherlock."

Ollie shouted, "All you people get out of here!"

People shuffled uncertainly, caught between fear of Ollie and morbid curiosity, until Aunt Connie raised her voice, "Everyone go home, please. Take the children and leave Trooper Moody to his work."

Ollie whipped out a cell phone and called in a suspicious death. He did not look happy. As the town's resident state trooper—lone-wolf master of sixty square miles of Connecticut turf, lord over all he could intimidate —Oliver Moody would rather slug it out single-handedly against raiding urban street gangs than have his territory invaded by the State Police Major Crime Squad.

‹›‹›‹›

In a sensible world the murder of Brian Grose would be investigated by the thoroughly competent Major Crime Squad that was on the scene within an hour. In a sensible world the responding officers, Detective-Lieutenant Marian Boyce, the best of the best, and her long-time partner Arnie Bender, far less pleasant to look at, but equally skilled, would have conducted their investigation while normal citizens went about their business building houses, teaching summer school, writing insurance policies, milking cows, repairing vehicles, mowing grass, and selling real estate.

But the next day, I got a visit from three guys I had known a long time who made it clear that it was not a sensible world, at least when it came to the war to control Newbury's Village Cemetery Association. Two bankers with whom I had grown up, pugnacious Dan Adams and easy-does-it Wes Little, and Rick Bowland—last seen wearing vest and shirt sleeves while reading the accounts of Newbury's first general store in a monotone—represented the original Village Cemetery Association, the pre-mausoleum, anti-mausoleum faction that had secured a sixty-day court injunction against new mausoleums. They wanted to hire me to investigate the murder.

I wanted the job, but all I said was, "Why?"

Dan said I was qualified.

"So are the cops. They sent the best squad in the state."

"It is important that we appear to take charge of the situation that affects the perceived integrity of the association," said Rick Bowland.

I knew enough about the struggle to ask, "Is this to influence the court?"

"The new people are attempting to get the injunction lifted."

"What does that have to do with Brian getting killed?"

"Quote: 'The security breach proves that cronyism has undermined the competence of the entrenched bloc who seized control of the Cemetery Association.'"

Everyone started talking at once.

"They're making us sound like Rumsfeld in Iraq."

"They're trying to steal the Association, Ben."

"Steal it?"

"Steal control, so they destroy the cemetery. They've got plans for fifty of them."

"Fifty what?"

"*Mausoleums.* It'll look like a Toll Brothers subdivision instead of our burying ground."

"They'll do anything to beat us."

"They're making hay out of this murder.'

"You know what we're saying, Ben?"

I said, "You are saying that you don't want anymore Hummer-house headstones in the burying ground. Neither do I."

"So you'll help us?"

I said, "This could get expensive, guys."

"Well, we're thinking you'll do it pro bono," they said, not surprising me a lot.

I wanted the job for numerous reasons. The money, of course. Unless the state police immediately turned up an obvious killer, then a man shot in his own mausoleum was a case to get the juices flowing. And I disliked gross mausoleums as much as my friends who were fighting to retain control of a beautiful burying ground that was my cemetery, too. But I had no intention of taking as deep a pay cut as they were plotting.

The Cemetery Association was solvent, and happened to own enough open ground right on the edge of the borough to bury Newburians until our next Tercentennial, because its trustees were tight-fisted, skin-flinty, penny-pinching Yankees and had been for the last three hundred years. If I allowed myself to get taken by a mob that regarded knocking my price down as a godfearing act, I'd get jerked around next time I negotiated a real estate deal with any of them.

I wasn't particularly worried: playing hard-to-get gave me an edge; that they felt under the gun helped; nor was it in their nature to hire an outsider.

Indeed, Banker Dan Adams, whose family had been around almost as long as mine, grudgingly sweetened the offer. "Maybe we could work out something where you'd get a free burial plot."

"I already have a burial plot," I reminded him. "In fact, I believe I have an extra one as my mother has announced she prefers to be buried in Frenchtown." Having fled "snobby" Main Street when my father died and left me the house, she was threatening to make the move eternal, even though it would mean leaving my father alone with his family.

Dan glowered. "Okay, how about we give you a break on your dues?"

In a sensible world a part-time private investigator would not have been invited to address the Cemetery Association's board of trustees that evening. But a town that's been home for centuries is not always a sensible world. Salary negotiation notwithstanding, there was no way I would dodge a request from any of the associations of volunteers that made Newbury work, be they firefighters, ambulance crews, Lions, Rotary, or custodians of the dead.

I promised the guys I would attend the meeting. I didn't necessarily buy into their reasoning about the court case. But I totally agreed that we should do whatever we could to prevent our burying ground from becoming a gated community for the eternally crass.

Aiming to wow the salary committee with clues the State Police would never turn up, I telephoned my sticky-fingered cousin Sherman Chevalley. None of the "Notables" pageants had been that close to Brian Grose's mausoleum. Brian and/or somebody could easily have slipped inside unnoticed. But Sherman had to have gone to the cemetery much earlier than the other performers to set up the complicated gas engine and weave a spider web of drive belts to his corn sheller, water pump, and buzz saw.

Alone in the cemetery, with an eye ever-roving for valuables not nailed down, Sherman could have noticed something like a car or a truck or someone lurking around the mausoleum— information that he was unlikely to share, voluntarily, with his nemesic foes, the cops, or even his parole officer. But he might talk to me if I bought him enough beers and promised to keep him out of it.

His cell phone rang and rang and rang. He didn't answer and it didn't take messages. I drove down to Frenchtown to his mother's house trailer, which huddled in the lee of a tumbled-down barn last painted by Sherman's grandfather. She was "Aunt Helen" to me, although there were several cousins once or twice removed between her and my mother, and she greeted me warmly. She was tall and skinny, like Sherman. Fifty years of mothering him would have worn most women to the bone, but in Aunt Helen a cheery optimism had somehow survived.

She sounded a little worried that he hadn't showed up for any free meals since Sunday morning. Which made me really worried. He could be off on an innocent drunk, but disappearing hours after a shooting where several hundred people had seen him all day was the sort of behavior that could pique the curiosity of the State Police.

"How did he do at the cemetery thing?" she asked hopefully.

"Star attraction," I assured her, thinking to myself, Sherman, what have you gotten into this time?

"Do you think Scooter McKay will write about him in the paper?"

I told her I thought he would, a safe bet. The Notables was big news to the *Clarion,* easily as big as Brian's murder—How many Tercentennials will most people experience? But even if Scooter neglected to mention his antique gas engine in the many pages of Notables coverage, Sherman's name would most weeks be attached to minor infractions in the Police Reports. I was just hoping that this time it wouldn't be a felony.

I asked her if the police had been by about Brian Grose's murder.

"That doesn't have anything to do with Sherman," she said with complete and utter faith in the boundaries of Sherman's criminality. With that she repeated one of those mottos that get a mother through the day: "I have always said that Sherman can't be all bad because animals and kids love him."

When I took Aunt Connie home Sunday, after we talked to the cops, I had pressed her about her Brian Grose gossip that would "curl your hair." She had alluded, tangentially, to what she called, "assignations." "With an 'S?'" I had asked. More than one? "'S' as in several," said Connie. When I asked if she had heard any names attached to the assignees, she reminded me that she did not repeat gossip.

Now I had to ask her again, and this time it was business. "I know that you don't repeat gossip, Connie. But in view of the circumstances, could you possibly tell me a little more about Brian Grose's 'assignations?'"

"You mean the assignees?"

"Their names."

We were having our regular Tuesday afternoon tea at a marble topped table set in the bay window of her dining room, as we had had the majority of Tuesdays since I was old enough to talk.

"No I can't," she said.

"Connie, I would not ask if it wasn't important. The Cemetery Association got the idea in its collective head to pay me to look into Mr. Grose's murder. It sounds a little loony, but they've got big problems with that court case. I have to meet with them tonight. The smarter I go in, the better I can serve them."

Connie looked away. Her jaw started to work. I could see frail bone press thin skin. When she turned back to look at me her eyes were watery. "I can't Ben. I would if I could, but I can't remember."

I could have cheerfully shot myself at that moment. Or shoved a rusty knife into my chest. One of the ways I dealt with Connie's increasing frailty was to pretend it wasn't happening. I was so successful at it that I could actually walk into her house and ask something truly stupid while totally missing every quiet signal she was sending about her fear and dread.

"I'm sorry. I didn't realize that was what you meant."

"Obviously, I heard it from someone. I can't remember whom. And I can't remember what she said."

"So you heard from a woman?"

That brought her back with a vengeance. She sat straighter than usual, which was very straight indeed and said, as crisply as a winter morning, "Well I certainly wouldn't listen to such talk from a man—well, maybe from a gay man—well, you know what I mean. But I don't think it matters, Ben. A name that would have led to a shooting, a murder for pity sake, would have stuck in my mind. Don't you agree?"

"Absolutely!" I lied to her and myself.

Connie squinted through me like a dirty window. "Do not patronize me, young man!"

"Sorry."

"Try some."

"Try some what?"

"Names, you ninny. Try some names, and perhaps they'll jog my memory."

I looked at her. She was perched on the edge of her chair, tea forgotten, the one cucumber sandwich I had persuaded her to try, half eaten. "Are you sure you want to do this?"

"You said it was important, for your sake. And it's now become important to me, for the sake of my old brain."

I started at the head of Main and worked my way down the street. "Mary…"

"No."

"Lori…."

"No."

Betty."

"No."

"Sydney…"

"No."

"Jeanne…"

"No."

"Anne Marie."

"No."

"Priscilla…."

"…Maybe."

Priscilla Adams, pugnacious Dan's wife. Maybe that's why he was so prickly, of late. Priscilla was a very nice looking blonde with the kind of glossy, straight hair pharmaceutical fortunes have been spent trying to replicate for ordinary mortals. But married to the sort of man who would not think twice about punching the interloper in the nose. On the other hand, love and sex make people brave, as well as silly. "Maybe?" I coaxed.

Connie nodded slowly. "Yes, I think so—Benjamin, this goes no further than this room."

"Of course not."

"Unless of course Dan was the one who shot him."

"Of course."

"I'm not positive. And when we're talking about angry husbands shooting, accuracy becomes paramount. More names, please."

"Lorraine."

"Oh yes."

"Lorraine? Lorraine Renner?"

"Definitely! I heard an earful."

"Do you recall any details?"

"Nothing true."

"What do you mean?"

"It was just silly gossip. You know, Ben, there are people who can't imagine a man and woman in the same room without ascribing all sorts of...activities."

"Wait. Let me get clear on this. The rumor was that Lorraine had a thing going—" Connie's eye fell bleakly on mine. "—an assignation, but there was none?"

"I recall every detail. It was claptrap. More names, Ben. Quickly, now, you've got me cooking."

We went down the rest of Main Street with no more hits, so I started tossing names at random. "Cindy."

"Cynthia. Cynthia Little."

Wes Little's wife. Another blonde. Not as pretty as Dan's wife; but I had seen the occasional predatory gleam in her hazel eyes that suggested a voraciousness that could make up for a lot in the looks department. We talked about Cynthia for a moment. Connie remembered no details, but neither did she remember disbelieving the gossip linking Cynthia Little to Brian Grose. "More names."

"Helen...."

"...No."

"Georgia."

"Yes!"

"Georgia Bowland?" A honey blonde.

"I think yes."

"Oh, God," I said, thinking, Poor Rick. And poor fragile Georgia.

"Do not leap to conclusions," said Connie.

"I'm trying not to."

"I mean, do not forget that I am merely repeating *gossip*. Not eyewitness accounts."

Maybe so, I thought, but her discerning ear had put no credence in the gossip about Lorraine Renner.

"More names," Connie demanded.

We ran through dozens, but produced no more hits, and I could see that she was growing tired. "Thank you, Connie. Thank you for your help."

"I must say, this has been rather fun. I mean gossip mongering is terrible, ordinarily. But there is nothing like a good cause to expiate guilt. Do you see the pattern? If three constitute a pattern?"

"Sure. Priscilla, Georgia and Cindy. All three of the possibly-seduced are married to Cemetery Association Trustees."

"Any one of whom could be an angry husband."

"Keeping in mind that all we know is gossip."

Connie smiled. "Shall we dub the possibly-seduced the 'gossiply-seduced'?

"But, seriously, Benjamin, why would such a husband want to hire a detective to solve the murder he committed?"

"He'd have no choice in the matter if the other two wanted it. At least he could console himself that a part-time detective would just get in the way of the police. Might even think he could pump me to keep abreast of their investigation in time to run for it."

The Board of Trustees of Newbury's Village Cemetery Association met in Grace Botsford's dining room. She lived in a large old saltbox, a beautifully kept gem of weathered shingles, twelve-over-twelve windows, and pale-green shutters. It stood half-smothered by a garden of roses on the edge of Newbury's central Borough, where the original settlement had clustered around Newbury Road, which we now call Main Street.

Rick Bowland introduced me formally to ten people I had known my whole life. Then he told them, "Ben is going to make an effort to find the murderer quickly to demonstrate to the court that the Village Cemetery Association took charge and did the right thing."

"That is absurd," Grace protested. "Let the police handle it. Why waste our money?"

"He won't charge a lot, will you Ben?"

I gave that the non-committal mumble it deserved.

Grace looked at the others, all men, most younger than she, and said, quietly and firmly, like the businesswoman she was, "I understand your strategy. But it will backfire. It will make us look like an entrenched faction so out of touch and mistrustful of the police that we conduct our own investigation led by a real estate broker. No offense, Ben, but that has been your primary occupation since you were released from the penitentiary."

That gratuitous shiv in the ribs really surprised me. And everyone else in the room, judging by their expressions. They all knew I had done time for Wall Street crime—falling in, enthusiastically, with the wrong crowd and then refusing to rat them out—but it tended not to come up in conversations where my face was present. I had never thought of Grace Botsford as a nasty person, so I figured she was extremely upset with the young ones who wanted to hire me and probably feeling a bit outnumbered since her father had passed on.

Before an embarrassed or voyeuristic silence could lock down the meeting, I said, "Actually, Grace, I'm running almost fifty-fifty, lately, half houses, half investigations. And, as Rick says, I am qualified. Even licensed." (I had resisted getting a license to avoid the risk of losing it. But clients liked labels, and I liked clients because the income I earned as a private investigator allowed me to sell houses I admired and decline to list ugly ones I did not.)

"But," I added, turning to the others, "Grace raises an excellent point. The State Police have a good record of solving murders. They're well-trained and well-equipped, if a little understaffed. Plus, as Connecticut doesn't have all that many murders outside of the cities, the occasional upscale country killing gives them something to sink their teeth into. You can count on their enthusiasm. So I think you should listen to Grace."

Grace said, "Thank you, Ben."

Rick Bowland said, "Ben, you want to excuse us a minute while we hash this out?"

"I'll be on the porch, for a while. Then I'm going home. The cat wants a drink and I'm hungry."

I sat in a fine old wicker chair, enjoying the perfume of ancient Louise Odiers and Reine des Violettes that Gerard Botsford had devoted half his life to. I had taken my best shot. I would either not get the job, or I would get it at the pay rate I wanted. Pretty soon I heard raised voices through the thin walls. It sounded like half were on Grace's side, half on Rick Bowland's. As it got noisier I heard Grace say, "Dan Adams, you tried to depose my father back in the nineties. He didn't let you then, and I won't let you now."

Instead of letting that water continue over the dam, Dan shouted back, "Your father drove my father out of this Association. I was just trying to get a little for him."

Grace was cold as ice. "If you don't think that our responsibility to the dead and Newbury's future is more important than an old feud over who runs things, let me remind you that your father tried to drive *me* out of *my* position."

"Jesus Christ, Grace, you were a twenty-year old college kid."

"Do not swear in my house."

"You didn't deserve to be treasurer."

"Dan, you were not yet three years old at the time. I do think you are complaining about things you do not understand. The board would not have gone along if they did not believe that I deserved the job."

All this time, Rick kept saying, louder and louder, "We have to appear to make the effort. We have to show we're rightfully in charge." Eventually he came out and got me, and I went in; and Grace, who had two red anger dots on her cheekbones said, speaking formally for the secretary taking notes, "The trustees of the Cemetery Association have voted to hire you, Ben Abbott, to investigate the murder of Brian Grose that occurred on Cemetery Association property."

I said, "I'll give you a cut rate of a hundred and fifty dollars an hour."

"Ben!" chorused an abruptly unanimous board of trustees.

I turned to the recording secretary and whispered, "Jeannie? Would you please put down your pen and cover your ears?" Jeannie looked at Grace. She had been the office manager/assistant/receptionist at the Botsford Agency since insurance was invented. Grace nodded, and Jeannie put down her pen and covered her ears.

I said, "You have to appear to pay me decently. Otherwise it won't look like much of an effort. Just between us, I won't keep such close track of every hour. Besides, this will all be moot the second the cops nail the killer, and all you will owe me for is an hour of time for attending this meeting." I raised a hand to quell howls of protest. "My *first* conversation earlier today with Rick and Dan and Wes was on the house."

Dan said, "Wait a minute. Nobody charges for the first conversation."

"Architects do," I said. "So do some lawyers. And if you ask Pinkerton Chevalley why your car's making that clunking noise, Pink's reply will cost you."

Rick Bowland offered to drive me home. I said I'd rather walk. It was maybe five minutes from Grace's place on the edge of the borough to mine on Main Street.

"So I'll walk you home."

"What about your car?" I had had enough cemetery chatter for one evening. Also, to do a proper job for them, I had to get out of their mind-set and into my own.

"I'll get my car later."

The old Borough has sidewalks, uprooted by aggressive maples, and narrowed by hedges. The houses are smaller and mostly lived in by long-time residents whose kids have grown up and moved away because they couldn't afford to buy in their home town with new house prices going nuts year after year. There was no traffic on the side streets.

"So what do you want to talk about?" I asked Rick.

"What do you mean?"

"You're walking me home. I'm relieved you didn't offer to carry my books."

"Huh?"

"What's up, Rick?"

"I was just wondering if you have any idea who killed Brian."

"I doubt he interrupted a burglar."

"Meaning he knew the guy? The guy who killed him?"

Curious, wondering was he toying with me, I asked, "What makes you think that?"

"They were alone in the mausoleum."

"Not necessarily. There was room for several people." The list, which I kept to myself, would include Donny Butler, Sherman Chevalley, or a blonde's husband who was also a Village Cemetery Association trustee like Dan Adams or Wes Little. Or you, Rick Bowland.

Rick stepped off the sidewalk where a hedge leaned close and called from the street, "What do the cops think?"

That was a good question; almost as good as: Why did you or Dan or Wes fight so hard to hire me to investigate? Was one of you really hoping a half-assed amateur would throw dust in the cops' eyes?

I said, "Beats me. But I would guess that they are looking for witnesses who might have seen Brian go inside with someone. Or seen someone go inside who wasn't Brian."

"How would he get in without a key?"

"Maybe Brian lent him a key. Maybe he picked the lock. Maybe they went in together."

"But the cemetery was full of people for the tour and setting up the tour."

"You can be sure the cops will be talking to them."

Which was why I wanted to talk to Sherman as soon as I found him.

Rick said, "You should talk to Donny Butler. He might have seen something. He's there all the time."

"Since Brian Grose pressed charges against Donny for creaming his Audi and punching his eye, you can bet the cops are grilling the hell out of Donny."

"Donny wouldn't shoot Brian."

"Probably not."

"Who do you suppose Brian would take into the mausoleum?"

"Someone he wanted to show off to, or someone he wanted to do some work on it—fix something; or install something. He already hooked up audio. Maybe he wanted running water or a barbeque or high def video. Maybe it was just someone he wanted to get laid with."

"What?"

"Private. Quiet. Cool stone under a beautiful skylight."

"It's weird to joke about it, Ben."

"I am not joking.

"The man is dead, Ben. Murdered."

"I am aware."

I wondered why he was so clawing so hard for the moral high ground. On the other hand, I had forgotten how buttoned down a fellow Rick Bowland really was. He had worked for IBM since college, and he actually sounded shocked by the concept of two adults sneaking off to a cemetery.

"Are you really suggesting Brian Grose took a woman into his mausoleum?"

"Could have took a guy. Could have took a *dog*. Who knows?"

"But—"

"Rick, one more dumb question and I will charge the Cemetery Association an hour of my time for this walk home."

"Sorry, Ben. I just was trying to get a leg up on what's going on."

"Turn on your radio in the morning. You'll hear the cops have solved it."

Except they didn't. Not by morning. Not even by lunch.

I telephoned Sherman Chevalley's cell phone for the fourth time. He was still not answering.

I walked to the cemetery. The grounds smelled of sweet, cut grass. I traced a distant diesel whine and roar up the slope to Donny Butler maneuvering among headstones on a Kaboda riding mower. Brian Grose's mausoleum was cordoned with yellow crime scene tape. I made sure that neither Trooper Moody nor Major Crime Squad cops were watching, slipped under it and tried the battered bronze door. Locked. I spotted the Kaboda pounding down a distant slope and I ran a broken field of headstones to cut it off at its next turn. Donny Butler saw me coming, idled back the engine and waited.

"You got a key to Brian's mausoleum?"

"The cops taped it."

"I noticed."

A wide stick-it-to-the-man grin crinkled his wrinkles. "Last time I looked, there was a key in the maintenance shed."

"Shed locked?"

"Not by me."

"Thanks, Donny." I started down the slope, then turned back before he could rev the machine. "Hey, Donny?"

"What?"

"The other day you told Ollie you didn't have a key."

"I didn't have one on me."

"But there was a key in the shed?"

"I didn't notice."

"But there's one there now?"

"Maybe Grace got a new one cut at Mike's."

As in Mike's Hardware, sacred ground for those who found Home Depot too far away or too big and were not adverse to taking out second mortgages to pay Mike's prices.

"Would I be wrong in guessing that you told Ollie you didn't have a key so you could watch the Chevalleys wreck Brian's door?"

"Could be."

"How many keys were there?"

"I don't know. One at Grace's office. The one in the shed. Plus how many with the asshole."

"Was the shed locked on Sunday?"

"No. I kept running back for stuff. You know, helping everybody set up. Besides, who was going to steal a mower in front of all those people?"

"Hey, Donny, could I ask you something?"

"Sure."

"Did the cops ask you about the key?"

His smile got ragged. "Yeah. Among other things. Sons of bitches."

"Wha'd you tell them?"

"Said I didn't notice if it was in the shed." He reached for the Kaboda's throttle. Before he could drown me out I asked, "Did they believe you?"

He looked annoyed, pissed off, and maybe a little scared. "I'm still here," he said, revved the machine, whirled it on a dime and roared away, spitting grass. I walked to the maintenance shed, found the key hanging on a hook with keys for the cemetery's backhoe and the pickup truck, and one marked, "McKay Memorial," and another marked, "Front Gate," which they locked at night, forcing the amorously inclined to climb the fence, which reduced traffic to a volume that could be ignored.

Back at Brian's mausoleum, I made sure, again, that neither troopers nor anyone else for that matter, was watching, pulled on disposable latex gloves, unlocked the door, stepped inside and closed it behind me. I found myself in a pleasant space larger than I had imagined. It was about the size of the guest room in my house on Main Street.

Some of Brian's blood had been swabbed off the marble—for lab samples, I supposed, and to expose two gouges in the floor for photographs. Dark fingerprinting dust lay everywhere. I saw no prints on the dust, though I did find a forgotten photo marker, a yellow card they had placed beside a piece of evidence to ID a picture.

It looked like someone had bashed the floor twice with a ball-peen hammer. The bashes marked where the bullets had exited Brian's head, which suggested he had been flat on his back on the floor when those shots were fired. A dent in the bronze door had probably been made by the bullet that had passed through him, the first shot, the one in the back that had killed him. The dent was deep. The cops would have the slug, along with the two that had pocked the floor, which meant they would know what I could only guess: that the weapon had been heavy enough to throw him on his face, judging by the dent in the door, which meant the shooter had turned him over to shoot him in the forehead. Why bother? Two shots in the back of the head would have the same effect.

What I had not seen, peering over Trooper Moody's shoulder at the body Sunday, was the marble throne. It was tucked in the alcove behind the door, situated in such a way, I discovered when I took a seat, that the not-yet-dead owner could enjoy views of his stained-glass skylight and his marble floor. As I had said to Rick Bowland the colored stream from the stained glass would make an enchanting bed on which companions could cherish each other. My mind wandered to such a companion smiling in the light. Not surprisingly, considering this was a crime scene, I recognized the face of an adventurous peace officer I had once known well.

The throne also afforded a view of four wide drawers in the back wall. Two were at floor level, two above in a second tier. I un-throned myself to pull on one of the lacquered bronze handles and a massively heavy crypt rolled out, gliding easily on ball bearings and steel rails. It was empty, lined with dark steel, and big enough to hold a corpse and the coffin it came in. Or a live person with a gun.

All four were empty. All had been dusted inside with white power for finger prints. Otherwise, they were clean as a whistle, not surprising as the crime scene guys would have vacuumed them for fibers and hair. Again I saw no prints.

I sat in the throne again. Had anyone hidden in there, he had worn gloves like mine. I imagined being Brian sitting on my throne, contemplating immortal privilege in my private final resting place when suddenly a crypt slid open. I imagined someone stepping out with a gun—no, sitting up with a gun. Someone I knew or didn't wouldn't matter. I imagined jumping off the throne to open the door. I imagined realizing that the door was my last sight on earth.

When by lunch the next day, the cops still hadn't solved the murder of Brian Grose, I dialed Major Crime Squad Detective-Lieutenant Marian Boyce's cell, punched in my call-back number and said, when my phone rang a moment later, "I see your vehicle still prowling the town."

She said, "I see you got lucky."

"News to me."

"The woman—or should I say, girl—whose baby blue Mustang is sitting in your driveway?"

"No, no, no. It didn't come with a girl. I have to replace the Olds. Pink rents me different cars to test drive to see what I like."

"What happened to the Fiat?" The Fiat was a slickly curvaceous, twenty-seven-year-old Spider 2000 racing green roadster my mother had left with the house.

"Italy is sending a part. By sailboat."

"Since when does Chevalley rent cars? Wait! Chevalley's renting you his *customers'* cars?"

"I don't ask."

Chevalley Enterprises drew repair customers from far beyond the town lines thanks to an eight-bay garage built by my favorite cousin, Renny, who had been an automotive genius. It had a dozen skilled mechanics who were disinclined to disappoint their enormous boss, Pinkerton Chevalley. Renny's widow Betty ran the office and shielded the public from her brother-in-law.

"So what's up?" Marian asked.

"Do you have time for lunch?"

"If it includes wine."

"Aren't you on duty?"

"I'm taking the afternoon off."

"In that case, I've got a Gascogne Rosé in the fridge."

"Lunch only. And not in your house."

"I'll set a table downstairs."

"No."

"Yankee Drover?"

"Half an hour."

I put on a tie and a linen jacket and walked the convenient short stumble between my front door and the Yankee Drover Inn with its excellent bar downstairs and decent restaurant up. In the dining room, I kissed various up-tilted cheeks of Main Street matrons, returned the smiles of some McMansion Moms (while marveling, not for the first time, how much prettier they were than their houses) shook hands with a jolly table full of Realtors and mortgage brokers, and a sterner one of bankers and lawyers, asked Anne Marie for a table in the window, which overlooked the tree-shaded lawns of Main Street, and ordered a bottle of Lasendal, a Spanish contribution to world peace.

Marian Boyce came in briskly, looking gorgeous.

For whatever reason, probably because I became friends with Aunt Connie at a very young age, I have always enjoyed and admired ambitious, intelligent women. For reasons I can't fathom, I find heavily-armed ambitious, intelligent women even more attractive. Marian, whose father had been shot on the job down in Bridgeport, packed a minimum of two sidearms at all times, concealing them ingeniously. Gray, wide-set eyes and an expressive mouth were icing on a very delicious cake.

I stood up. She extended a strong hand, then leaned in to brush cheeks. "Just because I won't sneak off for lunch in your house doesn't mean we can't have a dark booth."

"I wanted to see your face in bright light."

"Checking out wrinkles?"

"It looks like you left them in the car," I said, surprised. Even kidding around she was never one for self doubt. Something seemed a little off today. "How are you?

"Great," she shot back. "How about you?"

"Doing all right....How's things at home?"

"Not bad. Not bad at all."

"Good," I lied.

At home were a cheerful six-year old boy from her marriage to a state trooper that had not survived her remarkable career, and a pleasant Pratt and Whitney engineer who was good to the boy, and as good to her as a dull man could be. She did not appear to be losing any sleep over the problem, if it was a problem; and when she reported, proudly, that she was still top of her class in law school, which she was attending at night, I concluded that she had found a productive outlet for the sexual energy she used to expend so generously on me.

"I have a question for you," she said after we touched glasses. "Before my afternoon off begins."

"About the late Mr. Grose?"

"You ever meet him?"

"Around town. At a couple of parties. And a P&Z hearing."

"What did you think?"

"Type I used to know on the Street. Couldn't be bothered to hide his conviction that superior money skills made him a superior person."

"So you didn't like him?"

"I'd have been surprised if we became friends. On the other hand, people change. He did bail out of California real estate to make a home in Newbury."

"Quite a change."

"Of course, once he got here he started throwing his weight around, more like a California condo *macher* than a country gent."

"Maybe he thought Connecticut had entered the 21st Century?"

"Actually, I take that back. Brian was less *macher* than hyperactive. He did do the right thing after tangling with the Forest Association—you know about that?"

She nodded.

"Though not, from what I hear, with the Cemetery Association—you know about that?"

She nodded, again. Of course. And she had probably spoken with some if not all the trustees, including the possible gossiples.

I said, "I found it hard to believe he had retired. He was high energy. And very smooth—getting himself invited into the Cemetery Association, which is not usually open to outsiders."

"Who is it open to? Just old families?"

"And committed volunteers. You know, people who serve on commissions and join Rotary, but not the same year they arrive. Somehow, he charmed the old crowd. Though I must say, Gerard Botsford was no fool. He must have seen something solid in Brian to invite him onto the board."

"So maybe you could have become friends?"

"I don't think so. Not after railroading that mausoleum into the burying ground. Plus," I said, shifting what had become an interview (cop talk for interrogation) toward an issue I considered more important, "I thought that pressing charges against the cemetery groundsman for backing into his Audi was harsh."

"It wasn't your bashed-in Audi. Or your punch in the eye."

"Does that make Donny Butler a suspect?"

"Stupid question." She opened her menu and perused.

"Even though you know that a fracas like that doesn't usually escalate to shooting somebody months later in cold blood?"

"Prisons are full of people who didn't usually do what they were convicted for doing."

"Does Donny have an alibi?" I asked, afraid that poor Donny had wound up in a jam he wouldn't understand until they threw away the key. I knew that he could be hot-tempered with a couple of beers in him and that he owned some guns. And if I really pushed it I could imagine him shooting Grose in the middle of an argument. But I found it harder to imagine Donny shooting Grose in the back. Not to mention pumping a double *coup de grâce* into the man's head.

"Does he?"

Marian was gauging my reaction.

I repeated, "Does he?"

"Your friend has a fairly decent alibi."

"How decent?"

"Fairly."

"So who shot Mr. Grose?"

"Who do you think?"

"Well he pissed off everyone in the Cemetery Association. But I don't see any of them shooting him for it. In fact, I can't see any of them even owning a handgun."

"How about a rifle?"

"Inside the mausoleum? I doubt it. It's big on the outside, but kind of cramped inside. Besides, would he have turned his back on a guy with a rifle?"

"You think he got shot in the back?"

"If that wasn't an exit wound in his chest, you should be looking for the owner of a cannon."

"Two head shots," she said, still gauging.

"I can't imagine shooting a guy in the back *after* two head shots. Anyway, to answer your question, I don't know of anyone in town mad enough to shoot him. Including—especially—the guy with the 'fairly decent' alibi."

"So why did the Cemetery Association hire you?"

"I tried to talk them out of it," I said, telling myself that was more a fib than a lie. I did try to talk them out of it, but only to maneuver them into meeting my price.

"Not hard enough."

"They're running scared. I even told them you would nail the killer any second."

"I hope not to disappoint you."

"Got a suspect?"

"Yes."

"Does this suspect have a name?"

"Not before I have cuffs on him. What's for lunch?"

"BLT salad. Or the smoked wild Sockeye salmon."

She looked at the menu, again. "I don't see Sockeye."

"It's in my refrigerator."

"No way, Jose."

"Smoked it myself. Applewood. That fell off Scooter's tree when he wasn't looking."

"Sorry."

"Can't hurt to ask. So when are you cuffing this suspect?"

"Soon as we find him."

"Funny time to take the afternoon off."

"I'm learning to delegate."

I looked at her closely. Something was definitely off kilter. I was usually the one who asked questions, hoping she would toss me a crumb of a crumb in exchange for a crumb or two. Now she was asking questions. The change did not make either of us comfortable. I said, "Let me make a wild guess."

"About what?"

"Your suspect."

"What about him?"

"You don't like him. You don't think he's the guy."

"You're dreaming, Ben."

"I've never seen you doubtful before. It's a shocker. Like discovering that Superman can't fly."

Her smile got a little tight. Something else I had never seen before. Normally Marian smiled like she meant to or didn't smile at all.

"What's his name?"

"You know I can't tell you that until we go public."

"So why lunch? Other than the pleasure of our company."

"I thought maybe you might have some take on Grose. Different than everyone else's."

"Which is?"

"What we just said. Unpleasant rich outsider with no respect for traditional values."

"People don't get murdered for that."

"I *know.*"

"Happen to interview my cousin Sherman?"

"Why do you ask?"

"I can't find him. I was wondering if maybe you were looking to interview him and he got scared."

"He has no reason to be. Arnie talked to him Sunday."

"No reason? You're telling me Arnie didn't bring up his parole?"

"I am not going to discuss interview ethics with you, Ben. But I will tell you that your cousin Sherman has never struck me as a killer…Even though prisons are full of people who didn't usually do what they were convicted for doing," she added with a smile that said that she was a pro who regarded me as a vaguely-amusing amateur.

"Who do you like better than your suspect? Sherman or Donny?"

She shook her head.

"How soon before an arrest?"

"I don't know, Ben. He's hiding and he's good at it."

I sat up straight. "A bad guy? A genuine bad guy?" Instead of three "gossiple" husbands who were friends of mine, or a thief who was a cousin, or a grave digger whom I had always liked.

"As opposed to what?"

"A pissed-off, disgruntled whatever. You say he's good at it, like he's some kind of a pro. Doesn't that make the shooting a professional job?"

"No. I don't mean it was a hit."

I said, "When the Navy trained me for ONI, no one passed Assassination 101 before he mastered double head shots."

She said, "I don't want to talk about this anymore.

I said, "And since nobody heard a shot, maybe a silencer?"

She said, "This was a bad idea."

"Did he leave any prints or was he too slick?"

"I'm outta here." She started to stand.

I said, "Back to the menu....And I'm sticking with the BLT salad. Though the mushroom omelet is excellent."

"Thank you, Ben." She settled down, reached across the table and clasped my hand.

I said, "That feels wonderful," which it did—an electric tingle like champagne bubbles on the tongue—wonderful enough to seriously consider slinging her over my shoulder and carrying her upstairs to the Yankee Drover's famously romantic B&B room, the Organza Suite, in hopes of getting her clothes off before she located a pistol. But even though I thought I saw a look in her eye that said she wouldn't hunt too hard, and even though it seemed reasonable to wonder if she too was considering a second chance for us, I had to say, "Wonderful, but...."

"But, what?"

"But I'm afraid we have company."

Out the window we could see her wiry, little partner Arnie Bender alight from an unmarked State Police Crown Victoria. Behind it was a "company car," a dinky Ford Focus with government plates and two suits inside who looked like some kind of low-rent Feds. Immigration, I guessed, or DEA bureaucrats. Across the street Oliver Moody sat in his cruiser, expressionless as a coyote counting house cats.

"Oh shit," said Marian. "Ben, I gotta go. I'm really sorry."

I watched from the window as she hurried down the Drover's front walk and shook hands all around. Then everybody piled into the cars and drove off quickly, while I wondered what in hell was going on.

I was halfway through my BLT salad when Dan Adams rose from the bankers' and lawyers' table and walked across the restaurant to mine. At the meeting at Grace's house Dan had been strongly in favor of hiring me. I motioned to Marian's chair and invited him to sit.

"Your date left early." He looked nervous and his nervousness made him more than usually combative. In high school basketball, Dan had always been the kid that the Newbury Colonials could count on to foul out.

"That was no date, that was a peace officer."

"Really? With a behind like that?"

"And a very good friend. How are you doing, Dan?"

"Is she really a cop?"

"She is a State Police detective lieutenant, a walking arsenal, and possesses a mind quicker than anything you can buy from Dell. How are you doing, Dan?"

"Shouldn't the guy paying you be asking how you are doing?"

"Oh I'm doing very well, thank you for asking."

"Come on Ben."

"I predict, as I have been predicting all along, that the cops will announce a suspect soon. Either a name we all know. Or a stranger in town."

Dan did not react to that, saying only, "I thought we were paying you to get him first?"

"Tell me something, Dan?"

"What?"

"Is there something you guys aren't telling me?"

"No!"

"But you and Rick Bowland do seem obsessed."

"We already told you we're just afraid that they'll fool the judge into thinking that we are incompetent cronies who will destroy the association if the insurgents aren't restored to power."

I almost repeated Henry Kissinger's nasty take on academia: 'The infighting was so vicious because the stakes were so small'. But Dan looked so unhappy that I could not quote such meanness. Particularly when he said loudly enough for the whole dining room to hear, "I mean I've got family in that ground, Ben. *You've* got family in there, too."

"Rick doesn't," I advocated for the Devil.

Dan climbed very high on his horse. "The insurgents are pushing the kind of change that would change the cemetery forever. Rick Bowland is the kind of newcomer who works hard to keep this town the way it should be, not change it."

I said. "I would believe that sentiment more from a banker who had *not* jumped from Newbury Savings to the new national outfit that hands out mortgages for over-size McMansions to every bozo who pulls into town with zero down in his pocket and interest-only for the first two years."

Dan's face got red. "Goddammit, Ben, it's not my fault the town is changing. And you know that damned well."

"But that is not what is really troubling me."

"What's troubling you?"

"I've got friends jerking me around and I don't like that."

"What?"

"Since Brian got killed I've got friends lying to me, which I like even less than being jerked around."

Dan looked ready to throw a punch. Anne Marie started toward us, looking concerned about her glassware and crockery. I said, "Here comes Anne Marie. Maybe you and I should step outside?"

"I won't get in a fight where I pull my punches."

"I won't ask you to pull your punches."

"But I will," said Dan. "I'll think what happens if you fall down and crack your skull, or a punch I could have taken ten years ago knocks my brains loose—it's all right, Anne Marie, we're just talking—and end up getting my head handed to me because that's no way to win a fight." He sat down in Marian's chair and looked me in the face. "These changes you don't like aren't my fault, even if I am making a buck out of them. If I didn't, someone else would. But it's different in the burying ground, isn't it? I mean that's a place we should stop change. The town is our children's town—they'll live their lives as soon as we get old. Changes we hate they'll take for granted. But the burying ground belongs to our parents. We owe protection to the people already there."

I had to smile. "We'll make our last stand in the graveyard?"

"And hope our children will do the same for us."

I offered my hand and said the only thing I could, "You're a smarter man than I am, Dan."

‹›‹›‹›

Back in my office, I telephoned Sherman. No answer. Only after I had settled back with my feet on my father's desk, did I realize how smart Dan Adams really was. He still hadn't told me what they weren't telling me.

I called him in his office. "Did Brian bank with you?"

"Yes."

"Was he as solvent as he looked?"

Dan hesitated a moment. "You got me in a conflict of interest, here, Ben, not to mention privacy issues."

"The way I see it, Brian's dead. We're alive. We're not leaving an email trail. And unless you switched religions and didn't tell anybody, neither of our phones are likely to be tapped by Homeland Security."

Again Dan hesitated. I heard his computer tell him, "You've got mail."

"Still with me Dan?"

"What?"

"At the rate I'm charging the Cemetery Association, checking your email while talking to me gets expensive."

"Yeah, yeah, I hear you. I can do both."

"The question was: 'Was Brian as solvent as he looked?'"

"Not quite."

That was a fairly common answer to a routine question I had learned the hard way to ask in both my businesses. There was a ton of money around these days. But not everyone had as much as they pretended. So maybe Brian Grose had not retired quite so comfortably as his fancy house implied. In theory he could have been in hock to nasty sorts. Or working some scam to get out of trouble that got him deeper into trouble.

"How much less than he looked?"

"I don't know the whole picture. I don't know where else he maintained accounts."

"But you have a gut feeling about his circumstances, Dan."

"You're asking me to speculate."

"I'm asking you to help me 'get him—meaning the killer—first.'"

Dan said, "Let me put it this way and then I'm hanging up the phone: I don't believe that Brian was ready to retire."

It made we wonder what Brian had been working at to stay afloat or build for the future. But it still wasn't what Dan and Rick weren't telling me.

Chapter Four

According to a lady I occasionally spoke to who worked in Superior Court over in Plainfield, the county seat, Brian Grose's murder wasn't a hit. At least not in the sense of a professional murderer for hire. The troopers were telling the Connecticut State's Attorney it was personal. As in three gossiply-cuckolded trustees or a hot-tempered gravedigger.

"A love thing?" I asked

"Pissed off employee thing."

We were drinking coffee in a quiet booth in the Courthouse Diner, before the lunch rush started. I said, "I wasn't aware Grose had employees."

"Do you mow your own lawn?"

"As a matter of fact I do. My lawn, and sometimes the lawns of deceased owners whose houses I'm trying to sell for far-away heirs."

"Yeah, well you're in the minority."

"I've been accused of that before."

"I'm not accusing, I'm just saying."

"Understood." I kept forgetting that the lady who worked in Superior Court had no sense of humor. Every word and every fact carried the same weight, and whatever witticisms I managed to toss out dribbled down her metaphoric front like Halloween eggs lobbed at plate glass.

"My lawn isn't that big—my house is right in town. Besides, the perennial borders hi-jack grass every time I turn my back.

"Hi-jackers?"

"So are you saying his lawn guy did it?" In which case my vague suspects were off the hook again.

"I'm not saying. They're saying."

She was a skinny, leggy little thing, quite lovely in her own way, a way that included hiding her hair under a scarf most of the time and made the occasions she took the scarf off a pleasant surprise of honey-toned curls laced with silver. I had met her while filling out paperwork to interview a client on the wrong side of the bars, and we would have coffee now and then. I sometimes wondered why she was so generous with her inside information except I think she got a little kick out of having a secret. She was married. Whenever I planned to see her, I updated my vows not to get involved with other men's wives and the one time it might have gone that way—we were drinking wine instead of coffee—I said to her, "These things usually end in tears," and she looked relieved.

"'They' being the major crime squad?"

"Sort of."

"Sort of?" She was not a "sort of" person.

"Homeland Security wants him, too."

Why would Homeland Security want a "lawn guy?" Simple—ever since someone had gotten the bright idea to fold the Immigration and Naturalization Service—which was supposed to keep out impecunious migrants—into the Homeland Security Department, which was supposed to protect us from murderous Muslims.

Few Yankees still made a living mowing grass in our patch of Connecticut. Those who did employed immigrant help, because teenagers and college students were getting fatter and lazier every day. A recent phenomena had the first of the immigrant owned lawn services cropping up, with a Ecuadorian or Guatemalan or Mexican name proud on the pickup truck door. But not many. All of which suggested that the low-rent Feds I'd seen with Detective Marian were Immigration agents.

"What's the lawn guy's name?"

"Charlie something. I can't pronounce it. Here, I wrote it down." She handed me a paper napkin which spelled out "Cubrero."

I couldn't have pronounced it either, except I knew the guy. Sort of.

I drove a subcompact Toyota Yaris, Pink's latest entry in my find-new-wheels contest, back across the county to Newbury. Didn't love the name and thought the color would look better on a polo shirt, but it was a cute little thing if you liked cute little things in automobiles, which I did not. Pink didn't either, but he was having fun jerking my chain since I had expressed an interest in sensible gas mileage.

I drove up and down some long driveways looking for the assistant chief of Newbury Volunteer Hook and Ladder Number One—Jay Meadows, proprietor of Meadows Landscaping—and finally found him on the Cruson place, mowing Dr. Dan's croquet court. Jay shut down the machine and pulled foam plugs from his ears.

I said, "Hello, Boss."

He's the first boss I've had in years, but I had joined Hook and Ladder Number One, and Jay knew a lot more about fire fighting than I, the new volunteer. Although, in fact, so far I'd attended a lot more car wrecks than fires.

"What's happening?"

"I'm looking for Charlie. I thought he'd be with you."

"Quit. Some rich guy up on Morris Mountain is paying him the same as me and guaranteeing forty hours a week winter and summer."

So I drove out to the Morristown district and nearly to the top of Morris Mountain where a failed dairy farm was being transformed by a Seventh Avenue garmento who had sold his handbag company to a frozen food conglomerate. Up until then, the garmento's idea of "the country" had been the northern half of Central Park, so he had not been deterred from plowing his profits into stony ground that had bankrupted the last four generations of farmers who had tried to eke a living out of the place. Too ignorant to believe in failure, and too rich to fear it, Fred Kantor and his wife Joyce were already winning prizes for their artisan cheese, organically-raised knitting wool, and grass-fed beef.

On this summer day, the results looked magnificent: reddish-gold hayfields rippling in the breeze, emerald pastures, pristine white fences, happy horses, contented cows, decorative sheep and cheerful goats. They had painted the old barns barn red and moved a bunch more barns and outbuildings Fred had purchased around New England onto the property and painted them barn red, too. They had added a kitchen and dining room to one side of the old farmhouse and guest suites to the other, each bigger than the original, which huddled between them like a small bird with big wings.

I had sold them the land and they greeted me, as always, with huge smiles, that got wider when I repeated the phrase I always did: "Money well spent." I loved them for it. Not only was it beautiful, but they had saved a hundred acres from development.

"Guess what Fred bought," said Joyce.

"A general store."

"How did you know?"

"I'm in real estate."

Truth be told, I knew by sheer coincidence. An email from a friend in Montana mentioned that a local general store had been bought lock, stock, and barrel by somebody in Newbury, Connecticut. With Scupper McKay busy dodging the Feds, the only other likely candidate had to be Fred Kantor who had been collecting so many old buildings there were rumors he was starting a folk art museum. But today I was more interested in a white clapboard dormitory he had built for his immigrant farmhands. Competition for reliable manual labor was getting fierce and Fred had triumphed over the lawn mowing guys like Meadows by hiring year round with two weeks paid vacation.

I asked, "Have you seen Charlie Cubrero?"

Fred and Joyce's smiles dimmed and their sun-leathered faces wrinkled up like 3D topo maps.

"You're not the first to ask."

"Immigration?"

"Trooper Moody was just here looking for him."

"Ollie? Did he say why?"

"No, but he reminded me—threatened me—that quote, 'Harboring a fugitive is a crime.' The guy's a real charmer. I called our attorney right away."

Resident State Trooper Moody ruled his vast domain by terrorizing the terrible, brutalizing bullies, whacking wife beaters, reining in the rambunctious, detaining drunks, and luring the law-abiding into his radar traps. The second son of a dairy farmer, and a former U.S. Army MP, Ollie knew how to defer to the grandees of the old social order without losing an ounce of his authority, but he got a little confused by the recently-very-rich like Fred and Joyce who reached for lawyers like shotguns.

"Our attorney is writing Trooper Moody a letter."

"On the assumption," Joyce interrupted, "that Trooper Moody can read."

"What about Charlie? Have you seen him?"

"Not since Thursday. He disappeared. All of a sudden. Took one of the boys with him and split."

"I heard he wasn't like that."

"You're telling me? He was the best man on the place."

"Jay Meadows swore by him. Before you hired him away."

"Yeah, well, Jay couldn't pay him in the winter. I offered a better deal than washing dishes for six bucks an hour."

I refrained from explaining that grass didn't grow in the winter and that the ground was frozen too hard for a landscaping guy to dig holes for plants. Fred had been farming in Newbury long enough to know that.

He said, "Obviously an immigration problem."

"Ollie doesn't have time for immigration."

"Yeah, but the immigration people were here yesterday."

"Really?"

"Trooper Moody was following up—we've got a screwed up scene, Ben. The only people who want to work on the place are criminals? Come on. To treat a guy like Charlie like a criminal is—well—criminal."

"And Trooper Moody didn't mention any other problem? Any other reason he was looking for him?"

Fred Kantor gave me a look that reminded me that he had not gotten rich by accident. "Jay Meadows wasn't the only person Charlie worked for before me."

"He mowed Brian Grose's lawn, I was told."

"Well until they arrest somebody for shooting Brian Grose the cops are going to talk to everyone who knew him. Right?"

Right, of course. Except that one day last fall Jay Meadows brought Charlie and a tractor out to my mother's place in Frenchtown to help me pull some stumps. I had never seen anyone handle a machine better than Charlie, not even my Chevalley cousins who could drive backhoes before they could walk. I had also seen few people work as hard. And fewer still were as sweet-natured and gentle as the twenty-one-year-old kid from Ecuador who carried Spanish-English phrases on a sheet of paper in his back pocket and smiled like I had given him the stars and the moon when I slipped him an extra twenty at the end of the day.

Driving back to Main Street, I resolved to persuade my lawyer friends and acquaintances to take his case pro bono when the cops caught him.

Chapter Five

But they didn't catch him.

Next day—Wednesday, three days after Brian was shot—they went public.

Immigration and Customs Enforcement (ICE) of Homeland Security and the Connecticut State Police held a joint news conference in Hartford, the state capital. Their purpose was two-fold: to show that Federal and State authorities were cooperating to capture the worse kind of dangerous fugitive alien; and to ask the public for help tracking down Charlie Cubrero, an illegal immigrant they wanted to interrogate about the murder of Newbury resident Brian Grose.

The re-capped press conference led the Hartford TV station's evening news.

The ICE spokesman explained that the ICE "fugitive team," was one of seventy established around the country to hunt an estimated half-million fugitive aliens who had been deported but hadn't actually left America, or had snuck back. As three hundred officers clearly couldn't catch all half-million, they were "concentrating on getting the more dangerous people off the street."

How dangerous was Charlie Cubrero? Very. According to Homeland Security, Charlie was leader of a slum gang in Quito, the capital of Ecuador; such gangs were establishing themselves in the United States. According to the Connecticut State Police, Charlie had argued with Brian Grose over money, bought a gun, and was thought to be hiding in the Hispanic communities of either Waterbury, Danbury, Hartford, or Bridgeport—cities scattered widely around the central and southern parts of the state. The TV station showed file footage of a neighborhood of two story houses in either Waterbury, Danbury, Hartford, or Bridgeport with small, swarthy people on the sidewalk and low-riding automobiles with black-tinted windows, dual exhausts, spoilers and xenon headlights in the street.

It was a pretty good press conference. The troopers and Homeland Security did seem to be co-operating. Charlie Cubrero sounded like the fugitive alien from Hell.

I switched channels to a New York station and it got even better. Newbury got its own version of vid-scrutiny. File footage borrowed from the cable company's public access station (their loyal viewership of six allowed the cable folks to retain their monopoly) showed a Main Street sweep of colonial houses, Federal mansions, Second Empire extravaganzas, clapboard churches, the Yankee Drover, our red general store, our sturdy white bank, and our famously tall flagpole.

They even showed my Georgian colonial, a tidy medley of white clapboard and black shutters, and the camera lingered— God bless a certain lady who volunteered at the station—on my Benjamin Abbott Realty sign, which was sure to draw some business from the city. But my favorite part of the press conference was the way they kept cutting to close-ups of Marian Boyce, who was standing shoulder to shoulder with the feds and troopers in the back row. The comely detective-lieutenant revealed none of her doubts, of course, but the fact that she was as stone-faced as her law enforcement colleagues did nothing to discourage the camera man or the news director back at the TV station; professionals who recognized telegenic cheekbones, which boded well for the political career Marian was aiming for in the future.

I kept waiting for some reporter to ask, "Why did a Quito slum gang leader fugitive stealthily establishing his slum gang in the small town of Newbury draw attention to himself by shooting a rich American who had stiffed him for fifty bucks?"

No one asked.

Or, "Why would a Quito slum gang leader stealthily establish his slum gang in the Newbury in the first place since small towns are impossible places to do anything stealthily?"

No one asked.

"I have a third question," I yelled at my TV which was usually shut up in a cabinet in the library in the oldest part of the house. "If he did murder Brian Grose for stiffing him for fifty bucks, why did he set the surround-sound timer to turn the music on full blast?"

No one answered.

I telephoned Sherman Chevalley, again. He didn't answer, either. As I hung up the phone rang in my hand. It was Rick Bowland. "I just saw the news."

"Me too."

"There's something you should know."

"I'll get a pencil…All right I have a pencil."

"This Charlie Cubrero?"

"Yes."

"Well he, uh, shall we say, worked for us, a little."

"What us?"

"The Cemetery Association."

So much for Dan Adams vehement "No!"

"Off the books?"

"Well…"

"How dumb could you be?" I asked. "You hired an illegal and paid him cash?"

"Everybody does it."

"It's not like a homeowner slipping him a couple twenties to split firewood. You're an institution. You're an organization—"

"I know. It was stupid."

"I can't believe Grace Botsford allowed it."

"I never told her. I just paid him myself. If I asked to be re-imbursed, she would have gone ballistic. Like you are."

In other words he had known it was stupid from the get go. "Why'd you hire him anyhow? Doesn't Donny Butler do everything?"

"Remember when Donny got arrested?"

"Yes."

"When Grose pressed charges for blasting his Audi?"

"And punching him in the eye."

"That made it assault and it took Tim two weeks to get him out because there was some history of similar—"

"Twenty years ago!"

"Anyway, the grass was going crazy—the place looked like hell—and I had already had Charlie digging out my pond for me, so I—"

"Who else knows?"

"It's those insurgents I'm worried about. If they get wind they'll take it to the judge, and even though it was just me, the entire association will look...."

I waited, but he couldn't finish, so I did it for him. "Stupid?"

"Like incompetent cronies who will destroy the Association if the injunction is not lifted."

If I were the sighing type, I would have sighed. "What do you want me to do?"

"What we hired you to do. Find out who really murdered Brian Grose."

"The judge that issued the temporary injunction against more mausoleums doesn't care who killed Brian Grose."

"If our guy—you—solves the case, the cemetery comes out smelling like a rose."

"What if Charlie is the killer?"

"Charlie Cubrero wouldn't hurt a fly."

I hooked my legs over the arm of a short, cracked-leather sofa crammed into the library, ordered my thoughts a little better, thought of former acquaintances still locked up in Leavenworth (one hoped), and said, "Mothers routinely make such claims about the accused. Just the other day I heard one say, 'He can't be all bad because animals and kids love him.' What's your connection, Rick?"

"What?"

"There is something about Charlie that you are not telling me."

Rick was silent.

I said, "You're too smart, and certainly too cautious, to hire an illegal for the Cemetery Association even with Donny Butler in the hoosegow and the grass getting messy."

I waited awhile.

Rick said nothing.

Finally, I said, "I'm walking over to the Drover to sit downstairs at a private corner table and have a private glass of wine."

Anne Marie hadn't even taken my order when Rick hurried in, glowering suspiciously at the bar crowd as if they were only pretending to watch the Red Sox get pounded so that they could spy on a trustee of the Newbury Cemetery Association. He sidled across the room and took the chair I would ordinarily hope a date would take to make it easier to hold hands or whatever under the table.

Anne Marie came and went and returned with red wine for Rick and Rose' for me.

"What's with you and Charlie?" I asked.

Rick drank deep. "Georgia," he said, referring to his wife, "is…"

I waited a full minute and finally, again, finished it for him. "…a handful."

Rick flashed me a grateful smile. "Some people just find it very hard to just get through the day. Nothing is simple. Nothing is easy. Nothing has value if it isn't a struggle. Very little ever gets done."

Now he looked me straight in the eye. As is common, the first person he met in Newbury was his Realtor. So I had known him and Georgia since they came house hunting.

"But when very little gets done, it all gets even harder because there's no sense of purpose to bounce off of. Most of us take purpose for granted. I drive down to the office every day. I do well, or I don't. I do better every day, or I don't. I do my work, I fend off the corporate BS, I destroy my enemies, I drive home.

I may be tired. I may be frustrated. But I've done a day's work. Georgia never has that. Her old man gave her everything. Left her plenty—you know, we live a lot better than we would on just my salary—not that I'm doing badly. But the one thing he didn't leave Georgia was a purpose—you know Ben, not just a purpose, but a *belief* in purpose. I mean I very rarely question when I get up in the morning why am I going to work. I'm going to work because that's what I do. I mean, hell, at the end of the day it's fun. And if it's not fun, it's more fun that not doing anything. I'm sure you do the same."

He looked to me for agreement, and I nodded heartily. Juggling two careers, I was having twice the fun and glad of it.

But I wondered where Rick was going with this. We had never spoken so intimately. And yet, he wasn't telling me much I didn't suspect. Georgia drifted from brief interest to brief interest. She was charming and stylish, but brittle in the sense that no one would be totally surprised to discover her on Main Street in her bathrobe directing traffic with a bourbon bottle.

Rick took another slug of wine and looked away. His eyes were glistening.

"Charlie?" I asked.

"He was working at my place. Spring cleanup on a Sunday. His day off from Jay. I had to run down to New Milford to the Depot. When I got back, he comes running out of my house yelling, 'Mr. Mr. Come quick.'

"Georgia's lying on the kitchen floor throwing up."

Rick sat there shaking his head.

"It took a while to figure out what was happening. There about a hundred pills on the floor, floating in puked up wine. I don't think she really tried to kill herself. I think she was pretty high, forgot she had already taken some pills, took some more, forgot, took some more. All pretty quick. Then she must have gotten scared and staggered to the door with the wine bottle in one hand and the pill bottle in the other looking for help. Forgetting I was gone. Well Charlie took one look—got the whole scene—and acted so quickly he saved her life."

"How?"

Rick laughed. "I don't know where he got the smarts. Or the guts. But when Georgia pieced it back together and figured out the sequence of events, she told me that Charlie rammed his fingers down her throat and made her vomit up the pills.…

"Think of this twenty-one-year-old kid, with almost no English, no white folk friends except Jay Meadows who wasn't there, a rich white lady in a big house turning blue in front of his eyes. Instead of running for help, or running for his life, he thinks fast and violates her space, as it were. I mean would you stick your hand down some woman's throat? I sure as hell wouldn't even think of it. Point I'm trying to make, Ben, is that everything else aside—fast-thinking, decisive, brave—Charlie Cubrero was *compassionate*. He saw a human being in trouble and he helped. He is not a man to shoot that asshole Brian in the back. Much less drill two holes in his head."

"Didn't Immigration and the troopers say he's a gang leader?"

"Bull. He's no more a gang leader than I am. Besides, where's the gang? How come he was living in Newbury and working all winter for six bucks an hour? How come he took the job with Fred Kantor?"

"Steady work."

"Why would a gang leader take steady work, Ben?"

I did wonder. But while "compassionate" was not a word I associated with the gang leaders whose acquaintance I had made, "fast-thinking" was. So was "decisive." They had to be. The gang world—prison or slum or criminal enterprise—is not big on bureaucracy, so the slow-witted have no place to hide.

"So what he did for Georgia is why you hired Charlie to fill in for Donny Butler?"

"I tried to thank him with money. He wouldn't take it. When the cemetery job came along, I thought I could do him a favor."

"How's Georgia doing?"

Rick brightened. "A little better, actually. It was a kind of a wake up call. Like discovering that she is not indestructible. That acts have consequences."

"She looked great at the Notables."

"She's like a child, Ben. But maybe she's growing up."

I said, "Good luck," instead of "maybe."

"So you'll keep trying to find out what the hell really happened?"

I said, "I thought I would lean on Tim or even Ira to represent Charlie pro bono when they catch him. Could you contribute to expenses?"

"Of course—but privately. I can't get the association involved."

"You know it will come out, somehow, that he worked for the cemetery."

"That's why I'm hoping you'll find out who really killed that son of a bitch before they catch poor Charlie."

"Rick, they have two powers I don't—manpower and the power of arrest."

He went home to Georgia.

I didn't feel like going home to an empty house—by this hour the cat would be out hunting for things to kill or mate with—so I ordered another glass of wine and stepped outside to phone Sherman Chevalley getting, again, no answer. Back at my table I took out my note pad and made a list of plans for tomorrow, starting with the people I could call in New York to turn me on to a Spanish-speaking investigator.

"Hey!"

I looked up into the angular face of Lorraine Renner, noticed that the hair she had collected into a bun to keep out of the camera while video-ing Scooter's graveyard pirate act, was long and loose, and said, "Hi, how've you been?"

Though Newbury was small, and we had been born when it was smaller, we knew *of* each other more than we *knew* each other. We had older fathers in common—hers and mine had swung the occasional joint real estate deal and had served side by side on the Board of Selectman. One time when I was home for Thanksgiving we had talked at some family and friends gathering about the pleasures of leaving home to go to college. But she was eight years younger than I, which meant that when

I was in high school she was a little kid in elementary school, and by the time she graduated from high school I was a lieutenant in Naval Intelligence. When she was in college I was on Wall Street, and when she went to film school in Los Angeles I was in enrolled in Leavenworth. Still, it couldn't have slipped either of our minds entirely that we represented a very small set of Newbury citizens: youngish, single, never married and child free. And in fact, as she stood there smiling in dark jeans and a white blouse, it occurred to me that features I had thought a trifle austere formed interesting planes. And the long hair that framed them looked more reddish brown than brunette in the soft light of the Yankee Drover's cellar bar.

"Would you like a glass of wine?"

She held one up half full. "I'm okay, thanks."

She folded into the chair opposite and looked me over the way you might look at a bush that had been in your yard for years and discovered one day it was covered in berries. But curiosity was cloaked in wariness. Newbury was way too small a town to dodge each other if curiosity worked out badly.

I said, "I saw you taping Scooter at the Notables. "

"He wanted a fifteen minute DVD."

"Fifteen minutes of 'Yo ho ho?'"

"I added some of the others for context."

"Did you shoot my cousin Sherman?"

"Shot, digitized, edited, and entered in the New Haven Shorts Festival."

"That was fast."

"Popped some speed. Stayed up all night. Poor Scooter thought I was going to enter him, but documentary judges go for the gnarly types....I heard you're investigating Brian Grose."

"You did? Where?"

"Around."

Ten trustees of the Cemetery Association. One had to be a blabber mouth. "Well, I'm not exactly investigating Brian."

"Being dead and all."

"Right."

"But you are investigating who killed him?"

"Why do you ask, Lorraine?"

"I worked for him."

"Really? Doing what?"

"I was his videographer."

"Video-graphing what?"

"His death video."

"I beg your pardon."

She had a fun grin. "Don't you know what a death video is?"

"You've never struck me as the type of woman to make a snuff flick."

"Not a *snuff flick!* It's like a bio. Like you have at your retirement party? Except they show it at your funeral."

"Why was he planning his funeral?"

"That was my first question. Why did he want a death film at age forty-whatever? He said it went with the mausoleum. It was like, now I have my mausoleum, I might as well get the rest of the stuff out of the way and done so it's ready when I pop off."

"Was he sick?"

"He wasn't psycho. He was just trying to get the job done."

"I meant was he ill?"

"I don't think so. He looked fine."

I took a sip of wine and watched her face, wondering how close she had been with him. I couldn't say she was grieving. And Connie had said that the rumors about her and Brian were "claptrap."

"Can I ask you something?"

"Sure."

"Do you think Brian had a feeling he was in danger?"

"Like a premonition?"

"Or actual knowledge that someone was after him. Wanted to kill him?"

Lorraine shrugged bonily, all shoulder blades and clavicle. "I don't know. I don't think so. But I don't know. I mean he never said anything to me."

"Would he have?"

"What do you mean?"

"Were you close?"

She shrugged again. "I guess when you're making a movie about somebody's life maybe they tell you stuff they don't tell other people."

"Did he tell you anything?"

"Like what?"

"Like what he wouldn't tell other people."

She hesitated. "Not really."

"How did he happen to hire you? Saw your wedding ad in the *Clarion* and figured, what the heck, weddings, funerals, same thing?"

"No. I got the job from the mausoleum company. The film was part of the package—tomb, film, funeral services, etc."

"The mausoleum builders sell a package? Including embalming?"

"One stop shopping. They'll even hire mourners. Anyway, the mausoleum company Googled for a videographer in the area and Google sent them to my website. They tried to knock my price down, but I checked out *their* website, saw that Brian probably paid them six-hundred thousand dollars so they could afford my measly ten."

"Did you finish it?"

"I'm still editing the rough cut. The company says they'll put the DVD in the mausoleum."

"Did Brian see any of it?"

"Are you kidding? He was all over me like a cheap suit. He would have vetted every frame if I let him."

"Could you show it to me, sometime?"

"Sure. Why not?"

"When would it be convenient?"

She swigged her glass empty. "Now?"

We walked. Another thing we had in common was I lived in what had been my parents' house and Lorraine had moved into hers' when they retired to Lake Champlain. It was set back a few steps off Main Street and was probably the oldest in town, a 1710 colonial with a massive center chimney, a beehive oven in the kitchen and, like mine, home to numerous deferred maintenance projects like woodwork to be painted and floors replaced.

Eighty years older than my Georgian, it had fewer straight walls, bigger fireplaces, and smaller windows. Unlike my parents—my father having died, my mother having fled—her parents had taken most of their furniture with them. Some of the rooms appeared empty, or nearly so, and the living room was decorated in a style I'd have to call, "Moved from dorm rooms via condo apartments." Since she was tooling around town in a brand new Saab convertible, I guessed that the sparseness was due more to a shortage of time than money. What surprised me was her television set, the only object in the dining room. "Your TV's even older than mine."

"After staring at a screen all day I'd rather read a book or drink wine. Would you like some red?"

"Love some."

She poured from a dark jug into sturdy glasses and led me into the birthing room which she had converted into her editing studio. In that small back room near the kitchen, she had three computers with serious monitors on plywood work tables, banks of multi-gigabyte storage on the floor under the tables, and several hundred miles of wire connecting them all. She indicated a stool to sit on and began turning on machines. A zillion green and blue lights began blinking like a runway glide path on a dark night. A pair of square windows appeared side by side on the center monitor. Under them a wide window indicated a multi-layered time line. Lorraine caressed a roller-ball mouse, and Brian Grose *jumped* out of the right hand window.

"He wanted it to begin like this. It's so corny, but he wanted it and it's kind of like he was. Running around all the time, always in motion. I'll shut up, now….Oh, just so you know, there's no music. He didn't want music until the end. Said it would distract from the message…."

Brian walked quickly up his lawn in close up.

"He insisted on this shot. Paid two thousand extra for a steadicam. What the client wants—I'll shut up now...."

Now the camera pulled back, and we saw him open the ghastly front door of his stucco mansion. The next shot picked him up inside. He was striding along a row of French doors, looking out at his lawn and the Forestry Association trees he had not been allowed to cut down.

"Does he ever speak?"

"Not yet. He said he wanted to create a visual impression of what it was like to be alive at his age at this time."

"Do all your clients do their own direction?"

"Most. But I don't listen and they don't notice."

"Why'd you make an exception for Brian?"

"Shhh. Watch the film. Talk later."

I shut up and watched a fit, handsome guy in his forties rush around his house showing off the many rooms from kitchen to billiard rooms, to basement swimming pool, to screening room, to dining room, to den, to drawing room, to living room, to many bedrooms reached by multiple staircases.

I said, "Whoever gets the listing to sell Brian's house should pay you for a copy of this."

"Excellent idea."

He was smiling happily. He had brown hair and no hint of balding. And he had a face that looked warmer than the full-of-himself hotshot I remembered. "The camera loves him," murmured Lorraine. "He didn't look half that great in the flesh."

"Could have been a movie star."

"Not that jerky way he moves. Handsome, but too jumpy."

I found myself wondering two things. Why was he alone in that huge house? And why had such a high-energy guy retired? Three things. Why would he stiff a immigrant lawn guy out of fifty bucks? Speaking of whom...I leaned closer to the monitor; deep in the background three little guys were carrying tools and trundling a wheelbarrow across the lawn.

"Is that Charlie Cubrero?"

"The guy they think shot Brian?"

"Is that Charlie pushing the wheelbarrow?"

Lorraine shrugged bonily. "All I know is I had to cut this scene short because the wheelbarrow guy turned around and ran away like we were chasing him."

"Did Brian call him Charlie?"

"He just called them 'the Ecuadorians.' Like they were a unit. Watch the film, talk later."

The camera had moved elsewhere. A title superimposed said, "Ed Kelman: Brian's California Business Partner." A prosperous-looking tanned middle-aged gent in a book-lined law office was saying, "I had the pleasure of working with Brian on a some very big projects; and I have to tell you, he was *the* 'go-to guy.' What Brian Grose said, it was as good as done. There are so many phonies in the development business, but this guy was the real deal."

The next scene was shot inside the raw lumber colonnade of a new house being framed. I could hear staple guns in the background. The title said, "Horace Pinchot: Architect." Mr. Pinchot was clutching a roll of blue prints and he said, "I designed Brian's house in Newbury, Connecticut. Actually, by the time he got done showing me what he wanted, Brian designed the house and I just made sure we left enough bearing walls in place to prevent it falling down."

"Wait a minute. You started shooting this when he was still building the house? He had already bought the mausoleum?"

"No. That's not this house.

"But it seems to be."

"Artistic license. Stop talking."

The next scene showed his New York lawyer at the helm of a sailboat, smiling that when Brian structured a deal all he had to do was dot the 'i'-s."

Then we met his squash partner who said with a studiedly rueful laugh, "Brian plays a Rumsfeld game, if you know what I mean. Slow to clear, but not so slow you can call him on it." A bland smile learned young at Choate or a properly-laid dinner table, conveyed clearer than words: "The man cheats."

There were interviews with a chauffeur who drove him to and from New York, and the waiters at a lunch club, and his ski instructor atop a Killington peak. I said, "I'm surprised he didn't ski the Rockies."

"He said he liked ice. The challenge." Ice was plentiful on Northeast slopes. In fact, the surest way to make a seasoned New England skier crash was to cover a slope with actual snow.

A bright-eyed saleswoman at a glass desk addressed the camera: "The Bastian Mausoleum Company serves the rainmakers of our time. We are equipped with compassion, sensitivity, loyalty, intuition, and common sense in order to be successful in obtaining their trust and business." She uncrossed shapely legs and walked outside to a sturdy truck with a sign on the door that read, "Bastian Mausoleums. We Deliver."

I asked, "Did Brian really want a mausoleum advertisement in the middle of his death flick? Or was that part of the deal?"

"He loved being called a rainmaker."

The scene shifted and there was the rainmaker at a garden party. I recognized one of the finest perennial borders in Connecticut, if not the nation, aflame in forty species of day lilies. "I can't believe the Bells allowed you in with a camera— they even sent Martha Stewart packing."

"Babs made me hide in the woods."

"Wait, there I am." I was squiring Connie on a lily tour. "I didn't know you were filming."

"I rented a humongous lens and shot the whole party from the woods," said Lorraine. "Getting eaten by mosquitoes—you look good, there."

The elegant drape of my cotton suit last summer was a grim reminder of the pounds and bulges I had gained in one short year. I said, "I remember being surprised that Babs and Al invited Brian."

"I told Brian to write a huge check to Spay and Neuter."

"Slick move." Babs Bell's efforts to neuter and adopt Connecticut's feral and abandoned cats were legendary. She was currently on my case to de-ball Tom, who had arrived intact from a horse farm, and while I agreed with her in theory that the world had enough cats, I found myself putting it off on the grounds that Tom may one day be lured home by the ladies of the horse farm. But while it might be possible to buy into a (brief) social connection with the Bells, a family that had been doing well since the invention of the telephone, by supporting Babs' passion, I suspected that it was more that the Bells would have done anything to help their friends the Renners' daughter.

Lorraine's camera panned the party, which was set on an emerald lawn in front of white porches and sunrooms. The mostly older crowd were dressed for a summer event, the ladies in white cotton dresses, the gentlemen in the pastel colors that well-off retirees get talked into. The focus closed in on Brian Grose who was gesticulating at a group of men who listened with polite expressions. They looked relieved when Gerard Botsford approached in his trademark seersucker, bow tie and straw hat. Grace Botsford glided into the frame and handed Gerard a tall glass.

"Beautiful, isn't she?" asked Lorraine.

"Grace?" I had never noticed, before. Staid, even matronly, she had always dressed older than her years, and while old-fashioned could have an allure, her old-fashioned seemed more like a barrier than an invitation to admire.

"Do you see how she stands? Do you see how still?"

She did stand tall and straight. And now that Lorraine pointed it out I could see a powerful stillness about her that captured attention. She seemed to dismiss the motion of the video camera and the other people, especially Brian's gesticula-tions, as if they were superfluous.

The scene faded to the green of the Bells' lawn, and suddenly we were on Main Street watching Brian walk briskly up the steps of Town Hall to greet a puzzled-looking Gerard Botsford, who was standing beside a marble column in a business suit. I found myself leaning forward. It was a strange moment, both men in the picture now dead.

They shook hands. Gerard gazed toward the camera, then looked away, hurriedly, as if remembering he had been told not to look at it. But he recovered with aplomb, gazing down at Brian Grose as if he were a new species of wildlife. This went on for a few moments with no sound except for cars passing along Main Street and birds singing. The pillars of Town Hall went fuzzy and re-materialized as the bronze gates that Aunt Connie had contributed to the Village Cemetery back in the '50s.

Brian Grose walked briskly into ground and opened the gate. Just inside was Grace Botsford. A superimposed title filled the screen:

Grace Botsford, Treasurer of the Village Cemetery Association,
and
Newbury's Official Town Historian

Grace greeted Brian with a handshake and said in her dry Yankee tones, "Afternoon, Brian. Ready for your history lesson?"

Grose said he was.

"In the beginning," said Grace, "Newbury's churches were built in the middle of the road."

"In the middle of the road?"

"The proprietors listed in the original charter were entitled to share in the 'common land', and they had no intention of giving up any of it for 'churchyards.' So the selectmen voted to approve the expense to buy some ground for burying the dead, which would be open to all "admitted inhabitants.""

"As opposed to un-admitted inhabitants?" Brian interrupted with a broad smirk for the camera.

Grace was not to be derailed. "As opposed to undesirables," she answered with a singleness of purpose. "Those not welcome to live in the town were not welcome in our burying ground."

They commenced a slow walk through the cemetery, trailed closely by the camera, while Grace gave him a capsule history, illustrated by who was buried beneath each headstone. It was a sort of private version of the "Newbury Notables" tour, just for him.

Describing the McKay Mausoleum, she pointed out the Greek Cross on the roof and displayed an understated sense of humor that went right over Brian's head. "Of course in those days, no

Newburian was Greek, or had ever met a Greek, but the builder had seen a tomb like it for sale at the Chicago World's Fair.

"The word 'cemetery' is a 19th Century euphemism, Brian. The 'resting place.' The old word goes back to the Roman catacombs, of course, but by the 19th Century, people were looking for a new word to imply less death than sleep. Our older forebears said "burying ground." Mortality was brief then, death offered the possibility of eternal salvation. You'll notice that the old headstones are facing east. So when the Christ rose with the sun at dawn He would reach for your hand and pull you erect."

"So if they made a mistake and buried you facing west," Brian said to the camera, "you would end up for all Eternity on your head."

Grace gave that a thin smile and said, "Cotton Mather suggested stopping by the burying ground to contemplate your mortality. We are here are only briefly and our bodies will soon be dust. But attitudes toward death keep changing, as you will see here when you read the inscriptions. Around the middle of the 19th Century people preferred to think that the dead were only sleeping. These days, we regard death as a terrible mistake: if only we had worked harder or smarter we would have prevailed."

"I didn't know Grace was a philosopher."

"Brian wanted me to edit out that last line about the mistake. If he hadn't made the mistake of getting killed I would have had to. Now it stays."

The camera followed them up the slope from the old section to the new area where lay Brian's plot.

"Before McTomb," I said.

"Grace would never have appeared in the film afterwards. I shot all this before they delivered the mausoleum." (It had arrived last March on two flatbed trucks equipped with cranes.)

"Did Grace know it was coming?"

"I don't think so. She was thinking it was something smaller. All I know is when they brought it, and I was shooting them unloading the pieces, Grace got really mad. For a while, she blamed me. Then she realized it wasn't my fault—shhh. It's almost over."

The camera lingered on Brian's grassy plot. And then it shifted to Brian who looked right into as if he was talking to Grace and said, "You look at where you'll be buried and you ask yourself, what is the secret to life? Here in this beautiful cemetery it comes up simple for me. The first thing you must do is stay independent, stay private, be master of your own destiny. Second thing, you have to hire good people. Third thing, you must always strive for perfection. Fourth is you never should be satisfied. Fifth is don't plan too far ahead. Sixth is have a sense of urgency. Seven is work like hell. And eight is be lucky. The secret to life is the secret to success."

"I've heard that somewhere," I said.

"Yeah, I thought I did, too," said Lorraine. "But it's just one of those things that sound so smart and clear you figure you've heard it before. He then went on and on about dealing with success and all, and a whole bit about dealing with adversity, but I cut it to this and it stands out better."

"It seems so familiar."

"Shhh." Now the camera swept the burying ground and then slowly tilted up a big elm and traced the branches to where the tree's crown anchored the sky. Music, at last. Up came Bach, the same Bach that had thundered the afternoon he was killed.

When it was over I asked Lorraine, "Was he a little lonely, maybe?"

"Lonely? I don't think so."

"No family?"

"He decided he didn't want family in it. That's why I had to fill it out with the driver and waiters at that club."

"No girlfriends? Wives? Brothers, sisters, kids? Nobody out in California."

"Just his business partner."

"But not his New York partners?"

"He never mentioned them."

It sounded to me like a deeply lonely life, and I wondered if he had always been that way, or slipped away from people when he retired so young. "What was his thing with death?"

Lorraine answered indirectly. "Before weddings, when I was still trying to make it out on the Coast, I did some 60th birthdays. Rich people who worked twenty-four/seven to make their pile suddenly shift obsessions. Suddenly, with time on their hands, they discover a world beyond the dwarf life they made it in. I did one film about a guy who bought a basketball team. I did another about a guy who got totally wrapped up in solar power. And one who bankrupted himself racing sailboats. Brian seems to have developed a passion for death."

"His own."

"So what do you think of the film?"

"I think you made a lot out of very little."

"I guess that's a compliment?" She looked away, as if afraid to be disappointed.

"I mean, what do you say about a lonely life?…I mean, you can have a 'rich' life—he was obviously a talented man with many interests, but so alone. Living a life where the only people you know work for you?" It felt uncomfortably close to my own situation. Certainly, I had a close circle in Newbury, friends I had known all my life. But at the end of the day they went their way and I went home alone.

"Would you please tell me if you liked it or not?"

"Definitely. I liked all the different settings. Great looking. What do they call it, 'production values?' I can't believe you did all of that for ten thousand dollars."

"It started at ten. It was nearer to sixty when I started editing. He spent a ton on my travel. And the steadicams. The whole cemetery walk was steadicam, too. That took days."

"I liked that. And I loved the stuff you got Grace to say."

"Grace was wonderful. She sat for an audio interview, after, so I could get clean sound for the cemetery scene."

"Any more death films lined up?"

"Could be. The mausoleum company says they're going to recommend me to their clients. What they've seen so far they think is great."

I thanked her for the show and asked her if she would like to come to dinner Friday night. She said she would, and I walked home feeling kind of lucky.

I turned on the eleven o'clock news to see if the fugitive alien from hell needed a lawyer, yet. He did not, and I lay awake awhile wondering what it felt like to be on the lam in a foreign land. Lonely, of course. Scary, too. But what were the odds of getting captured if you looked similar to twelve million penniless immigrants, few cops spoke your language, and citizens never looked you in the face?

Chapter Six

Of the three things that could happen to Charlie Cubrero, two were vaguely likely. The combined forces of the ICE and the Connecticut State Police and local cops might stumble upon him hiding in one of the urban immigrant communities. Or Charlie would light out for some far away community or even all the way home to Ecuador and disappear. (If Marian was right that he was "good at" hiding and ICE was right that Charlie was a gang leader, he might conceivably be snorting coke in a nice hotel in Bogota.) That I would find him first, was so unlikely that I wouldn't even bother.

Except that Marian Boyce thought Charlie might be innocent. Rick Bowland thought he was a hero. The Village Cemetery Association had its venerable tail in a crack. And a supposed gang leader was someone I knew only as a hard-working, polite kid who was about to be treated very badly. So I got on the horn with people I knew in New York.

A friend, a "buddy of mine" in Brooklyn-ese, steered me to a buddy of his, a private investigator who spoke Spanish. He was Puerto Rican, not Ecuadorian, and his accent was more Brooklyn than Caribbean, but he was guaranteed a stand up guy. Nor was he hideously expensive, which was an important consideration as I was not certain where the money was coming from. I gave him a bare bones situation report on the telephone, and when I was done Hector Ramirez confirmed that he was the straight shooter I had been promised by our mutual acquaintance.

"Sorry, Buddy. No way."

"Why not?"

"There is no way I can duke it with Homeland Security for a fugitive from a murder warrant."

"My clients believe the guy is innocent."

"Tell your clients to spend their dough on a lawyer."

I said, "It's possible he's so deep in the community we could find him before ICE."

"Believe me, Buddy. They got Federal funds paying Connecticut troopers and city cops to co-operate with Immigration, and paying ICE to be nice to the yokels. Wait 'til they nail the 'sucker. If they don't blow him away in the process, put your money on a lawyer."

Good advice. But it didn't quite fit the peculiar situation, which, as Ramirez had pointed out, included the grim possibility of what could be called a fatal arrest experience.

Stymied, I took another shot at my best possible witness, telephoned the White Birch biker bar and asked Wide Greg, the proprietor, "Has my cousin Sherman shown up yet?"

"Staggering in as we speak," said Greg, and hung up.

I drove down to the White Birch, in Frenchtown, at the foot of Church Hill. The only motorcycle in the parking lot belonged to Sherman Chevalley. Interestingly, the other vehicle, a rusty pickup truck, was Donny Butler's. (Even if Wide Greg owned a vehicle, no one could recall seeing him anywhere but inside the White Birch.)

It had been some time since Connecticut banned smoking in bars, but so many cigarettes had burned over the years that the stench of tobacco would never disappear. By contrast, last night's spilled beer smelled fresh. Decor consisted of an antique Miller High Life beer sign with spinning lights and a clock that didn't work, tables scattered sufficiently far apart to prevent overhearing conversations that should not be, knotty pine paneled walls blackened by the aforementioned smoke, a remarkable long bar, and very few windows.

It was early, well before noon. At the end of the bar nearest the door, the tall, angular Sherman Chevalley was nodding over his beer, apparently the latest in a long line of nightcaps. He seemed oblivious to his friend Donny Butler, Village Cemetery groundskeeper and gravedigger and puncher of Brian Grose in the eye, who was propping up the other end of the bar and yelling toward him. Wide Greg stood dead center the middle, reading the morning papers' police reports.

Sherman opened his eyes when I approached. They were broad slits of a hard green-grey color that resembled countertops in what my competitors called "gourmet kitchens." Sherman's hadn't been wiped in a awhile.

I said, "I've been looking all over for you. Got a minute?"

Before he could stir himself to answer, Donny shouted down the bar. "Ben! That trooper—that friend of yours?"

"Ollie's no friend of mine."

"You can say that again," Sherman muttered sleepily.

"Not Ollie, for Christ sake!" Donny yelled. "Everybody knows about you and Ollie. Ollie hates your guts, 'cause of the logging chain. The *woman*. The babe with the great ass."

"Well she's not exactly a trooper. She's a detective. And yes, she is a friend of mine, so let's leave her ass out of it."

"Yeah, well she's leaning on me."

"How?"

"Keeps asking questions."

I said, "Sherman, don't leave, I got to talk to Donny a minute," and walked to the Donny end of the bar. The redness of his handsome, weathered face suggested that he had had enough to drink to appreciate simple sentences. "That's her job, Donny. She's a major crime squad detective. Murder is a major crime. Brian Grose was murdered at the cemetery. She's asking everybody questions, including people who work there. You work there."

"I told her to get lost."

"What did you do that for?"

"She was bugging me."

Wide Greg, ever-wary of information he should be able to deny knowledge of under oath, sauntered to the Sherman end of his bar to polish a vodka bottle, and I asked Donny, quietly. "Do you have an alibi that will stick?"

"Not one I'm giving to her."

"Donny, she can make your life awful."

"I didn't shoot that freakin' yuppie!"

"You might have to prove that."

"That's crazy!" Donny bellowed, turning redder and pounding the bar. "I'm not a killer."

I glanced up-bar at Greg, who looked pleased that nothing Donny had shouted could not be repeated happily in court. "You got any coffee?" I asked. Greg poured some black in a mug from the pot he had going for himself. I walked to it, got it, and walked back.

"Donny. You know you're not a killer. I know you're not a killer. But they don't know you're not a killer, and they are looking for a killer—or at least someone they can convince a jury is a killer."

"You don't understand, Ben. I don't take that crap from anybody."

"She was just doing her job."

"Like I was telling Greg. Didn't I tell you Greg? I don't take crap from anybody."

Wide Greg was very good at ignoring such questions.

Donny asked me, "What are they bugging me for? I'll tell you why. I'll tell both you and Greg why."

"What about me?" Sherman called down the bar.

"I'll tell all a ya. They're bugging me 'cause they can't find that goddamned wetback."

I put down my mug. "Donny you keep talking about friends of mine in ways that aren't, shall we say, respectful."

"The wetback is your friend?"

"He worked for Jay. He's a good kid."

"So why doesn't he turn himself in?"

"So why don't you answer Detective Boyce's question?"

"Because I didn't do nothing—Greg! Another beer!"

"I don't think so," said Greg.

"What?" Donny half rose from his stool. "Are you cutting me off?"

"Yes."

I said, "Donny, let me drive you home."

Donny got redder in the face. He started to set his jaw. Then his eyes went a little fuzzy and his cheeks a little slack and he said, "Oh come on, guys."

"Toss me your keys," Greg said conversationally. "I'll get one of the boys to drop your car off later."

Donny stood there a moment, swaying on the rungs of his stool. "Do I owe you anything?"

"You're fine." This was not kindness. The White Birch was pay as you go until Greg extended a dispensation as rare as one papal.

As I walked Donny out I said to Sherman Chevalley, "I got to talk to you. I'll buy you a beer when I get back."

"Buy me one now so I'll stay."

"Greg," I called, "A beer for my cousin, please."

Instead of saying thank you to me, Sherman looked Donny in the face and said, "Pussy."

"What did you say?" asked Donny.

"Pussy. Takin' all that crap."

I got quickly between them and said, "Back off, Sherman."

My cousin, a man of few words, immediately threw a punch, which I slipped while managing to kick his feet out from under him. He landed on his back with a crash that shook the building and laughed. "You see that, Greg? The kid's growing up."

Knowing Sherman too well, I was backing away as fast as I could, though not fast enough. Sherman sprang quick as a cobra, wasting a mere giga-second to pick up a bar stool to swing at my head. But if Sherman was a cobra, Wide Greg was a broad-shoul-dered barrel-chested mongoose. If you were to gather a hundred warring Hells Angels, Pagans, Mongols, and Devils Disciples in a parking lot, the rivals would all agree on one thing: Wide Greg was the fastest biker-bar proprietor on the planet.

His sawed off baseball bat materialized in his hand. Before Sherman could hit me with the stool, he went down for the second time in two breaths, popped hard, but not so hard as to be concussed thanks to Wide Greg's fine-tuned sense of proportion. Flat on his back, holding his head, groaning, his eyes grew large with terror. For how many weeks would Wide Greg bar him from the White Birch? How many long, lonely nights would pass alone with the History Channel?

But Wide Greg did nothing to excess. Order restored, justice dispensed, he slipped his bat back in its scabbard of PVC pipe nailed under the bar, picked up a towel, and resumed polishing.

I walked Donny out to my car.

He looked around blearily. "What is this piece of crap?"

"Rented from Pink. Put on your seat belt."

I got him home and up his front steps, in the door and up the stairs to his bedroom. When I came back down, his mother, a white-haired lady in her seventies with whom he moved in after his last divorce, was in the front parlor wiping her hands on dishtowel. "Oh it's you. Hello Ben. Donny okay?"

"Touch of flu."

She looked at me. "Yes, it's going around this summer."

Mercy Mission accomplished, I went back to the White Birch where I found Sherman yawning over a new beer. "What was all that about?" I asked. "What were you on Donny's case for?"

Sherman shrugged.

"And why'd you take a swing me? Donny's your pal, I'm your cousin. What's going on?"

"Stressed, man."

"Over what?"

"Stress."

"You're stressed out by stress?"

"Big joke. You'd be stressed too."

"Parole officer on your case?"

"Naw. He don't have anything on me....Nothin' that'll stick." He glanced over at Greg polishing and lowered his voice. "Thing is, man, somebody's leaning on me."

"Who?" I asked, wondering who would dare.

"I don't know."

"Well, what do you mean leaning?"

"Tried to kill me."

"What?"

"You heard me."

"Someone's trying to kill you and you have no idea who it is?"

"Nope."

I looked at him. He looked back.

Sherman was a first class liar. His vast arsenal of mendacity had been honed in prison where congenital prowess takes on a professional edge. It made him an excellent judge of character and a keen observer of motive. I did not doubt that someone was trying to kill him. Several of the worlds he inhabited could generate enemies; some, for sure, who regarded death as an appropriate closing argument. But I did doubt that he didn't know who.

"Something from inside?"

"Naw. I didn't have any problems inside."

That I believed. Sherman was just too ornery for fellow prisoners to bully and too anti-social to hook up with a gang.

"So how'd they try to kill you?"

"Hack-sawed the brake cables on the Harley."

"Are you sure?"

"You'd be sure if you lost both brakes doing 90 on Route 7, came round a bend, and found a semi jackknifed across both lanes."

"How come it didn't work?"

"What do mean?"

"You're still living."

"Oh. Yeah, well there's more than one way to skin a cat."

"How'd you stop?"

"Couldn't stop."

"Then what happened?"

"I went under him."

"How?"

"Slid."

I tried to picture Sherman and seven-hundred pounds of motorcycle sliding sideways under a trailer truck like a runner stealing second base. Failing, I asked, "How did you pull out of the slide?"

"Got lucky," said Sherman.

"So you're still a little shaken up."

"I ain't shaken up."

"You just said you were stressed."

"I'm stressed, 'cause I don't know what he's plannin' next."

"Did you tell Ollie?"

"Yeah, right. Tell Ollie."

"Could I see the cables?"

"Already changed them out."

"Where'd you put the broken ones?"

"On the junk pile."

"Let's have a look."

"You don't believe me?" Sherman asked dangerously.

"I want to see for myself."

We said good-bye to Wide Greg and drove to Sherman's junk pile which contained enough parts to build half of many vehicles and machines. It was in and around the sagging barn behind his mother's house trailer. Any Chevalley worth his name had a heap like it, though rarely as deep. Sherman's had been started by his grandfather, who had inherited items from *his* grandfather, so that the green 1975 Jeep pickup front fender visible under a defunct cement mixer represented a mid point in a buried time line that probably originated with a chrome bumper from a '37 De Soto. We found his discarded Harley brake cables tangled in a coil of copper cable that looked suspiciously like a grid element strung between poles to transmit electricity. "Aren't you taking a chance keeping this 'scrap?' What if Connecticut Light and Power comes looking?"

"I gotta sit on it. Copper just took a nosedive. Goddamned commodity speculators, biggest thieves on the planet."

We untangled the Harley cables and had a look in the day-light. There were three lines, two for the front brake calipers, one for the rear. Sherman showed me where they had snapped. If it were only one I would have suggested they just broke from wear. But all three had broken. "See this little nick?" said Sherman. "That's where they cut it—you see here's the cut, here's the break. And look at this scrape. The saw slipped, and he went back and finished here. Right?"

"You really ought to show this to Ollie."

"I'll handle this myself."

I asked how, if he didn't know who was after him. But there was no talking to Sherman when he made his mind up. I was quite sure that he knew exactly who had done it. I asked again who it might be, but he still wouldn't tell me, so all I could say, "If I were you I'd keep my eyes open."

Sherman yawned and pressed large fingers to his temples. "Man, my head hurts." Then he changed the subject. "Wha'd you want to talk about?"

"Remember Sunday you had the gas engine at the Notables?"

"Notables?"

"In the Cemetery."

"Sure. I had the saw, too. Really cool. Did you hear that sucker screaming?"

"Sherman. The guy was killed. Remember? Shot? In the mausoleum?"

"Yeah? What about him?"

"You were there, early. Right. Setting up the engine?"

"And the saw. I figure they shot him when I had the saw running loud. You think?"

"I don't know. Steve Greenan told me he was maybe dead longer than that." Steve was a retired doctor who worked part time as an assistant medical examiner. Aunt Connie having helped him pay for medical school, and he, having attended my mother and father, and delivered me, Doc Greenan was generous with information. "Sherman, did you notice anybody at the mausoleum?"

"I saw the guy who got shot. Freaking yuppie who gave Donny Butler a hard time."

"You saw Brian Grose go inside?"

"Yeah."

"Alone?"

"Yeah."

"What time?"

"I don't know. Right after I got there."

"What time was that?"

"About ten."

"So you're saying Brian Gross went inside around ten in the morning?"

"About."

"Did you see anyone else?"

"Latino dude was hanging out."

"Charlie Cubrero?"

"I don't know one of them from the other."

"Did you tell the cops?"

"I don't talk to cops."

I said, "Sherman, please stop bullshitting me. You're on parole. When the cops questioned you they surely reminded you that you are on parole, and they probably leaned very hard on you to tell them what you saw being there early. What did you tell them? You must have told them something just to get them off your back."

"I told them I saw a Latino dude."

"Did they show you a picture?"

"Yeah."

"Did you recognize the guy in the picture."

"Nope."

"You told them nope, or you didn't recognize the guy?"

"I told them nope I didn't recognize the guy."

"Did you?"

"Did I what?"

"Recognize the guy."

"Nope."

"So it wasn't Charlie."

"I don't know Charlie."

"Works for Jay."

"I never looked at him."

"So you didn't give the police a positive ID?"

"I couldn't have dropped a dime on the guy if I wanted to. I didn't see his face."

"How'd you know he was Latino?"

"Stood like one—little guy, you know how they stand, low to the ground, but kind of loose like they could move real fast if they had to. Strong little bastards, too. You ever seen them lift stone? Those little guys are something else."

"Sherman let me pop a thought on you. Is it possible that whoever you saw hanging around the cemetery wants to knock you off before you tell the cops you saw him?"

"No way, man. No way! I told you, I didn't see him."

"What if he thinks you did?"

"Then he's got his head up his ass. Later, Ben, I gotta get some sleep."

‹›‹›‹›

I drove to Grace Botsford's office to ask her if she could try to talk sense to Donny Butler who had worked for the Cemetery Association since high school.

Inside, the Botsford Insurance Agency office was a wonderful throwback to the days before plastic and Formica. It had paneled walls, heavy rails supported by turned balusters, and etched glass in the wooden doors. Behind the railing was a magnificent quartered-oak and rosewood partners desk that Scupper McKay would have bid his eye teeth for if the antique cops weren't on his trail. Grace sat at it, alone, eying a pair of sleek, black flat-screen monitors as she typed on a keyboard on a low table beside the desk.

Gerard Botsford cast a thin, knowing smile down from a oil portrait of the two of them in business attire standing in front of that same desk. Grace wore the same smile in the painting and on her present face as she stood and extended her hand. Their smiles said, "Life is unpredictable, but you can count on Botsford Insurance. Just don't miss any premiums."

Grace did not seem surprised that Donny Butler would strike a self-destructive posture with the cops.

"Dad always said that two circumstances shaped the Yankee character. Donny is an example inscribed in stone: fixedness and resistance. Fixedness because for three-hundred-and-forty years after the boat landed at Plymouth Rock, most New Englanders moved West. Those whom the pioneers left behind represent three and a half centuries of inertia."

"I don't know about that, Grace. I mean I'm still here. You're still here. We're not inert."

"No, you're wrong about that," she said with the same purposeful single-mindedness that she had dismissed Brian's lame jokes in Lorraine's video. It was not that she was humorless, but utterly absorbed and completely confident in her opinion. "We went off to college. We saw the larger world. We chose to return for whatever reason." She blinked, looked a bit surprised for a moment as trying to recall her reason to return. Then she laughed. "Dad was absolutely spot on. If it weren't for immigrant Irish, Italians, Poles, and Portuguese, the entire region would have reverted to forest."

She held up two fingers like an umpire counting strikes. "The second and more important facet of Yankee character is resistance. What Dad called, 'Dodging the Puritans.'

"We started as a strictly-managed theocracy. For generations, the Puritans and their blue-nose predecessors ruled—organizing, writing the laws, enforcing ordinances, implementing an entire way of life—demanding by law and example that everyone behave like them. Human beings being human beings—a favorite phrase of Dad's—many resisted. An anti-Puritan, anti-establishment culture took hold from the day after Plymouth Rock. Resistance was bred and re-bred among those who remained for twelve generations. That's why a real Yankee would rather put one over on you than do a good job."

"Pretty harsh, Grace," I said with a smile, because it rang kind of true.

"Not at all. It's part of the game. It's how people maintain their dignity." She named a carpenter I knew, a craftsman who took pride in his skills, yet always found a way to screw up a job, whether by disappearing in the middle of it or introducing an exotic new material that he knew in his heart would not work as well as old-reliable wood.

I argued back with the names of electricians who did precision work.

"They have to or the house will burn down," said Grace. "But have you ever met an electrician who wasn't at least slightly psychotic?" Again, I could not deny a ring of truth. Both of us, she selling insurance and I selling houses, butted up against the material world on a daily basis. She named plumbers who would find any excuse to tear out a ceiling while hunting for a leak, and couldn't leave a job happy until at least two rooms looked like Baghdad.

"Bet you can't tar stone masons with that brush. At least not always."

"Stone masons are sometimes the exception," Grace admitted. "Ours is a harsh climate. Anything but stone will rot."

"Frost will kill a wall."

"Not a good one. The masons know that they're not bucking the establishment. They're vying with weather and each other. And physics. Masons love physics."

"It doesn't fit farmers, either. They work too hard."

"What happens if you're driving down the road at the speed limit and a farmer is coming out of his driveway in a pickup truck?"

"He pulls out right in front of me, and then drives fifteen miles under the limit. But the truck is old or he's old and—."

"What happens when you come to a straight where you could pass?"

"The farmer speeds up. Okay, but—"

"Do you recall what Scooter and you did at the General Store when you were ten years old?"

"What do you mean?"

"You know what I mean. When Gordon Williams installed the new Coca Cola machine?"

"I only stood lookout. Scooter did it. Oh, my god, I'd completely forgotten."

Grace said, "As I heard it, Scooter had figured a way to pry two bottles out of the old machine for one coin, but you couldn't do it to the new one."

"We spent the entire summer sneaking in there trying to fox the machine. That second bottle just stayed locked. One day Scooter figured out all he had to do was pop the cap off and suck it up with a long straw. You win, Grace. Yankees are perverse."

"Not perverse. Resistant."

"How'd you hear about that, by the way?"

"Gordon Williams told Dad he billed Scooter's father for every bottle."

"Will you talk to Donny?"

Grace stood up and called to her Jeannie, "I'll be back." To me she said, "I'll stop by his house, call on his mother—we'll double-team him."

I walked home, pondering what next.

I knew that I really ought to put some time into investigating who exactly Brian Grose was: what anomalies in his life might have led to his murder, what enemies he had made. The means of doing that offered a secondary pleasantry of having an excuse to see Lorraine Renner. I continued up Main to her house.

She came to her door with her hair wild and looking mad as hell. "Oh. It's you. Hi. Come in!"

"What's wrong?"

"I have just had a visit from the goddamned cops, and I am really pissed."

"What happened."

"That bitch practically threatened to arrest me if I didn't hand over my tapes."

"What tapes."

"From shooting Scooter at the Notables."

"Was this cop a State Police Detective-Lieutenant named Boyce?"

"Bitch."

"Actually, she's kind of a good friend of mine."

"That's your problem."

"She probably wants to scan the tapes for witnesses and suspects."

"Well she could have been a little nicer about it."

"I think she's under the gun. There's a lot of pressure from Immigration, and I got the impression"—I wanted to say this carefully, without giving anything Marian had entrusted to me—"that she's feeling backed into a corner. I gotta tell you, she's really a good person. You would like her under different circumstances."

"What's up? What did you come over for?"

"I'm trying to remember something you told me about Brian's film."

"My film about Brian."

"Right. You said you had to fill it out with a waiter and a ski instructor or something."

"His driver."

"Because you dropped some material?"

"He changed his mind about having family in the film."

"That's it. Had you already shot family?"

"Oh God, yeah. I was down there for three days getting bit by chiggers."

"Down where?"

"Arkansas. I stayed at his brother's. They were good people."

"Could I see what you shot?"

"All I've got is partially-edited raw footage."

"Could you show it to me?"

"I'll set you up at a screen. I'm busy. I've got to do other stuff." She opened a file drawer and fished out a couple of mini DV tapes. "Here. Actually, it's kind of cool. Very WPA Okie-project, if you know what I mean."

What she meant was that Brian's family were small time cotton farmers in the Arkansas Delta. She had shot beautiful scenes of machinery crossing land as flat as the ocean and truly wonderful portrait-quality shots of Brian's cousins and brothers dressed in khaki work clothes with their shirts buttoned to the throat. The young were reddened by the sun. The older brown and crinkly-eyed. They looked into Lorraine's camera with polite, indulgent expressions that seemed to say, "Don't know why you all are wasting video tape on me, but if that's what you want, Ma'am, you all go right ahead."

His oldest brother was named Chance. He led Lorraine on a tour of the farm where they had grown up. The frame house, which looked sun-faded and wind-battered on the treeless field, had been converted to migrant worker housing. An overgrown kitchen garden was surrounded by broken picket fences, but they still kept machinery on the place. "House was six hundred square foot." said Chance. "Tractor shed and shop are almost six thousand."

Chance's new house up a dirt road was only a little bigger than the old. His pickup truck was beat up. But the tractor, which was about eight times bigger than any in Newbury and carried chemical tanks big as Volkswagens on front and back, looked brand new, as did a huge large backhoe and a two-story tall cotton picker.

"Does Brian visit?" I heard Lorraine ask off camera.

"Yes, Ma'am. He come by, three-four years back."

"What's it like when you visit him?"

"We never made that California visit. But we're fixing to drive up to Connecticut, after the crop's in, one of these days."

I watched an hour and a half of tape and decided I'd seen enough. I called into the room where she had retreated. "Hey, thanks a lot."

"No problem."

"See you Friday."

I walked back to my office, doubting that Chance Grose's family visit to Connecticut would have occurred even if Brian hadn't been killed. I felt a little guilty charging the Cemetery Association for my viewing time. All I knew now that I hadn't known before was that Brian Grose was a self-made man who had left his roots in the dust—which I could have guessed looking at his over-size house and flashy mausoleum.

Better to fix on Charlie Cubrero?

How well did I know Charlie? What do you know in eight hours? And glimpses over the months of seeing him mowing lawns with Jay. Body language showed how much he loved machines. Jay said the kid could drive anything. But that could be said about a murderer. One thing did not fit, and that was the look in Charlie's eyes when I slipped him a measly extra twenty at the end of a long day's work: gratitude, not for the money, which surely he needed, but for the fact that I had noticed how hard he had worked.

I kept thinking about the loneliness suffered by the hunted. And the fact was the cops were looking for him. And the fact was that my employers in the Cemetery Association wanted to look good. And if I brought Charlie in with a lawyer, they would look good and the kid would get a break and I could concentrate on who actually killed Brian.

So I went looking, sans Spanish-speaking detective.

I started at the Newbury Funeral Home. Mortician Brooks, a calm, gray-haired gent who was president of the Ram Pasture Photography Club had let himself be conned into volunteering to edit a coffee table book that would be a photographic record of Newbury's Tercentennial year. The club had fanned out around town shooting everything that moved. Don himself had come by my mother's with his camera the day Jay brought Charlie out to help pull stumps. We went through a slew of shots he had scanned into his computer under the heading "Newbury Workers."

Don said, "Do you notice how he always turns away from the camera?"

Or hides in the shadow under the brim of his cap.

Or casually shields his face with his hand.

I did not recall that Ecuadorians were among the people who feared that photographs would steal their spirit. But that didn't make him any more a gang leader than any illegal immigrant dodging cameras just to be on the safe side.

We found a wide shot of Jay's tractor backing up, pulling a huge octopus of a stump at the end of a chain. Don had taken it from the other side of my mother's pond and had achieved an arty reflection in the water. He had been so far away that Charlie Cubrero, concentrating on the machine, probably didn't realize he was facing the camera. He had both hands on the controls, and he was looking over his shoulder with the late afternoon sun angling under the bill of his cap.

Unfortunately, the shot was so wide that his face was little more than a dot. Don blew it up and up and up on the computer, and we watched Charlie's face grow broad cheekbones, a handsome hawk nose, dark eyes, and a smile that suggested he was having a fine time on Jay's tractor.

It's a long way from the computer screen to paper, and I held little hope for more than a blown up blur. But Don printed me a color three by five that was as crisp as any portrait in the high school yearbook. When I marveled at the miracle, he explained, very proudly that he was an anti-digital troglodyte who still used 35 mm film.

As I was leaving I asked if he knew when Brian's funeral would be. Don looked annoyed. "I have no idea. The mausoleum company contracted a mortician from Waterbury. Not someone I would have hired, but nobody asked."

Next, I dropped in on my twelve-year-old friend Alison Mealy, who had until recently lived with her mother in the old stable hand's apartment over my barn. Her father had returned after a long absence, stone cold AA sober and working hard to rescue his family from the destruction he had visited upon them. They lived down in Frenchtown in a tiny rented ranch house that had a shed out back big enough for Redman, the horse I had given Alison.

I missed the kid, and found what excuses I could to visit. Alison was usually busy doing kid stuff, of course, school, computer, music lessons, biking with her friends. I got lucky this summer day and found her at home on her horse. She demanded I watch Redman jump a fence, which I did with my heart in my throat as she was small for her age and the horse was very big.

While she brushed him down she told me that come Fall the school was assigning her a more advanced flute teacher. She grabbed her flute and played me an air from the "Magic Flute," which impressed me mightily. Then she showed me the used computer her father's boss had passed down to her. Then she asked about Tom. The cat had originally come with Redman but had decided to stay with me when the horse left. Then, she told me that she had had tea with Aunt Connie last week and that Connie had invited her to come every Wednesday after school. (Just as Tuesday after school had been my day to learn the manners that would make me comfortable anywhere.)

Then Alison asked, as always, if I had seen First Selectman Vicky recently. I said no, running the town and Tim was keeping her very busy. Alison made a face. She adored Vicky and harbored fantasies of Vicky and me getting back together. Finally she asked, "What's up?"

"How are you doing in Spanish class?"

"Okay."

"Can you print me a sign in Spanish?"

"I got Spanish software. What do you want to say?"

"I want the sign to say, 'I am not a cop.' That's *policia* right?

"Yeah," she said dubiously.

"Yes, not yeah."

"Yes."

"And then I want it to say, 'I am a private detective.'"

"*Detective privado.*"

"Great. Then I want it to say, 'I want to help this man.' And I'll show them this picture."

"That's Charlie Cubrero."

"How do I say I want to help him?"

"*Desear…socorrer,* like save. *Por que?*"

"What?"

"Why?"

"Even I know *por que?* means why."

"Why would they trust you?"

"Why not?"

"Charlie's *lo busca la policia.*"

"What is that?"

"Wanted by the police."

"That's the problem. So how do I say, Trust me?"

"*Esperar en alguien.*"

"Put that on the sign, too."

"If you say so."

I did and she did.

As I was leaving, climbing into the car, reaching for the key I had left in the ignition, she said, "Guess what."

"What?"

"My father?"

"How's he doing?"

"They made him manager."

"Good. He said he was hoping that would happen." The hope was if it worked out the boss could buy another store, leave Alison's father in charge of the first store, and give him a break buying the ranch house, which the boss owned.

"He got a raise." It meant, she explained that her mother could cut back to only three days a week cleaning houses.

"Ben?"

I let go the key. "What?"

"Do you think it's hard for him working in a liquor store?"

"Yes, I do."

"So why does he do it?"

"Have you asked him?"

Twelve years old, she looked me in the face like a veteran State's Attorney investigator and said, "I'm asking you."

"Well…well, your father told me it was like a test. It kept him strong—No, actually, I think he meant it kept him alert—you know, aware of the problem….Of drinking."

"Do you believe him?"

"I believe he believes it. And he said his sponsor had done something similar."

"Yeah, but…."

"Yes, but what?"

"Yes, but isn't it like a pothead selling grass?"

"Not at all," I shot back without even thinking. I didn't know where such certainty had come from, but I was glad it had, although I knew now I had better be prepared to flesh out my meaning.

Alison looked intrigued. "What do you mean?"

I reminded myself that, thanks to the Internet and cable TV, a small-town, twelve-year old child knows more of the world than I did before I was processed into Leavenworth. "It's more like a mid-level drug dealer. Not the pothead dealer at school, not his supplier, but the next guy up, or the one above him, who can't stay in business if he uses their own stuff."

"Really?"

"Sort of."

"But Dad's not a drug dealer."

"No. But a liquor store manager does sell a product that some people can't handle. And he knows he can't survive if he uses it himself."

"Because he can't handle it."

"Which he knows."

"Now."

I said, "Your father came home, didn't he? He came home clean. With a job. He found this house. He's made a wonderful place for you and your mother."

"For now."

She was an intensely observant kid, and I worried that she was seeing some sign that Tom might be heading for a fall from the wagon. I said the only thing left to say. "You know the story. One day at a time."

She brightened, willing to hope or just trying to make me not worry. "Hey, good luck with the sign."

It wasn't the brightest idea. But it wasn't the dumbest, either. From talking to Fred Kantor and Rick Bowland and Jay Meadows I knew that the Ecuadorian immigrants were a close knit community from a small country. Many were related by blood, or at least came from the same village or city neighborhood. Last year, when a boatload of illegals trying to board a smuggler's freighter had drowned in the Pacific Ocean, every Ecuadorian in Connecticut lost somebody he knew. So if I got lucky and somebody who knew Charlie trusted my sign, fine, but even if they didn't trust me, I had reason to hope someone would pass my card to Charlie or to someone who knew where Charlie was hiding. Meantime, the second I met someone who could speak enough English to translate for me, that someone had a job with no heavy lifting.

I went looking in the places I was accustomed to seeing immigrants who were probably illegal and most likely penniless: street corners where contractors and homeowners cruised by to hire them for the day, the lumber yard parking lot, car washes, large lawns tended by mowing crews.

I was driving a Scion xA this morning—courtesy of Pink who was still in his blue phase; "Indigo Ink Pearl" according to the spec sheet he had purloined from somewhere for my benefit—and while it handled relatively crisply, I did not believe that it made me look like a cop.

"*Policia?*"

"*¡Yo no!* Not me! *Detective privado. Esperar en alguien* trust me."

"*Por que?*"

The guys building the stone wall didn't trust me. They were courteous about it, but their eyes dimmed down and they backed away. Neither did the demolition crew knocking down an old gas station in Brookfield; they just kept swinging sledge hammers and throwing scraps in the Dumpster. I showed Charlie's picture to people who were lugging grocery bags on foot where everyone else drove. I showed it to a crew of roofers broiling in the midday sun. I climbed a ladder to show it to three guys painting a church steeple. And I showed it to weary men scarfing down a cheap Chinese lunch at an all-you-can-eat buffet where it was cheaper before it was re-named-and-priced "dinner" at three-thirty.

Nine o'clock that night I called it a day when I was asked politely, but firmly, to leave a Ecuadorian bar on a back street of Waterbury. I drove the Scion home, drank some wine, and fell into bed at midnight telling myself that tomorrow was another day.

Chapter Seven

Deeee-Dahhhhh. Deeee-Dahhhhh.

I was up out of bed and on my feet before I realized that was exactly what I should be doing because the Plectron bleating its duo-tone *Deeee-Dahhhhh. Deeee-Dahhhhh* was saying, *Firehouse, now! Put gear on first.*

I let it keep bleating while I climbed into my overalls, boots, and rubbery coat. One time I had squelched it while heading for my clothes and fell straight back to sleep, leaving my fellow volunteers to fight a house fire without me, which was not a way to their hearts. One reason why I was still on probation.

My watch on the night table said it was three minutes to three. If there was any good news at all it was that I had poured myself into bed three hours earlier with wine instead of martinis. As I grabbed my helmet, the duo-tone was interrupted by a mechanical voice that pinpointed the call: "Vehicular accident. Mount Pleasant Road."

I ran out of the house and up Main Street toward Town Hall, behind which stood the firehouse. By the time I had galloped past the Drover, the flagpole, the churches, the bank and general store, pickups, trucks and cars were converging from three directions, flashing blue lights in their windshields. Most of the volunteers lived too far away to respond on foot. In fact I was the only one who lived on Main Street, except for seventy-eight year old Chuck Adams, Banker Dan's father, who clumped around on a cane but managed to get to the firehouse ahead of me anyhow, and was hobbling quickly toward his position in the cab of Engine 112, the all-wheel-drive attack pumper favored for motor vehicle accidents.

Chuck held the door so the new guy could squeeze in the middle between him and the driver, Wes Little, with my feet on the drive shaft hump and chin on my knees. We all buckled in, and 112 lurched out of the house, ahead of the rescue truck which carried the lights, cutters, spreaders, rams and first aid, and behind a red SUV driven by Chief Eddie Thomas, who was wearing the kind of smile you smile when you have just returned from a tour of the Middle East funded by the National Guard and have every reason to believe that angry Muslims will not be shooting at you on your way to this fire.

We tore off of Main Street onto Mount Pleasant.

My grandfather, who apparently had more of a sense of humor than my father had ever displayed, had invented the name Mount Pleasant in 1950, hoping to sell house lots on a slope known for centuries as Slut's Hill. The Board of Selectman had approved the change, impressed by his successful re-naming of Carcass Street—the route that had served the abandoned slaughterhouse, as Rose Lane.

Mount Pleasant veered away from the head of Main Street and up a long, tall hill of the steepness that used to mark the boundaries between towns that no one would climb on horse, wagon, or foot except for special events. For modern vehicles, Mount Pleasant Road offers a precipitous grade on a sharp curve halfway up the hill that guarantees at least one wreck a season. The most recent had been fatal: Grace Botsford's father Gerard.

Trooper Moody was there ahead of us illuminating an upside down SUV with more candlepower than a Rolling Stones' concert. Red and blue strobes flashed in his cruiser's light bar. White takedown and alley lights glared. Road flares pillared smoke into the night, blocking both lanes.

Wes Little wondered aloud what we used to when we were prowling teenagers, "Does Ollie ever sleep?"

The trooper was crouched on the asphalt shining his five cell Mag through the SUV's shattered windshield. We joined him with extinguishers. "One man, alone," said Ollie. "Get him out as quick as you can. I want to breathalyze him."

We could hear why. The victim flailing among yellow airbags was singing an inebriated attempt at a hymn in a voice as tuneless and flat as a garbage truck that needed a brake job. He was too big to crawl out the window. His doors were jammed and the frame around the former windshield had been squashed to half its normal height.

While I stood guard with the fire extinguisher, the guys got the Hurst kit, started our portable hydraulic pump, hooked up a spreader and pried open the passenger door. Out crawled Alison's father, Tom Mealy, blinking at the lights and yelling, "Son of a bitch cut me off."

Ollie helped him to his feet, more firmly than kindly. "Tom, have you been drinking?"

"I haven't had a drink in one year, one month and seventeen days."

"I want you to walk toward my cruiser nine steps, placing one foot directly in front of the other, heel to toe, turn when I tell you and walk back."

"I can't walk like that. My leg hurts like hell."

"Are you refusing to take a field sobriety test?" Ollie asked ominously.

Tom looked afraid. "But I haven't been drinking. This guy cut me off."

"Then walk the line."

I said, "You don't have to, Tom."

"Butt out, Ben!" said Ollie, and one of the guys took my arm, saying, "Stay out of it, Ben."

Tom said, "Yeah, but then what will he do to me?"

"They'll test you at the barracks," I said. "It's a better test. More accurate. If you haven't been drinking."

"I ain't been drinking."

"Then you are better off doing it at the barracks. They can't use the road test as evidence, but a false positive still looks bad to the jury. If," I repeated, again, "you haven't been drinking."

"I want to go home. It's three o'clock in the morning. I gotta go to work."

Betty Butler, the EMT crew chief stifled a yawn. "Come into the ambulance, Tom. We better look at that leg."

"It's okay. It just hurts. Can somebody give me a ride home?"

"We'll take you home," said Betty. "Just get in the ambulance—Okay, Ollie?"

Trooper Moody looked about to detonate. Betty added in a low voice, "I don't smell alcohol."

"He's a drunk."

"Not tonight."

"When I got here he was hanging upside down from his seatbelt singing. You heard him."

"I was singing a hymn," shouted Tom. "I was scared and I was grateful to be alive. I was singing a song from church." He burst back into song and treated us to a couple of bars vaguely reminiscent of "A Closer Walk With Thee."

I shook off the hand restraining me. "Ollie, you know damned well if Tom was drunk he'd have come out of that wreck swinging." We had both had set-tos with Tom, Ollie armed with pistol, handcuffs, five cell flashlight and fists, me with fists and good intentions. When he was drunk, Tom Mealy was the belligerent, nasty sort who gave bar room brawlers a bad name.

"If he's not drunk?" asked Ollie. "What's he doing out at three in the morning?"

"I was down in Danbury, helping a friend."

"What were you helping him do at three in the morning?"

"Get through the night."

Betty Butler said, "I'll pull some blood, if he lets me. Would that be okay with you, Tom, if I draw a blood sample?"

Tom looked at me. I said, "Ask Betty for a second sample, sealed, in case your lawyer wants to get it tested yourself."

"Okay, I'll let her. But I don't need no lawyer."

"Ollie?" asked Betty.

Nobody likes to argue with a nurse, particularly with a dedicated volunteer who may be your first responder the night you wrap your cruiser around a telephone pole in a sleet storm, or get ambushed by an armed meth addict tweaking a fifteen day binge. Ollie finally did the intelligent thing, took Tom's statement—"Son of a bitch cut me off!"—and let Tom climb into the ambulance with Betty and a brace of EMT trainees.

Scooter pulled up in his Range Rover with a blue light flashing and took a bunch of pictures for the *Clarion*. Then the Chevalley wrecker arrived and they tipped the SUV onto its wheels and hauled it away. We hosed down a smidgeon of spilled oil and spread kitty litter on the slick that remained.

I helped Chuck Adams drain and stow the hose. He looked troubled and kept stopping to stare at the side of the road. I asked him what was wrong.

"This is where Gerard died. You weren't here that night."

"I was in New York."

"Yeah, well, just like what happened to Tom tonight. Fell asleep at the wheel."

"Tom said he was cut off."

"Ninety-five years old. Doc Greenan told me his heart was fine. Autopsy showed no heart attack. Fell asleep at the wheel. Veered onto the curbing. Maybe woke up and tried to steer out of it. Spun out, instead. Do you see those skid marks?"

They were clear as day in the lights of the attack pumper. "Looks like Tom did a full three-sixty."

"Skidded just like Gerard. Hit the curbing again. Caught a tire. Rolled over."

"Tom said he was cut off."

"I heard him. I think he fell asleep, just like Gerard. Or passed out. In my opinion. Not that anyone's asking it."

"I didn't smell any booze on his breath."

Chuck said, "When we were kids, we used to chew privet hedge to fix our breath."

"Wasn't that for cigarette smoke?"

"Worked for hooch, too."

"Well, maybe that's what happened to Tom."

"What do you mean?"

"Reached out the window for a privet hedge and lost control."

Age had not mellowed Chuck and it was clear from whom his son Banker Dan had inherited his pugnaciousness. He counterpunched with a familiar Main Street rumor as silly as it was nasty. "Maybe you're defending Tom Mealy because you were friends with his wife."

Not in the habit of poking gentlemen forty years my senior in the snoot, I spoke the truth in mild tones. "Actually, I was—am still—friends with his little girl, Alison. Mrs. Mealy is very shy." (Too shy and frightened for a conversation, much less a love affair.) Besides, she had never stopped hoping that Tom would come home sober.

⟨⟩⟨⟩⟨⟩

The next day, woozy on a short sleep, and surprised that the Feds still hadn't captured him, I resumed looking for Charlie Cubrero showing his picture and my Spanish signs at every lawn I saw being mowed. As had been the case yesterday, the Ecuadorians were polite, but totally unhelpful.

Heading down toward Danbury, I found a immigrant crew working for one of the national lawn care chains. They were spraying a yellow chemical, and I stopped to speak to a guy who was covered head to toe in yellow powder.

"You really should be wearing protective gear," I said.

"The boss says no. It scares the customers."

"What is that stuff, a cholinesterase inhibitor? Or 'pre-emergent' herbicide?"

"He says it's not supposed to hurt me."

"Your lungs—Hey, wait a minute. You speak great English."

"What?"

"I'm looking for this guy and—"

Well I blew that one. He backed up like I was a snake.

"I'm not a cop."

I heard him say something like "*Nada Ingles*," as he vanished in the yellow mist.

Brilliant.

I continued driving south figuring I'd try the Danbury street corner where Brian Grose had picked up workers. I stopped to talk to a painting crew, who were no help, and some guys with loud leaf blowers, who were less. I spotted a car wash in Brookfield and tried it, but they were Israelis or Russians, I couldn't tell which. Then, nearing Danbury I pulled into another car wash where a crowd of short, slim Ecuadorians were drying the finished product. Waiting for a break in the action, I noticed a guy propped against a wall watching his friends work. His foot was in a cast and he had a beat up pair of crutches beside him. When he nodded in a not-unfriendly manner I said, "Por que," pointing at his crutches. He answered in English, "Ramp slipped. Loading the mower? It dropped on my foot....The mower."

"You speak good English."

"A little."

I spoke very slowly. "My name is Ben Abbott. I am a private detective. I'm trying to help a man named Charlie Cubrero."

He spoke quickly. "I don't know him."

"Would you like a job?"

"I can't walk."

"Translating. Spanish to English. English to Spanish."

"How much?"

Minimum wage was seven dollars and sixty-five cents an hour then. Immigrants hired off the street were getting nine. A decent glass of wine in most restaurants cost eight. A decent martini—hard to find—ran around ten. Jay Meadows had paid Charlie fourteen. Fred Kantor had stolen Charlie for fifteen with guarantees.

"Eighteen dollars an hour."

He stood up on his crutches.

I told him, again, that my name was Ben Abbott. He told me his name was Henry. His English was meager, but far superior to my Spanish signs. Between us we could order a meal from a

Spanish coffee shop. I helped him into the car and we headed into Danbury, the old hatter's city whose industry had gone up in smoke after John F. Kennedy was inaugurated without a hat on and combustible chemicals in bankrupt fedora factories mysteriously caught fire. For many years its once-fashionable shopping district had been a ghostly thoroughfare, abandoned for a mall. Today, Main Street bustled with Brazilian and Ecuadorian and Mexican restaurants and shops, while neighborhoods that hadn't seen fresh paint since 1962 were swarming with do-it-themselfers fixing up houses. This made the mayor of Danbury so angry he gave speeches denouncing illegal immigration.

Henry, who was leaning against the passenger door like he was calculating his chances of surviving a thirty-mile-an-hour jump on crutches, said, "I heard you were asking around."

"What did you hear?"

"You're a cop."

"Well, I'm not."

"Okay," he said, not sounding convinced.

"Why did you come with me?" I asked. Stupid question for a man who was broke with a broken foot, but I wanted to open him up and get him on my side so people would see us as a team they could trust.

Henry said, "My friend said maybe you're the guy who says hello."

"What do mean?"

"He see you in Newbury, right?"

"Someone I met?"

"When you see a guy mowing lawns what do you do?"

"What do you mean?"

"When you see us, what do you say?"

"I say hello."

"Why?"

"Why?"

"Why do you say hello? Nobody says hello. You say hello."

"Well, I suppose I assume you are country men—from the farms? Where people say hello."

Henry's face closed up a bit. He hadn't the faintest idea what I was trying to say. So I said, "Why do I say hello? I think it must be lonely to be so far from home."

Henry nodded and looked out the window. I cruised by the bus station and Henry spoke to people he knew without getting out of the car, holding up his crutches, breaking ice with them, then asking about Charlie Cubrero. It seemed that Henry's presence was giving me a trust pass. People who would not have spoken to me, spoke to us. Unfortunately nobody told us anything about Charlie. Though, from their anxious looks away, they knew that Immigration and the cops were hunting him.

Suddenly, two men we were talking to made a quick goodbye and hurried down the street to a big van that had just pulled up. "Work," Henry explained and in seconds twelve men gathered around the vehicle. A pickup truck with a four-door passenger cab pulled up behind them. Before anyone could move, the van's doors burst open and out stormed six Federal agents, guns drawn. Four more pretend-contractors swarmed from the pickup.

"Drive!" yelled Henry.

I was already pulling a Uey. In the rearview mirror I saw Ecuadorians running from the Feds who were grabbing and cuffing them to street signs and lamp posts. A priest waded into the melee, signaling men to come with him. He got a bunch loaded into a little car and drove away before the Feds, who had their hands full, noticed.

"Out Reach Guy," said Henry. "From the church."

It was over in seconds. A Corrections bus with mesh windows swung around the corner. The prisoners were loaded. It drove away and then everything got quiet except for some women crying.

"ICE," said Henry. "I heard they do that. Never seen it."

We cruised another neighborhood, but the streets were empty, except for the occasional anxious woman on a cell phone. I asked Henry if he was hungry, and he answered like a man who definitely was and directed me to a convenience store that had a food counter and Formica tables in back. We were standing (Henry leaning on crutches and a pillar) at the counter perusing the menu, with Henry explaining dishes, when the place suddenly got very quiet.

I said, "Here we go again."

The glass door swung inward and the bulky shadow behind it materialized into a beefy, overweight unpleasant-looking fellow with longish, greasy hair and a bad-tempered face. He could have been a disgruntled biker, but was more likely a plainclothes Immigration officer.

The people eating stopped eating. The people standing around waiting for food looked like they wished the guy was not between them and the door. The cook looked worried and the guy at the cash register looked sick with fear.

"Listen up! Who's seen Charlie Cubrero? You? No? What about you? Nobody seen him? All line up there! Get out your papers."

Seeing a way to make friends in the immigrant community, I stepped past Henry and asked, "Are you an officer of the law?"

"Back off, Mister. Line up! Over there. Now. Now, now, now! Move!"

"Are you a peace officer?"

"I am warning you to back off, mister."

"I am asking you one more time, are you a peace officer?"

He stopped shoving the Ecuadorians against the grocery shelves to shove me instead. I said, "Thank you, that's all I need to know," and dipped a shoulder so he would think I was leading with my left. Orthodox stuff. A prize fighter would have handed me my head, but he didn't carry himself like one so I was guessing he was no more a prizefighter than a cop.

It did the job.

"Henry, please translate: 'Anyone who wants to leave, now would be a good time.'"

Several barreled out the door before the fellow got up off the linoleum, pawing a gun from somewhere and a badge from somewhere else. Right on the prizefighter, wrong on the cop.

Chapter Eight

He yelled at me to lay on the floor.

I definitely did not want to lay on the floor. I looked around for a way out without making things more unpleasant than they had already become. All I could think of was to put both hands in the air and call loudly to the store clerk, "Would you please dial 911?" on the theory that the more cops present to witness his behavior, the less likely he was to avenge his civil rights by violating mine.

The clerk was terrified. One of the Ecuadorians reached for his cell. The man with the badge yelled not to move, but he was too busy concentrating on me to intimidate all of them; and the guy with the phone slipped out the door.

"On the floor! Now!"

Slowly, very slowly, I started toward the floor hoping that he was not the sort of officer to kick a man when he was down. His gun, I noticed, was shaking. It was an awful sight as he had a finger on the trigger. Stupid way to hold the only gun in a crowded room. I looked closer at his badge.

It was handsome gold circle of Art Deco sun rays set atop a bar with a four digit cutout number, a dead ringer for an NYPD detective badge, at a distance. The giveaway was the tiny red, white and blue enamel American flag where there should have been the seal the City of New York on a field of black.

"Connecticut," I said, conversationally, as if he was not holding a shaky gun on me, "forbids police officers from moonlighting as bounty hunters. So you're not a cop. Bounty hunters are supposed to notify local police before making an arrest. But I don't see any local police. Nor are bounty hunters permitted to wear clothes or carry a badge suggesting that they are an agent of the state or federal government."

"I am a licensed bail enforcement officer," he said. "On the floor."

"You can call yourself what you want, but you're acting like a bounty hunter out of bounds. So put your weapon away before somebody gets hurt."

He didn't.

I said, "Or before the cops come along and take it away from you."

"Who the fuck are you?"

"I'm a real estate agent."

Bounty hunters, it turned out, were picking up extra income picking up illegal aliens who had been deported but had neglected to actually leave or sneaked back in. This was allowed in many states, including mine, but they did have to follow rules. Were he to bend them so sharply while apprehending a fugitive Greenwich hedge fund manager, he would find himself in hot water, boiled by the hedger's attorneys. But when it came to illegals from Ecuador, he could reasonably reason that if he dragged Charlie Cubrero in cuffs, an understaffed, overwhelmed Immigration Service might fork over the reward.

My standing in the convenience store would hinge on whatever personal contacts he had made among the various authorities. And, indeed, when two Danbury cops screeched up in their patrol cars, they did not appear pleased to make the gentleman's acquaintance. To be frank, they didn't look that pleased by me, either, nor struck with admiration for my PI license; but I at least was not carrying any weapons, which reduced me from potential threat to minor annoyance. The bounty hunter was carrying. But he was licensed to chase bail jumpers, and he was also licensed to carry the gun that he had managed to pocket before the cops walked in on him waving it around. It looked like a draw, with all but the most illegal free to leave the convenience shop. But then the Feds marched in.

I recognized the two I had seen outside the Yankee Drover. They hadn't seen me sitting inside the restaurant, of course. But they knew the bounty hunter. One said to him, "Hey, Al."

The other said, "How you doing, Dude?"

"My Man," said Al, cementing a warm relationship that probably centered around disappearing lunch checks.

"What's up?"

Al gave me a hard stare. But all he said was, "I got a tip Cubrero was hanging here."

I gave Al a polite nod, relieved to learn that he was not as stupid as he had acted earlier. Or at least not about to waste hard-earned favors on the pleasure of giving me a hard time.

"You know you got blood on your lip?" asked one of the Feds.

"Cut myself trying to open a CD jewel case," said Al, and I found myself starting to like him.

"That," said the Fed, "is why everybody bought an iPod." His partner and the younger Danbury cop nodded. The elder asked, "Who called in the 911?"

"Not me," said Al.

The cops looked at me. "Beats me," I said.

"Sir, may I see your cell?"

"Sure."

He checked my number and handed it back. "Al?"

Al handed over his cell. So did everyone else in the shop, with the cheerfulness of people not worried since the guy who had stepped outside to make the call was by now stepping toward Bridgeport. Done with phones, the cops and Feds checked everyone's ID and eventually left with a guy who had wandered in with a driver's license that looked like something off a cereal box.

I said to Al, "Thanks for standing up."

"Gotta tell you, Dude, I haven't been hit that hard since my old man caught me humping his girlfriend."

That was a picture tough to contemplate, even subtracting twenty years from his greasy, beefy bad looks and assuming the girlfriend was drunk. I gave him my card. "Call if I can return the favor up my way."

He read it and said, "Dude, you're in the boonies."

"If you get a lead on Charlie Cubrero, I'll make it worth your while to talk to me first."

"I don't get paid if I don't bring him in."

"We pay cash on delivery in the boonies." I could talk Tim Hall into turning Charlie over to the cops pro bono. But Al's money would have to be pried out of the parsimonious, not to say cheap, Cemetery Association. "We won't hassle you with paperwork. We won't even ask to see your license."

He liked that. He gave me his card. Richard Albert Vetere. "You don't pronounce the last 'e.' 'It's V-Tear.' Like rip. But you can call me Al."

His card said he worked for a Brooklyn-based Bail Bonds company called Out Now! At the bottom it read, "Big Al's Discrete Investigations."

"You're a PI, too?"

"Starting up a little sideline," he said. I didn't have the heart to ask if he meant to be discreet. We shook hands, and he left.

The cook meanwhile had spoken quietly to Henry. He wrapped a couple of sausage sandwiches in foil, poured us coffee in take out cups, and refused money. I tried to tip him and he refused that too. In the car, as we chewed sausage and drank coffee, I asked, "What was that about?"

"He thanks us."

"For what?"

Henry smiled. "For punching out the bounty hunter."

"What did he say to you."

Henry looked away.

"Come on, he told you something. Can't you tell me?"

"Why you want to see Charlie?"

"I told you. I'm trying to help him. I'm hoping to get him a lawyer. If he surrenders to the cops with a lawyer he'll be treated better. Maybe get a fair hearing." At least until Homeland Security got a hold of him.

"You really not a cop?"

"Did those cops treat me like a cop?"

Henry shrugged. "A trick?"

"Was punching that guy a trick?"

He shrugged again. "I saw you talking like buddies."

"He understood it was business. Maybe I can help him one day. Maybe he can help me and get paid for it." I put my hand on my heart. "Henry, I swear to you I will not do anything to hurt Charlie….What did the cook tell you about Charlie?"

Henry chewed awhile. "There's a guy in New Milford maybe knows where he is."

We found Tony Gandara picking tomatoes in one of the last fields left on Route 7 where so many box stores and subdivisions had been built that they had to widen the road. It had taken awhile to get there. Widened or not, the road was packed with end of the day homeward bound commuters and the traffic was brutal. And it turned out that Tony, who was covered in dust and tired from a long, long day in the sun, did not actually know where Charlie was. But he did know the car he was driving. And as a car nut, he spoke enough automotive English to describe in detail a 1993 Acura Integra that had been customized to a fare thee well.

Tony named each detail in precise English, then demonstrated its function with body language. The "Ground Control Coil Over Suspension kit," allowed the driver to spin adjustable springs by hand to raise or lower the ride height. The Street Glow under car lights floated the ride on a blue ocean at night. Projector headlights could illuminate the dark side of the moon. The "APR Performance Side View Mirror," was the first performance side view mirror I had ever heard of. "Carbon Fiber Canards" threw me for a loop.

I knew ducks and I knew hoaxes and I knew a shade of blue, but I didn't know they went on cars. It took awhile for Tony and Henry to explain that canards reduced lifting of the front end by wind pressure. (Later, my OED informed me that they had originally been installed on airplanes.) He showed them to me. He had them on his car, which was a very-fancied up 1991 Integra. They looked like little wings on the front fenders. Charlie's vehicle, he informed us, also had "Wind Splitters," a protruding flat surface at the lower edge of the front spoiler. His rear spoiler was a wing made of black anodized aluminum bolted to the trunk lid.

I shook my head.

"What's wrong?" asked Henry.

"No way Charlie's going to drive such a stand-out car when the cops are hunting him. They'll be all over it."

Henry spoke Spanish to Tony. Tony said, "Not Charlie's."

It seemed that Charlie had borrowed the hopped up coup from a cook in a Woodbury café who had gone home to visit his mother. And there was no way the cops could know that Charlie was driving it, Tony assured us. At least until the cops cuffed somebody on some unrelated felonious issue who asked, through a translator, "By the way, will you let me go if I tell you what car my old amigo Charlie Cubrero is driving?"

"So basically it looks like your car?" I was eyeballing it to commit to memory a vehicle that looked similar to many I had seen driven by young immigrants. From the side it showed a long nose, a short rear, and a short, chunky cockpit. The back was characterized by a fat, round single exhaust pipe and the spoiler elevated on twin stanchions. Head on, the sleek front resembled the snout of a crocodile pretending to sleep.

"Charlie's has carbon fiber canards. Mine aluminum."

That would be very helpful information at sixty miles an hour. "Any other difference?"

"Charlie's is burnt."

"Burnt?"

"How you say?" Tony turned to Henry and spoke Spanish.

Henry said, "Burnt orange color."

I looked at him. "*Burnt orange?* How many of those are around?"

"I never seen one."

Tony spoke again in Spanish and wiggled his fingers.

"What does he mean with the fingers?"

"Flame decals on the sides."

It was a nice break. And having done all I could for the moment to find Charlie, I headed home to Newbury, my sights set on the gossiply-seduced brides of the Village Cemetery Association.

Chapter Nine

"Benjamin," said Aunt Connie. "You look like you want something."

"I do."

Instead of asking what it was I wanted, she said to me, "Did I tell you that I looked up 'mausoleum?'"

"No."

She often browsed, feistily, in her own Oxford English Dictionary and had taught me the habit, which was why I had had little Alison help me install a CD version on my hard drive. I had paid full price, Connie having impressed on me as child that stealing was a terrible crime against both the rightful owner and the creator of the coveted object. But the entire dictionary was on one fragile disc, one scratch from oblivion, and encrypted so that no one older than fourteen could store it safely in his computer. Connie's edition occupied thirteen calfskin bindings on a shelf in her library. A mug's game, looking up words coined or changed since 1933, it remained the ultimate lexicon for centuries past.

"King Mausolus of Caria was buried in the first 'mausoleum.' In the Fourth Century BC—don't you detest the 'Before the Common Era' euphemism? BCE? Before whose Common Era? And who's common, for that matter?"

She was high as a kite on caffeine. Lately she had switched to chamomile, but this morning she was feeling good and living wild on Earl Grey.

"Apparently it was a magnificent tomb. The Ancients named it one of the Seven Wonders of the World. Mausolus' wife erected it, Queen Artemisia, who also happened to be his sister, but we won't talk about that—More tea dear?

"I think we've both had enough."

"Now what is it you want?"

"I'm concerned about this kid they're after. I haven't been able to find hide nor hair of him. Since I can't find him I should investigate who else might have shot the son—gentleman—so that when the kid is arrested I can help him. Which brings me back to the gossiply-seduced."

"Priscilla Adams, Georgia Bowland, and Cynthia Little. All married to Cemetery Association Trustees."

Which put me face to face with a downside of playing detective in my hometown. If I were investigating Brian Grose's murder in, say, Greenwich or Bedford, or Washington Depot I could knock on strangers' doors to ask the "lady of the house" how well she knew the deceased. The lady of the house, in turn, could tell me to get lost, or tell me she didn't, but her neighbor Sally did, or break down in tears on my shoulder and list her dead lover's best qualities. Out of such moments, cases are made, facts assembled. If an angry husband burst into the room and threatened to rip my lungs out, it wouldn't be personal.

But asking intimate questions in Newbury meant prying into the private lives of women I had known for years, smiled at in the Drover, nodded to in Steve's Liquor Locker, flirted with at dinner parties, and would have to look in the eye for years to come. As for their husbands, it would be hard to remain friends, much less do business together. All that would be the easy part.

The hard part would be causing pain and upset for people I cared about. I feared for Georgia Bowland, but I also liked her and admired the hope that kept her going. While *I* hoped that she would someday find peace or at least see Rick as more than her caretaker. I liked Priscilla Adams who was lovely to look at, and the kind of joke-cracking mother to her children we all wished we had had; I also admired how she deflected Banker

Dan's prickliness without ever allowing him to bully her. Cynthia Little I did not know as well; Wes had brought her home from college. But I knew that voracious look, had been its target once or twice, and had always harbored the dumb thought in the back of my mind: one of these days, who knew.

On the other hand, investigating Brian's murder in my own town gave me one clear advantage over a professional snoop who did not live in Newbury. Neither Brooklyn PI Hector Ramirez nor wannabe Big Al Vetere could ask a grande dame of Main Street, "Aunt Connie, what are you doing tomorrow night? What do you say we invite the gossiply-seduced for cocktails?"

Connie had fallen silent. Now her eyes tracked back from the middle distance and for a grim second I wondered if she was still with me. "Benjamin," she said. "I certainly don't know all that much about such things, but what makes you so sure they were seduced? Perhaps they were the seducers."

"And passed Brian around?"

"Doesn't it strike you that the gentleman would have made a conveniently unimpaired assignee? Not married, no jealous wife, living alone in an enormous empty house hidden in the woods—if the gossip is true."

"Possible," I conceded.

"Contrariwise," she conceded back at me, "whether or not Mr. Grose *was* the seducer, the distinction would mean little to a jealous, suspicious husband, would it?"

"From the husband's point of view, you're right. It would be as upsetting, or enraging, one way or another. But there is another way to look at it."

"The husband might be understanding. He might even be relieved. Who knows the strains in a marriage?"

"That is not what I mean."

"What do you mean, Benjamin?"

"If Brian Grose was the active seducer of all three women, it could mean that Brian Grose laid a lot of *groundwork*, shall we say, to get that damned mausoleum into the cemetery."

"'Laid,'" Connie said, with all the warmth of a February Nor'easter," is not the first word I would have chosen."

My cell phone had the kindness to ring in my shirt pocket and I said, "I'm sorry. I have to answer this." Young Henry the Translator and I had missed earlier when one of us was out of range. I walked into Connie's kitchen and said, "Hello, Henry. What's up?"

"Tony? Remember Tony?"

"Picking tomatoes in New Milford."

"I just got a call from Tony. He thinks he saw Charlie's car on Route 7."

"You're kidding."

That stretched Henry's English and I asked, "Which way was he heading?"

"Up."

"North?"

"Like to Newbury."

There was a lot territory between New Milford and Newbury and a lot of turnoffs.

I said a fast good bye to Connie, "Are we on for drinks tomorrow?"

"It's short notice for Saturday night. Surely they have plans."

"We'll make it six. If they're going out to dinner, they can stop on the way. Shall I call them?"

"Invite them here. If it's warm enough we'll do it in the garden."

‹›‹›‹›

I jumped in my latest rental, and headed down 7, eyes peeled for a burnt orange Honda Integra with flame decals coming the other way.

I drove ten miles, almost to the town line, just past a turnoff which offered a shortcut to Morris Mountain; and there I pulled over, thinking that Charlie would head for the nearest thing to home, the Kantors' beef cow and goat cheese farm. It was also possible that he had heard by now that I was offering to get him a lawyer. I turned the car around, got out, and made myself visible by sitting on the trunk. If anyone wondered what I was watching with my Swarovski birding binoculars, I was watching birds.

Late morning, after commuters and summer camp buses and before lunch, the road was not busy. A car or truck would come along every half a minute or so. On the unusually long straight where I had parked, I could identify an on-coming vehicle with plenty of time to wave it down. I could only hope he would stop as the piece of junk Pink had rented me couldn't catch a monkey on a bicycle.

And damned if something burnt orange didn't come along.

Head on in the glasses, it showed its sleeping crocodile snout. It was orange and it was moving fast. Its windows were tinted so I could not see enough of the driver to recognize Charlie. He didn't recognize me either, or didn't want to. He certainly didn't stop, or even slow down when I waved. I thought I saw canards in front as it roared by, and definitely saw the fat single round exhaust and a spoiler in back. I jumped into the rental and floored it with little hope of catching up anytime soon.

Standing on the accelerator, pounding the steering wheel, and yelling encouragement, I finally persuaded it past the speed limit. Two seconds later, a trillion- candlepower galaxy exploded in my mirrors. Under the galaxy, high beams flashing in syncopation, steamed a familiar, grim, gray profile.

"Son. Of. A. *Bitch!*"

Here I am trying to catch Charlie Cubrero's warp speed Integra and Trooper Moody nails me for speeding. His sirens shrieked and shrilled like demented crows. I signaled right, slowed, and pulled over.

Ollie passed me so fast his wind shook the car.

The Crown Victoria whipped around a bend and out of sight. I floored the piece of junk again, fumbled my cell from my shirt pocket, and thumbed phone keys. Somewhere in the far, far ahead Newbury's Resident State Trooper was about to get famous for pulling over a speeder who turned out to be an alleged Ecuadorian illegal immigrant gang leader wanted on suspicion of murder. Famous, or shot.

I had no love for Ollie, but dislike had its natural limits. If Charlie was what the cops said he was, even Oliver Moody might be caught flatfooted by a speeder who extended license and registration from the muzzle of an AK-47.

God knew if he would answer his cell phone while maneuvering at speed.

"What?"

The part of my brain that gets its hackles up at the mere sight of Trooper Moody wanted to ask if he was operating a handheld telephone while driving, which was illegal in Connecticut. The smarter part said, "The guy in that burnt orange Integra might come out shooting."

"I doubt that," said Ollie.

"Be sure," I said. "He could be a fugitive."

"I'm damned sure, Sherlock. He's a goddamned priest."

When I had finally squealed around a few more bends in the road; there was the cruiser, flashing red and blue and yellow a safe distance behind the Integra. And there was Ollie, glowering down perplexedly at a slim, smiling fellow dressed head to toe all in black, except for the white collar on his short sleeved neckband clergy shirt.

Chapter Ten

He wasn't carrying a Bible, but he should have been, smiling up beneficently at Trooper Moody who appeared to delivering a half-hearted sermon on the sins of speeding. Ollie interrupted himself to wave me along with a very stern arm. I stopped a respectful distance away and waited for the opportunity to ask him how a priest happened to driving a burnt orange '93 Integra with canards and spoiler.

Ollie stomped back to his cruiser. Instead of writing out a ticket, he drove off, fast enough to lay some rubber. He passed me, stone faced and roared toward Newbury. I jumped out and hurried back to the Integra. The priest stopped climbing into the car and watched me walking toward him. The beneficent smile he had used to talk Ollie out of a ticket must have cost him, because he was shaking with rage. Before I could speak, he said, "That cop pulled me over because I'm Latino."

His accent was Eastern Seaboard vanilla. Though up close, he looked as Ecuadorian as Charlie and Henry and Tony.

"I don't know if he could see you're Latino through the smoked glass."

"Yeah, well he thinks the car is Latino."

I said, "I'm surprised you're surprised."

I saw an explosion of fire in his eyes and had the novel impression that I was as close as I had ever been to being punched out by a priest. "How do you mean that?" he asked.

"You're driving a low-riding, burnt-orange-colored automobile with flame decals on the sides and slipstream-management devices usually found on craft that take off from military airfields. The vehicle is old but immaculate. And it's a Acura Integra, a type of car driven by nine out of ten Latino young gentlemen."

"Do you think they can afford Mercedes?"

"Actually, now that you mention it, I've just started to see young, prosperous Latino gentlemen driving newer BMWs. Only when their passengers look like bodyguards do I jump to the conclusion that they are drug dealers."

"You're just like that cop. What are you saying? A hard-working young man can't own a car he likes? He can't enjoy a small indulgence even when he's sending most of his money home and helping relatives get here to find work?"

"I didn't—"

"While living six to a room?"

"I didn't—"

"Driving a hot car is the only way a hard-working young immigrant gets to be a boy. Guys like you go off to college, you extend your boyhood into your twenties. These kids have to be men at fourteen. They have to work."

I said, "First of all, Father, it's clear you went to college, too. Second, what are you mad at me for? I didn't stop you for speeding, the cop did."

"I wasn't speeding."

"I don't know what they call speeding back at the seminary, Father, but you passed me doing seventy. But I gotta say I would love to hear you preach sometime because you must have been pretty darned convincing to talk Trooper Moody out of the ticket."

The priest gave me a thin smile. "Hey, don't mind me, man. I just get so wired up the way they treat people. I lead an outreach program for immigrants. I hear terrible stories." Suddenly his smile was as bright as his eyes had been fiery. "I'm Father Bobby," he said, extending his hand. "Who are you?"

"Ben Abbott."

Father Bobby looked my age or younger. His skin was smooth and dark, his hair was cut short. While his casual summer rig, including the well-worn New Balances on his feet, appeared designed to make both him and the people around him comfortable, he had the charisma of a man who could be counted on to lead. A nasty, wide, flat scar on his right forearm hinted that he, like the Savior, had known pain, if not violence.

"Wha'd you stop for, Ben?"

"A guy I know is driving a car like yours. I thought it might have been his."

"I wondered what you doing with the binoculars."

I watched his face and said, "His name is Charlie Cubrero."

"Did you see that despicable press conference?" he shot back at me. "They've practically ordered the cops to shoot to kill like he's John Dillinger in a Latino body."

The Dillinger reference sounded so odd, so out of place and time in the mouth of an Ecuadorian priest, that I said, "Do you mind me asking? Where did you learn English?"

"La Salle Military Academy."

"La Salle? I know La Salle." La Salle used to be a Catholic military boys school on Long Island that catered to wealthy South American families. Some famous dictators had gone there. It had closed some years back. "I played you in soccer when I was at Stony Brook." Connie had urged my parents to ship me off to the boarding school for my senior year. It would supposedly make it easier to get into Annapolis, but Connie told me privately, bluntly, it was to keep me out of trouble. I was hanging with the wrong crowd, my Chevalley cousins; though in fact whatever trouble we got into I had usually led the way.

"Your coaches were monks. I'll never forget the sight of monks running in long robes to break up a fight before the whole field joined the brawl."

"Before my time," Father Bobby said, looking me up and down. "I think you're a few years older."

"Do you know Charlie Cubrero?"

"You think every Latino knows every other Latino?"

"I think you are Ecuadorian. And so is he."

"Do you think every Ecuadorian knows every other Ecuadorian?"

"Do you think there are two cars like this one in the state of Connecticut?"

He said nothing.

I said, "And since immigrants seeking work tend to follow routes blazed by family and friends, isn't it likely that two Ecuadorians in one small state would be acquainted."

We looked at each other for awhile, looked away, looked back.

I said, "You want to get some coffee?"

"What for?"

"Confession."

"Are you a Catholic?"

"No."

Father Bobby looked down and scuffed the grass with his sneaker. After a while he said, so softly I could hardly hear him, "Charlie stashed his car with me for safekeeping. Mine's in the shop today, so I borrowed it. Thank God that trooper didn't ask me for the registration."

"Where's Charlie?"

"I don't know."

I didn't believe him. But if he was protecting Charlie, why would he trust me? I said, "The cops and Immigration are after him. I'm neither."

"Charlie was already hiding out before they started looking for him."

"What do you mean?"

"I don't know the whole story." He looked up and down Route 7, looked me up and down again. "He ran from a gang war back in Ecuador. He's been living here working hard, saving to bring his sister to America. Somehow they caught up with him. Some enemy spotted him. I don't know. But they're trying to kill him. That's why he's hiding."

"Are you saying he was already hiding when Brian Grose was murdered?"

"The white man? Yes. He was already hiding."

"Are the cops right? Is he a gangbanger?"

"Absolutely not. He's just a slum kid who got caught in a cross fire. You know, you stand up for a friend one day and suddenly you're in it."

"Could you get a message to him?"

"What message?"

"Tell him that I am convinced he did not kill Brian Grose. Tell him I will get him lawyers in Newbury. Tell him I will find out who killed Brian Grose so he won't be charged."

"Let's assume for a moment I could pass your message. I doubt he'd come in on your word."

"It's worth a try. Sooner or later, he's going to fall into a federal man-eating machine. He'll be better off with us. Will you help me?"

Instead of answering yes or no, the priest went off on another tear. "They're putting the pressure on illegals. They've got a new tactic: scaring them. People say the United States can't deport twelve million illegals. But they don't have to. If they deport enough of them, others will go back voluntarily because they don't want to live in these conditions."

"At this moment, Charlie's problems are a lot bigger than being illegal."

"Many people are counting on me," said the priest. "I have to be extra cautious. If I were jailed, many more people than I alone would suffer. So if I am going to help you help Charlie, you have to protect me."

"How? Name it, I'll do it."

He scuffed the ground again and looked away, shaking his head the way you do when you know something's not a good idea, but you're worried you have to do it because not doing it might be worse. Finally he turned back to me. "You have to keep my name out of it. Tell *no one* that I am helping you. Tell *no one* you even met me. No one."

"All right."

"Particularly no one at St. Peter's."

"I don't know anyone at St. Peter's. I don't even know where St. Peter's is."

"My parish in Bridgeport. The parish supports my outreach program program—but the parish should not suffer for it. The Federal authorities are itching to criminalize Christian sanctuary. Give me your word that you will never do anything to call attention to the fact that I am helping you help Charlie Cubrero."

"I give you my word I will do nothing to put you or your parish in danger."

"That could include lying if you are asked about me."

"I will lie to protect you."

"It is a crime to lie to federal agents. You could be charged, prosecuted."

"It's a hard crime to prove."

He looked me deep in the eyes. I had no trouble returning his gaze. I had told him the truth. I would lie to protect him from the consequences of helping me. He smiled, "Lying is a sin, too."

"I was taught to take lying very seriously. But I'm not religious."

"You don't believe in God?"

"I believe in God."

"But not in religion?"

"I'm a Miltonian Deist."

He looked baffled. As well he might. It wasn't taught in Seminary. "What on earth is a Miltonian Deist?"

"Miltonian Deists believe that God and Satan battle it out in Heaven and Hell while we stumble around here in the World. Sometimes when Miltonian Deists meet people like you who really make an effort to serve God, they even believe in religion."

Father Bobby looked at his watch. "The power of institutions, for good and evil, is a subject worth debate, some time—when we both have the time—but right now I have places to go and things to do."

"Wait. What about Charlie?"

"If I see him I will tell him what you said."

"Even if you don't see him can you get the word to him?"

"He will know my opinion and my advice. I really must go. Give me your cell number."

I gave him my card. "May I have your number?"

"I change it every day. Like a drug dealer." He looked weary all of a sudden, almost beaten down. Then he smiled, again. "Don't you worry, Ben, a Miltonian Deist sounds like an amigo. I'll be in touch. Maybe sooner than you think."

Chapter Eleven

Between one third and one half of first dates are broken. In my experience. Most, at the last minute.

Friday stayed busy all day. After parting from Father Bobby on Route 7, I drove home and invited the Adams, the Bowlands, and the Littles to Connie's for cocktails the following night; all could make it, though the Adams had to leave by seven-thirty to join a dinner party. Then I went food shopping at the Big Y. Then I showed a house to a couple who dreamed of owning an authentic antique colonial but were dismayed by the authentic odors brewed up in uninhabited, shuttered old rooms. Then I laid out the ingredients for a participatory dinner for two based on the *Cook's Illustrated* magazine recipe for Moroccan Chicken.

Cook's, which prided itself in meticulous analysis, bold re-thinking, and creative methodology, swore they had discovered ways to make the dish so simple that you could cook it in one hour flat. The first time I tried, it was ready to eat in a little under four hours. And well worth the wait. Next try, conceding that drinking martinis while reading and re-reading the instructions had been counterproductive the first time, I nailed it at three. I got the dish down to two and a half hours next time, but tangled ingredients unforgivably—it didn't taste terrible, but it was not the taste of heaven I had experienced.

My dream was to come in perfect at ninety minutes, and I felt I had a shot tonight with a partner like Lorraine Renner who, being a filmmaker, was a hands on person adept at interpreting technology. Such was my dream. I took the precaution of laying out the ingredients—half the spices in my spice rack, from cayenne through paprika, honey, lemon peel, onions, large carrots (for propping up the breasts, don't ask), chicken broth, olives, cilantro, etcetera. I even washed and dismembered the chicken to get that messy chore out of the way. Then I walked up Main Street to escort Lorraine back to my kitchen.

She was on the phone when I got there.

She waved me in through the screen door, held up a "one-minute" finger and said into the phone, "I'm really sorry. I would love to help you out.... But I can't.... Yes, I know I already have three cats. And that's the problem.... No. You're absolutely right. The cats would not mind. They would like your cat. Or at least get used to it. But—" She rolled her eyes and walked to a wine jug and splashed some in a glass and handed it to me. I mouthed, "Where's yours."

She pantomimed a steering wheel.

Wondering what that meant, I mouthed, "Cheers."

"But the fact that my cats would not mind, or adapt, doesn't change one big problem. I already have three cats—no, please, let me finish—I have three cats—Yes I know a lot of people have three cats. But four cats—a lot of people do *not* have four cats. Four cats would make me 'the cat lady,' and I may be a little weird in some ways, I may be known to drink and get involved with the wrong type"— she glanced my way—"and stay out later than I should, but I am way too young to be known as 'the cat lady.' Goodbye!"

She pressed Off on the phone, plunked it in its charger, and said to me, "You don't need a cat by any chance?"

"I am fully catted."

"They come at me like I'm Mother Teresa. Give me a sip of that!" She grabbed my glass, took a swig and said, "I'm really sorry. I can't do dinner tonight."

"You can't?"

"One of my G-D baby clients just called. They think the kid is going to walk tonight. I've got to shoot it."

"You're going to video a crippled child walking?"

"No, no, no, not a crippled child. A baby. A baby that's never walked before. It wasn't old enough, but they think tonight's the night and I've got to shoot its first steps."

"I'm a little confused. It's Friday. It's evening already. Won't the baby be asleep—wait. You're videoing a *baby*? Why?"

"I make DVD scrapbooks. You know, for people who are too busy to do their own home video? I take all the crappy stuff they've shot, and I shoot some good stuff myself; and then I edit it all together and they've got a home movie starring their kid."

"Why would anyone—" I started to ask.

"Five grand they pay me. I don't know about your business, but if someone offers me five grand to do what I do, and I don't even have to take my clothes off—to me that's serious money."

"I guess I'm just surprised people don't make their own home movies."

"I tried to get out of the walk-shoot, tonight. For all I know he will be asleep when I get there. But they just offered me another thou to be there—no way I could say no. Besides, if they like this, then I get to do the little bastard's pre-school DVD in eighteen months. And a tutor session. First ski run. Day one of kindergarten. By the time he grows up to become a documentarian with a trust fund I'll be able to buy some furniture. So I'm really sorry. But I can't have dinner, tonight."

"Don't worry about it," I said. "Work is work." Then I said, "Drive carefully," and started walking home, feeling a little disappointed and quite lonely.

I was passing Town Hall when who should come down the front steps but the First Selectman herself. Vicky McLachlan, who was walking proof of about the stupidest move I have ever made with a woman, favored long summery dresses, snug on top, flowing below, and they favored her. She has thick chestnut-colored hair with a lot of curls, and while her photogenic front-page smiles help sell Scooter's newspapers, she is thoroughly pleasing to ogle in person as well.

"Ben!" She stepped close, kissed my cheek; and she smelled so good my knees went weak.

"How are you doing?" she asked.

"Just got stood up by a date. How about you?"

"With whom?"

"Lorraine Renner—Just dinner."

We were standing a little closer than people tend to when meeting on the sidewalk in front of Town Hall. "Well, I can't think of anything I'd rather have at this very moment, than 'just dinner,'" said Vicky.

My heart soared in the general direction of the moon, a new sliver of which was settling in the west a couple of steps behind the midsummer sun. "I happen to have one started."

"Oh, I wish.…But Tim's already cooking at home. Want to come?"

"I better pass."

"Oh, come on. Spend the evening with us. You always say you're coming over, but you never do."

"No, no, no. Friday, end of the week, you two must have plenty of catching up to do."

She kissed me again, squeezed my hand, cupped my cheek, and hurried off to their cottage.

I watched her walk until she turned down her lane, rearranged my trousers, and continued on. Ahead, I saw two police cars stopped side by side at the Flagpole, Ollie's gray cruiser and an unmarked unit. Three Federal "company cars" whisked past. Ollie roared off after them and the unmarked unit pulled onto the shoulder. I kept walking—my house is just past the Drover, which shares the flagpole four corners with three churches—and as I reached the unmarked, saw that the driver was Marian Boyce.

No sign of her partner, Arnie. Marian was alone, drumming big fingers on the steering wheel and looking grim. Her window was open. She was watching me approach in her side mirror. I stepped off the sidewalk, crossed the tree lawn, stepped into the street and along the driver's side.

"Dinner?" I asked.

She gave me a you-never-stop-trying look and looked away. "Innocent dinner. I just got stood up."

"Who got smart at the last moment?"

"I have a kitchen full of ingredients for an amazing dinner for two. It will take ninety minutes to cook, with luck, if you help, an hour to eat what will probably be the most spectacularly delicious meal you have ever eaten in your life, and you'll be back on the case by nine-thirty."

I knew my girl: Marian was a woman of powerful appetites. She asked, "How would it taste with water? I can't drink tonight."

"Not a drop of wine will pass any lips."

"No reason why you shouldn't."

"No fun alone. Besides, it's an Arab dish. Poor bastards haven't had a drink since the Eighth Century."

Her generous lips began to the form the "O" of "okay." Before the word passed between them, her radio clattered. "Hang on," she said, closed her window and spoke so softly into her mouthpiece that I could not hear through the glass.

Down slid her window. "Sorry, Pal, gotta go," and gone she was in a haze of burnt rubber and gasoline.

I got home to my kitchen full of ingredients. The cat was out. My answering machine was not blinking. I was standing there, staring at things, when the telephone rang. The house felt so empty, it seemed to echo. I said, "Hello" expecting a telemarketer or somebody drinking Cosmopolitans in Manhattan who had a sudden impulse to go country-house shopping on the weekend.

"Hello, Ben. It's Grace Botsford. Sorry to call so late, I'm still at the office."

"How are you?"

"I thought I would call to see how your investigation is going?"

Why, I wondered, the sudden interest? She hadn't even mentioned it Wednesday when I asked her to talk sense to Donny Butler. Had Rick Bowland and Dan Adams fessed up about hiring Charlie Cubrero off the books? Had she known all alone. Or had she discovered more secrets buried in the Cemetery Association?

"As I told Rick and Dan I'm sure it's only a matter of time before the cops arrest somebody and that somebody looks very much like a Ecuadorian kid named Charlie Cubrero."

"Ben, I heard that three days ago on the news. What are you doing?"

"Nothing I want to say on the telephone."

"Then why don't you stop by my office tomorrow morning?"

I looked at the bowls of spices, olives, garlic, and wondered what was really on her mind? "Grace, have you had dinner?

"No, I didn't feel like cooking tonight. I was thinking about grabbing a bite at the Drover. We could talk there, if you prefer."

"I just happen to have the makings of a Moroccan chicken. If you like Moroccan chicken come over, help cook, and I'll tell you what I know. I've already got it started."

"I don't want to bother you at supper."

"There's plenty for two."

"Are you sure? I eat like a horse."

"There's enough here for a herd."

"All right. Thank you, Ben. I'll be there in fifteen minutes. Do you need anything?"

I looked over the simple ingredients, again. Last time I had forgotten lemon peel and it was sorely missed. But there was a yellow lemon beside a peeler.

"Bring reading glasses. The recipe is a bear."

She arrived in exactly fifteen minutes. I heard the front doorbell and when I saw her standing outside the screen I recalled her stillness in Lorraine's film. She waited for me to answer the door without moving, none of the shuffles and twitches most of us fill waiting time with. Even when she heard my footsteps, she did not move. Though as I opened the door her face opened in a pleasant smile that softened the lines that slanted from her nostrils to the corners of her mouth.

She looked tired. People have grown fond of saying that sixty is the new forty. But it was clear judging by the weariness in her eyes that at the end of a long week the strain of running a business that had always kept two hard workers busy, made Grace Botsford feel more sixty than forty.

She was dressed in dark office slacks and a white cotton blouse. She had exchanged the jacket she usually wore at work for a cotton cardigan against the evening cool. Her hair was pulled back in a bun, and she had slung reading glasses over her neck with a silk cord. I led her to the kitchen, gave her an apron to protect her blouse, and told her very quickly where I stood on the case, minus any mention of Father Bobby, and assured her I had not run up a huge bill.

"But I strongly recommend you spend your money on the bounty hunter if he gets to Charlie first. That way either you have caught the perpetrator yourselves, or if he didn't do it—which I am quite sure he did not—Charlie might be able to give us a clue about who did. Either way, we do the right thing, turning him in with a decent lawyer. I think I can get Tim to stand up for him."

Grace did not look thrilled. "So you have a gut feeling the boy didn't do it, but otherwise essentially, nothing has changed."

"Except that now we have a chance at least of getting to Charlie first. If we do, then we head off the problem of him working for the Association." I looked her in face. "You did know about that, didn't you?"

"Of course."

"I figured."

"No thanks to Rick Bowland."

"He's under the impression you don't know."

"How the devil could Rick and that fool Dan Adams—a bigger fool than his father, if that were possible—please don't repeat that—assume that I wouldn't see that immigrant mowing the grass. He was a foot shorter than Donny Butler and thirty years younger, not to mention being Hispanic."

"They must have figured you were looking the other way."

"I have never looked the other way and neither did Dad. Do you really believe the boy didn't kill Brian?"

"Yes. And I suspect that the cops are thin on evidence. But he's the perfect suspect because if he is innocent they can still arrest him for being illegal and pump a bunch more charges out that—document fraud, identity theft of et-damned-cetera."

Grace pursed her lips and blew through them. She shook her head. "We will not be party to railroading the wrong person for a crime he didn't commit. But if not him, who, then?"

I was not about to say out loud, Sherman Chevalley or Donny Butler or three of your trustees, so I said, "I don't know enough about Brian yet, and I've wasted a lot a time chasing this kid."

Grace shook her head, again. "I knew I should touch base."

"I'll write you an official report if you want."

"Monday will be fine."

"Okay. So, oral report ended, I can offer you a glass of wine."

She hesitated, looked like she wanted to rag on the case a bit more, then decided to drop it for now. "Would you by any chance have the makings of a vodka Martini?"

Silly me, offering wine to a Yankee on Friday evening. "Olives or twist?"

"Olives. Bad enough defying tradition with vodka, but I'm too old for gin."

"Most people are. Straight up?"

"Absolutely."

"I hope you don't mind Smirnoff. The *New York Times* swears by it."

"Dad's favorite."

I got out a pair of martini glasses to ice them, and Grace gasped. "Good Lord, Ben. That glass is enormous."

"It eliminates repetitive strain syndrome. I don't have to pour so often."

"Please don't pour mine anywhere near the rim."

"Wait."

I went out to the dining room to my grandmother's cabinet and returned with a 1920s martini glass. I had forgotten how small real martini glasses were originally. It made mine look like a horse trough. I went back and got another and dropped in small ice cubes to chill them.

When I finished shaking the cocktail shaker, Grace said, "Sixteen more shakes."

"I beg pardon."

"Thirty-three shakes is the magic number. Dad always said, A decent martini requires patience. Which is why they are rarely cold enough in a bar."

"You're very observant, Grace. I don't know how many people would count the number of shakes."

"I work with numbers. And I used to play the piano so I naturally count."

I shook sixteen more shakes, dumped the ice out of the glasses, dropped an olive in each, poured and handed one across the work table. "Cheers."

Grace took a sip that reminded me of Aunt Connie who could make one cocktail last until dinner. "Excellent."

"When did you stop playing piano?"

"Years ago."

"I'm curious why. I've been getting a yen to learn how."

"My father played like Bobby Short. I decided one day I would never catch up." She put down her drink and fished reading glasses from her purse. "Best read the recipe while I can still see straight." I gave her a stool, and she read both pages slowly, word by word, pausing at each ingredient to locate it on the table. When she was done, she rearranged the ingredients in a precise row.

"Now they are in the order they will be used. When you are ready for the next ingredient just take the lead dish."

"Brilliant. I should have thought about that. I was going nuts shifting between the page and the table."

"Shall I read?"

"Grace, do you want a little bite of something first? It'll be a while 'til we eat."

"I'm going to save myself for this recipe. Don't let me stop you."

I was starving already, just thinking about the final result. But I said, "No. Abstemious—food-wise. More room for the recipe."

"Brown the chicken," Grace read. "The oil should be smoking."

I turned on the exhaust fan, heated the oil in the Dutch oven, which I surrounded with a wall of tin foil to contain splatters, salt and peppered the chicken parts, and when white smoke rose from the oil laid them in skin side down.

"Five minutes," said Grace, setting her wrist watch alarm.

I told her a little more about my hunt for Charlie, again leaving out Father Bobby. Her watch beeped. I turned a thigh with a tongs. Grace looked over my shoulder. "The recipe says 'golden' brown. That's only tan."

While we waited I said, "I saw you in Lorraine's movie."

"Good God. That man took such advantage of Dad."

"I never thought of your father as someone take-advantage-able."

"Dad was too polite to turn him down."

"You mean about the film?"

"Dad could not figure out how to say no, and before he knew it Lorraine had him posing in front of Town Hall."

"I thought your father's expression said a lot."

"I'm sure it did. But subtlety only goes so far with someone like Brian Grose. You know Dad was a very sharp business-man—as 'Yankee Trader' as you'd ever meet—but a hot shot like Brian Grose would seize on decency for his own purposes….It's golden brown. Turn it."

I turned legs, breasts and thighs. Grace consulted the recipe and set an alarm for four minutes.

"Did you know Brian well?" I asked.

"I should hope not."

"But he got close to your father."

"He wormed his way in. If that's what you mean by close."

I tugged some loose skin from a thigh with a tongs and discarded it. Ordinarily I would have tasted the crisper bites. But even though I was starving, my gut said this would be the best

Moroccan chicken yet, and I honored my pledge to save myself for the final result.

"I was surprised when you brought Brian in as a trustee."

"That's what I meant," she shot back. "He used Dad. And no sooner had Dad invited him onto the board than Brian began recruiting allies.

"Who?"

"The younger ones."

"Dan Adams?"

"No, Dan stayed loyal—but on the fence, if you know what I mean. He supported Dad, but Dad feared he would suddenly switch sides. For all his hot-headedness, Dan Adams has a fine sense of which way the wind blows.

"But how did it get into the court?"

"Well." Grace took a sip of martini. "Dad was no sooner in his grave than Grose made his move."

"To get his mausoleum approved?"

"He had already pulled that off—talked a few fools into allowing some form of memorial. We had no idea how big it would be. If my poor father had lived to see that monstrosity, it would have killed him."

"Why did you go along?"

"*I* did *not* go along. Some of the others did. I've always suspected that Brian hinted to the fence sitters that he was terminally ill to get his way. I can't prove that, but I suspect it."

"But how did you end up in court?"

"Brian over stepped. When they saw the mausoleum they had voted to allow, even some who had voted approval turned against him. They voted with me to ban any more such monstrosities and that vote pretty much drove Brian out of the picture. That's when he sued. That's what got us into court."

"But with him permanently out of the picture, now, as it were, being dead, isn't it all moot?"

"Others who had joined in the suit, are continuing. They claim that as citizens of the town they have a right to be voted into the Association. If they get in, they will vote me out."

"I wondered."

Her watch beeped. "Take it off."

I heaped the chicken on a plate.

"Pour off the extra fat."

I dumped all but a tablespoon in the sink.

"Onions!" called Grace. "And two lemon zest strips."

I dumped in the sliced onions and the lemon strips. "Here's where it gets tricky. We're supposed to stir until the onions are brown at the edges, right?"

"Five to seven minutes."

"And then all hell breaks loose."

"Garlic thirty seconds til fragrant," Grace read ahead. "Then spices forty-five seconds, til very fragrant, then—"

"But I'm also supposed to let the chicken get cool enough to remove the skin, while stirring the onions."

Grace took her third miniature sip of martini—my glass was bone dry by now—and stepped to the stove. "I'll stir. You skin."

The skin on the drumsticks held tight. I used two tongs to prevent finger burns and snipped resistant strands with a scissors and had them skinned just in time to make first garlic, then spices, fragrant.

"Add broth," read Grace. "And the honey....Scrape the pot. Are you aware that this recipe is called 'simpli-*fying*, not simpli-*fied*?'"

"No, and that explains a lot."

At last we had the thighs and drum sticks back in the pot, simmering.

Grace took her fourth sip. I refilled my glass. "I liked the history lesson you gave in the film."

"I love history. And it's all there in the burying ground."

"Grace, will you take over the Association?"

"What do you mean?"

"Replace your father as president—if the court breaks your way."

"Good Lord no, Ben, though that's a big assumption. No, one of the young ones is welcome to that. I've got my hands full with the agency, now that Dad's gone. I'll just stay on as treasurer."

"Rick Bowland?"

"I don't think Rick has the time—commuting as he does."

I interpreted that as code for *No More Outsiders, Not Even The Best Of Them*, and said, "Dan Adams works right in town."

"Dan would have been all right. Before he joined the new bank. We've had a relationship for so long with Newbury Savings—now that Wes Little has joined them, he could step forward. Though I would prefer one of their trustees." Code for *Someone Who Has Been Around And Loyal Since At Least 1857*, the year of the bank's charter.

"An 'Admitted Inhabitant'?" I asked with a smile.

She give up no more smile than she had in Brian's death film. "A resident who can be counted upon to take care of it for the next sixty years, as my father did for the last sixty years. A young townsman, like yourself." Code for *You should volunteer, Ben.*

"Not too many people live as long as your father, Grace." Code for *Not every son is the man his father and grandfather were.*

"Your Aunt Constance is going strong." Code for *You've got the genes.*

Her watch beeped. "Carrots and white meat."

We laid a base of carrot rounds on top of the legs and thighs and laid in the breasts. "Simmer ten to fifteen minutes," read Grace. "What is this you've written here? Lid on?"

"They forgot to tell you to put it back on. It keeps the moisture in, like a Moroccan tagine."

"Is your thermometer ready?"

I got one out of the drawer. By then it was clear that Grace was not a woman to guess at temperature.

"So Brian was a really calculating guy."

Grace thought that over. "In theory. In practice he was too impatient. Ramming that monstrosity in the burying ground before he had really solidified his power on the board was counterproductive."

Twelve minutes and one-hundred-and-sixty degrees later we removed the chicken from the pot again.

Now Grace read from my notes in the margin. "Boil water for couscous. Chop cilantro."

Six minutes later, when the carrots were tender and the liquid thick, Grace said, dubiously, "I see you have edited the next step."

"If you put the chicken back in first you can't stir the cilantro and lemon."

She put on her glasses, again, and re-read the recipe. I said, "Grace, you look as skeptical as if I had requested liability insurance for an eight-hundred horse power motorcycle."

She kept reading and said, at last, "You know, I see your point."

Into the pot went cilantro, garlic and zest, and lemon juice. Then I returned the chicken, piece by piece, coating each with the sauce. "What time is it?" asked Grace. "I am suddenly starving."

"New world record," I said. "One hour and twenty-seven minutes. Can you imagine Arabs cooking this over a fire?"

"Why not?" said Grace. "They own slaves."

We carried our plates into the dining room, where I had already set the table and put a bottle of Lasendal in an ice bucket. After the first bite Grace closed her eyes and said, "I think this is the most delicious thing I have ever eaten."

I had waited to see her reaction, and now I raised the first fragrant fork toward my mouth. The miracle of the dish was that each and every spice—

Deeee-Dahhhhh. Deeee-Dahhhhh.

The Plectron's duotone echoed down the stairs. *Firehouse, now! Firehouse, now! Firehouse, now! Firehouse, now!* "

I stood up.

"Fire or accident?" asked Grace.

In answer, a mechanical voice pinpointed the call: "Structural fire. Morris Mountain. Kantor Farm.

"Fred's place," I shouted, running for my gear.

Chapter Twelve

We could see the sky streaming red long before we got up the mountain.

I was crammed into the jump seat of the older attack truck. Many bake sales and lobster fests from replacement, its tired diesel labored on the steep road far behind the light attack truck and Chief Eddie who had forged ahead in the SUV. Suddenly he radioed a warning to us and the pumpers behind us. He sounded less cheery than last time out, more in Iraq mode.

"Heads up. Some kind of police activity."

The volunteers crowded into the cab looked at each other. "Police activity" did not describe the routine presence of Trooper Moody, which would be related as a simple, "Ollie's here," or, "Doesn't Ollie ever sleep?"

The radio shrilled again. "They're all over the place. Try not to run over any cops." A minute later Chief Eddie had scoped out the situation up close and he radioed another warning. A ton of Homeland Security money had been spent to get all the first responders on radios that could talk to each other, and be overheard. But Eddie Thomas was not a man to self-censor himself. "You see any of these idiots draw a weapon, hit the deck."

In fact, we discovered when our truck had climbed high enough to see flames shooting from the roof of Fred Kantor's farm-hands dormitory, that various branches of Homeland Security had saturated the neighborhood with the automatic rifles usually found in a war zone. There were guns everywhere, not the sidearms cops draw from their holsters, but the heavy weapons that soldiers hang in front of their body-armored chests. They stood in the leaping shadows watching the building burn.

Nor was the smoke billowing into the sky the sort of smoke we expected. Spicing the usual mix of burning wood, shingles and insulation was the sharp sting of tear gas. It hung heavily in the air—the stink of street fighting, so unlike a hillside farm.

Garden hoses crisscrossed the barnyard between the dormitory and Fred and Joyce's house and the barns as if they had tried to fight the blaze before we arrived in the trucks. A private ambulance, not the Newbury volunteer's, was parked with its lights flashing. Hunched on its back bumper, an ICE agent was holding his foot. Just as we piled out of the trucks, the roof of the dormitory fell into the building, which erupted in volcanic sparks.

"Heads up!" Chief Eddie ordered. "The building's a goner. We're going to hose down the others before they catch too." He broke us up into teams to run hose from the pumpers to a pond. I ended up at one of the barns, humping hose for Wes Little who aimed the nozzle at the roof. When we looked next, the dormitory had burned to little but cinders and a charred wooden frame. At least it was replaceable. Not one of the antiques that we were soaking down to save. But Fred Kantor was not looking on the bright side.

"Monumental screwup!" he yelled at an ICE agent, who had a bull horn dangling from his wrist.

"Back away, sir."

"Don't 'sir' me you son of a bitch. You know goddamned well what happened, you so-called agent-in-charge."

The agent-in-charge looked even madder than Fred and completely discombobulated to discover that wealthy gentleman farmers were harder to bully than frightened foreigners. He drew himself up to his full height and yelled down at the much shorter Fred, "Operation Return to Sender raids are aimed at child molesters, gang members, violent criminals."

Fred pointed at a half dozen Ecuadorians sitting on the ground with their hands cuffed behind them. "Those aren't criminals. They're my farmhands."

"This raid sends a message: When we deport you, we're serious."

"Serious?" Fred hopped up and down and screamed. "My employees came out as requested, hands in the air. That idiot"— he pointed at the agent holding his foot— "accidentally shot himself. Your other idiots responded by shooting at my building. My farm hands ran for their lives. You picked up that bull horn and ordered the men inside the building to surrender. Since there was no one left in there no one came out. But that was a concept beyond your comprehension, so you fired tear gas into my building. Which started that goddamned fire. You're telling *me* to back away. *You* back away!"

"Sir, we guard America's borders from inside."

"Who needs borders when government runs amok?"

The heavy *thump-thump* of a helicopter interrupted Fred. He stopped yelling and threw an arm around Joyce, who looked up with a funny smile on her face.

The agent-in-charge whirled on a heavily-armed aide. "Who called in the chopper?"

"Not me sir."

The machine clattered out of the sky and landed by firelight. Prop wash scattered ash and cinders. The agent ran toward it, saluting. The blades stopped twirling. The racket ceased. The door opened.

The ICE agent's salute dribbled toward his knees. Out of the helicopter hopped two men and a woman in business suits. Each carried a double-wide brief case.

"May we have your name sir?" they chorused.

"Who the hell are you?"

"Mr. Kantor's attorneys."

〈 〉〈 〉〈 〉

The population of the barnyard fell by half as federal gunmen faded into the shadows leaving Newbury Hook and Ladder

Number One, the ICE agent-in-charge, Fred and Joyce, and their lawyers to contemplate the ruins. I spotted a familiar-looking bulging silhouette edging toward the dark road and ran after him. "Found your way to the boonies?"

"Hey, what are you, Dude?" asked Big Al Vetere. "Fireman?'

"Volunteer. What are you doing here?"

"Drove up to bag Cubrero. Walked into a m-effing ICE raid."

"What made you think Cubrero was here?"

"Does Gimbels tell Macy?"

"Gimbels went bankrupt thirty years ago."

"I heard somebody saw his car on Route 7."

"Really?"

"Yeah. So I headed up here, figuring he holed up in the nearest thing to home."

"How'd you find it?"

"Google Maps. Anyway I'm nosing around in the bushes, about to make my move, and I see a bunch of SUVs creeping up the road with their lights off. A mob of Feds climb down wearing those big Kevlar gloves and I think, 'Oh boy. It's a raid.'"

The Kevlar gloves, Al explained to the country bumpkin, were to protect the agents' hands from broken glass on window ledges and rusty razor wire. Another clue that tipped Al off, he admitted, were law enforcement IDs dangling on necklaces.

"They're going, 'Police! *Policia!* Police' at that house. Somebody pulls back a curtain and they flash their badges. Lights go out. Shooting starts. I'm like behind the fattest tree in the yard."

"The owner says the Feds just starting shooting."

"No way. That's not true. The first shot came from inside."

"You sure?"

"Damned sure. The guys inside shot first. *Then* the Feds opened up."

"Amazing they didn't get killed. Wooden building, and the Feds had some heavy ordnance."

Al rubbed his face. "Feds didn't start shooting right away. Someone in there let loose a round. Outside everybody froze. I mean these guys aren't DEA or special forces. They don't expect to get shot it. The fools they're after just run for it. So like for one second, they're all looking at each other, like, 'What the fuck?'"

"Is that when the ICE agent shot himself in the foot?"

Al chuckled. "You saw that, did you? Just like in the jokes, the dumb fuck. *Then* they started shooting."

I went back to helping the guys roll hose. Dan Adam's father Chuck—of all people—said to me, "Think how scared they must have been in there."

"Who?"

"Fred's hands. Guns everywhere all of a sudden. Probably thought they were dead men. I would have run too."

Chuck Adams had a point. I would have run too. Unless I was more complicated, shall we say, than an ordinary illegal farmhand. If I were a seasoned street fighter or a gang leader, accustomed to police raids, I would have squeezed off a shot in the air and slipped away in the chaos I had started.

As we headed back to Newbury, the attack pumper's headlights swept an unmarked State Police Crown Victoria parked at the foot of the Kantor's drive. Detectives Marian and Arnie were standing outside the car, so still and unhappy they looked like the sculptor George Segal had wrapped them in plaster.

I walked home from the fire house, too hungry to even shower the smoke off first. Grace had covered my plate with plastic wrap, cleaned up the kitchen and left a note. "It was delicious, thank you."

A gentle nuking in the microwave warmed my plate. I sat to it with a cold glass of Vouvray, took a sip and reached for my fork. Someone started knocking on the front door. Very odd, so late; a friend would have tried the kitchen door; a real estate client would wait til morning. I hurried through the house and opened the door. It was Al Vetere. A beat-to-death Crown Victoria that he must have bought at a used police car auction was parked at the curb.

"Hey, Ben, Dude, can you tell me someplace to stay around here? I was just at that Yankee Drive place, and they want a fortune for a room."

"It's kind of a honeymoon suite," I explained. "They assume the guests are pooling resources."

"Any idea where else I find a room at this hour?"

The nearest motel was a long drive and a rat hole, so I said, "Come on in, you can crash in the guest room."

He lumbered after me through the living room and dining room—"Hey, Dude, some digs."—and into the kitchen. "Oh man, that smells good."

"Have you eaten, Al?"

"Kitchen was closed at that Drive place."

"Welcome to the boonies. Here, have some of this."

Al sat. I went to get another plate. The phone rang. "Excuse me a second."

Rick Bowland wanted to talk. He said he knew that it was one in the morning, but he had heard there was a police raid at the Kantor farm and wondered had they arrested Charlie Cubrero. I told him no and good night and hurried back to the kitchen where Al removed a tooth pick from his mouth to say, "Hmmmm, hmmm, that was good. Got any more?"

With murder on my mind it was easy to say, "In return for a place to sleep tonight, and in return for me not *killing* you for eating my dinner—no, no, not to worry, a straight answer will hold me 'til breakfast—what did you mean when you said, 'I heard somebody saw Charlie Cubrero's car on Route 7'. Who? Where? Why did you come here?"

"Well, Ben, I'm not sure I can flip a source."

"The only motel that might still be open tonight is frequented by deer hunters. The beds are crawling with deer ticks that give you Lyme Disease." It wasn't deer season, but I doubted Al knew that. "I'm not taking anything away from you, Al. I'm not moving in on your case. I just want some help. Tell me who, where, why? Or sleep in your car."

"Okay, okay. I ran into a priest."

"A priest? What kind of priest?"

"A priest priest. You know like a Catholic?"

"What's his name."

"Gave my word I wouldn't rat him out."

"God forbid."

"The priest is doing an outreach—for the illegals? Lot of 'em do that. They got a lot of Latinos. Replacing Italians like me who stop going when our mother dies. The Irish, too, same problem. Nobody goes to mass except Latinos. So anyhow, he's outreaching these dumb illegals and we got to talking."

"But you're on the other side, catching illegals."

"Well he don't know that. I give him a card that says I'm a social worker."

"And the priest bought that?"

"Damned straight he bought it. I can be very convincing."

"How did you get to talking to the priest in the first place?"

Al lowered his voice and looked around my kitchen. The cat was out. We were alone. "I got a tip a wheelman was at this diner, in Bridgeport?"

"A wheelman?" Where did Al get his words, I wondered. Hundred year old TV movies.

"Yeah, you know. A guy who drives the car when you do a drive-by hit."

"Oh, a *modern* wheelman."

"Yeah, what do you think? Anyhow, this drive-by dude told me about a guy who drove for him. Best driver he ever saw. They did a couple of shootings down in Norwalk."

"Why is a hitman talking to you, Al? I think you're jerking me around."

"No, man. I took a page from your book. I helped a guy get away and he figured I was his pal. Like you did with those illegals when you slugged me."

I looked at him in disbelief, but Al was not kidding. Without even trying, just by setting an example, I had become mentor to a half-assed bounty hunter who wanted to become a PI.

"You saved a hitman from the police?"

"No. Some guys were chasing him with baseball bats. I gave him a hand. Sure, enough, he's my buddy. Just like you did."

The short of it was that Al's new best friend, a supposed drive-by shooter who I suspected was inflating his resume´, turned Al onto an Ecuadorian driver who sounded very much like Charlie Cubrero who was expected to show up in a diner where Al met an Ecuadorian outreach priest instead. Father Bobby did get around.

"And the priest sent you to Newbury."

"Said somebody told him they saw his car heading that way. Orange 'sucker. You couldn't miss it."

"Presumably a different vehicle than the one he used for drive-by shootings?"

I was finishing my first cup of coffee early the next morning, when I heard giggles, and grunts and heavy breathing in front of the house. I looked out the window and saw Dennis and Albert Chevalley carrying a blue Smart Car around Big Al's fake police cruiser and up my front walk. It was the size of a mature Blue Angel Hosta in Aunt Connie's garden, big for a Hosta, small for a car. Albert held the front end. Dennis the back. Their cousin Anton, who had married into the felonious Jervis clan and was rarely seen in daylight, was holding up the middle.

I opened the front door.

"Uh oh," said Albert. "We're in jail."

"If you put that car on my front step I will tell Pink I saw you do it."

Anton let go the middle to scratch his nose and the brothers staggered under the additional weight of what was, while a very small automobile, still an automobile. Itch satisfied, Anton lit a cigarette and grabbed the middle again.

"What do you think Pink will do to you?" I asked.

"We was just kidding, Ben."

"Put it in my driveway and go tell Pink that tomorrow I need something bigger and faster."

They huffed and puffed across the lawn, stomped through a lily bed before I could stop them, and dropped it in my driveway.

Al came down, inquiring about breakfast.

I was recommending the Frenchtown Diner, while steering him out the kitchen door, when the phone rang. I reminded him quickly that I would pay cash for Charlie Cubrero, no waiting, no paperwork, no hassles.

We shook hands goodbye. I picked up the phone. It was Aunt Connie. "After you bid good morning to your overnight guest, could come you over for a moment?"

"Before you get your hopes up, my guest was a gentleman—a term I use in the loosest sense—who was in town on business."

"I am so sorry. I thought I recognized a prowl car belonging to a state police detective with lovely gray eyes."

"He drives a similar looking car so that he can appear to be a policeman without actually impersonating one. And his eyes are beady. Anyhow, he just left. I'll be right over."

The phone rang again. Actual house business. I chatted up the client, a not unattractive divorced lawyer from New York who was seriously considering my advice that she was better off sinking her considerable disposable income into an antique house instead of another husband. She wondered aloud what she would do on the weekends in a house alone. I suggested she make friends with the locals, and we made an appointment to see a couple of properties tomorrow, right after I walked Connie home from church.

Then I hurried across the street and found Connie outside in the old-fashioned perennial border behind her house, dead-heading spent blossoms into an English trug. She was dressed for gardening in a cotton dress, a stand of pearls, and a broad brim hat. Despite our kidding around on the phone, she wore a troubled expression, one I had come to recognize as set off by a memory problem.

"Good morning."

"Good morning, Ben."

"I thought I would just stop over," I lied.

"Benjamin Abbott, what are you talking about? Didn't we just get off the telephone?"

"Sorry, yeah, got distracted, had another call." Good, she remembered telephoning me. Sometimes she didn't. I hoped she would correct me with, "Yes, not Yeah." Instead she glanced into the arborvitae hedge that bordered the back of the place, and her gaze locked there.

Finally, I broke the silence. "What is it?" I asked.

"Strange," she murmured. "Ever since we talked about Mr. Grose's assignations."

"Gossibles included Cynthia Little, Georgia Bowland, Lorraine Renner, and Priscilla Adams if I recall."

"Not Lorraine."

"Right. That's what you said. Only blondes. Anyway, minus Lorraine, the blondes and their husbands are coming by for drinks this evening."

"Yes, yes, I know that. Everything is taken care of. Mrs. Mealy will bring hors d'oeuvres. But we don't need her to serve."

"Six guests, no need."

"But ever since we talked about Mr. Grose's relationships I've had all sorts of strange words running in my head."

"What words?"

"Honor. Mercy. Kindness. Charity."

"Strange?" I asked. "They sound more like good causes. Except that contributing to Newbury Forest instead of getting sued is the only good cause I've heard in the same breath with Brian Grose."

"Constance...."

"Your name," I said. And when she didn't answer right away I started getting scared.

Finally, she said, "I think I know my own name, Ben. It's the other names I wonder about. I mean, there was a time when names that conferred qualities were common. Honor. Charity. Faith. Hope. Constance. My friend Bishop Marsh's daughters were named Patience and Prudence. We used to joke that he'd name a third Perspicacity. And a fourth, Purposeful." She smiled, but her smile faded quickly and she looked up at me and raised both hands as if extending a tangled skein of yarn. Help me, please untangle strands of Honor, Charity, Faith, Hope, Patience, Prudence, Perspicacity, Purpose and Constance.

"Grace?" I asked.

Connie's face clouded.

"Three wives of Association Trustees and the daughter of the president?"

"Oh good lord, Ben, what a thing to think. She's twenty years his senior."

"More like fifteen."

"But if there was ever a constant woman, it was Grace Botsford."

"Grace isn't married. Neither was Brian. What was unconstant?"

"But the age. Not to mention background. I mean, really Ben. Grace is…and Grose was….Well, you know what I mean."

She meant, although she would never permit intuitive distinctions to sink so low as bigotry, that Grace was "Grace Botsford of Newbury," while Brian was "Brian Grose of God-knew-where." In the democratic republic of New England, "of Newbury" was not quite translatable to a German "von Newburgh" or a French "de Newbrie," shall we say, but it carried more weight on Constance Abbott's Main Street than "of, von, or de God-knew-where."

"Actually, I found out he's from farm people. Grew up down in Arkansas. Cotton farmers."

"Ah, the long arm of the Department of Agriculture. The ugliest house in Newbury paid for by Federal cotton subsidies."

"No. Small family operation. Just working farmers. Salt of the earth."

"Well, he certainly put on airs."

"Do you recall gossip about him and Grace?"

"No."

"No?"

"No, I don't."

"But, then what do you suppose prompted this connection? If there is a connection."

Connie sighed. "I suppose that I have eyes as well as ears. Perhaps I noticed something. Something different than the ordinary. After all, I've known Grace since Gerard used to bring her along when she was a little girl. Maybe I saw....God knows what. A blush where there'd been no blush?"

She shook her head. "Pretty girl, when she was younger. Lovely posture—all the Botsfords have that....Sad, Mr. Grose's passing, when you consider that with Gerard gone Grace is free to marry at last." She looked at me, suddenly, head cocked like a blue jay. "How do you feel about asking Grace to join us this evening?"

Chapter Thirteen

From Connie's, I hurried up Main Street and knocked on Lorraine Renner's door, hoping nine-thirty in the morning wasn't too early.

"In here," she called through the screen. She was in the birth/editing room, working in a fuzzy bathrobe.

"Is this too early? Should I come back later?"

"No, I haven't gone to bed. Didn't get back from New York until one. I was wired from the drive, so I just went to work."

"Did the baby walk?"

"His parents think so. I got great footage of a dangling infant. How you doing? I heard the fire trucks coming back late. Was that you?"

"Fred and Joyce's dormitory. Huge immigration raid. It ended up like the Branch Davidians. Miracle nobody got killed."

"So what's up?"

"Tell me to go to hell if it seems I'm too nosy. But I am asking for a reason."

"Asking what?"

"The thing is you're the only person I know who spent a lot of time with Brian Grose."

"It happens with the subject of your film."

"Did Brian ever put any moves on you?"

"Just the typical."

"Typical?"

"Typical 'I'm a guy, you're a woman, we're alone,' syndrome." She re-tied the belt around her robe and said. "No big deal. It's just a guy impulse. Like you looking down the front of my robe—Don't apologize—It's hormones and genes and chromosomes. Most men grow out of it when they turn ninety-five."

"I'm not looking forward to that."

"Most men, not all. I don't think you have to worry."

"Could I ask your reaction? I mean to Brian. Like was he really smooth?"

Lorraine gave me a look. "To somebody else, maybe. Not my type."

"So you wouldn't call him a Don Juan?"

"Are you wondering if he got shot by a pissed off girl friend?"

"Yes. Which I would appreciate your keeping between us."

"Like I say, he wasn't my Don Juan type. But everybody's got their type, right?"

> > >

I was back in my office failing to imagine Brian Grose successfully seducing four women linked to the Cemetery Association to erect his mausoleum when I got a call from Sherman Chevalley. A *blatting* noise in the background indicated he was on his motorcycle.

"Hey, Ben?" He sounded as if he were asking for something.

"What's up?"

"Why don't we go have a beer?" It was almost noon.

I wondered if he was going to come clean about who was trying to kill him and if that someone had something to do with Brian Grose getting shot, so I said, "Sure, where are you?"

"Right outside your house."

I parted the sheer that covered the window. On the sidewalk, mothers walking their children to the library for Saturday Story Hour gripped small hands and quickened their pace as the scarecrow in boots, jeans, and mottled tee shirt that was Sherman Chevalley swooped his Harley into my drive. Stringy hair trailed from the do rag and cell phone headset that he wore in lieu of a helmet.

"Come on in. I got some Rhode Island Red in the fridge."

"That's okay. I'm little greasy. Let's go out."

I was too busy to waste the afternoon in a bar. "I'll cover the floor with newspaper."

"Naw, why don't we hit a joint."

"White Birch?"

"I was thinking somewhere more private?"

More private than the White Birch? As far as I knew, the popular line about what happens in Vegas stays in Vegas was originally coined in Wide Greg's establishment.

Sherman said, "They re-opened the Hitching Post."

"You're kidding. They get a new bar?"

"Naw, they nailed the old one back together. So you'll follow me up there, right? I might have to see a guy. Won't take long."

"Hang on one sec, I got another call coming in," I lied, put the phone down, walked into the kitchen and dialed Chevalley Enterprises on my cell. "It's Ben, Betty. Pink in yet? (Not a money bet Saturday before noon as the name "Pinkerton Chevalley," the time "Friday night," and the phrase "riotous debauch" could easily be imagined in the same sentence.).... Pink, got a question for you. Did Sherman just ask you to go drinking?"

"Yeah."

"Why didn't you?"

"Cause the weasel was banging me."

"Did he want to go to the Hitching Post?"

"That's how I knew he was banging me."

"You mean you think he's meeting somebody and wants backup?"

"You going deaf, Ben? Listen, I don't mind going along as a guy's hitter if a guy is straight with me. I'll back up any man who asks. Ever turn you down? But if he's weaseling me—like surprise, Pink, look at all them dudes with baseball bats, wonder where they came from—I'm not interested."

"Thanks, Pink."

"Watch your behind. He's probably buying meth."

"Sherman is not stupid enough to do meth—oh, you mean stupid enough to sell it?"

Pink said, "You shouldn't be allowed out," and hung up.

I went back to the office phone and told Sherman, "Hitching Post it is." My gut told me this was not about meth. If it was, I was outta there so fast they would hear me whiz.

"You want to ride on back?"

I weighed for a moment of fleeting youth the pleasure of blasting north on a summer day on a back road on the back of very fast Harley versus wearing a seatbelt surrounded by Smart Car steel and plastic. I leaned to the former, until I imagined walking twenty miles home from the Hitching Post after Sherman rolled off without me for what seemed to him like a good reason at the time.

So I said, "I've got people coming over. I better follow you so I can leave early." Which turned out to be a very wise decision.

The Hitching Post was a long ways north of Newbury on a remote country road that skirted lands that belonged to the Jervis clan—from whom Sherman might buy meth, if meth was his goal—and the Indian reservation. We headed out of town, me trailing, up Route 7 for eight miles, and cut off onto a narrow paved road that wound through farm land into a broad reach of state forest. I had my windows open to enjoy the clean crisp rhythm of motorcycle exhaust from a perfectly tuned machine. The sound of manhood, I was thinking, rhapsodically (almost kicking myself for not riding along with him) when suddenly I heard a loud *bang*, which I thought was the bike backfiring.

Sherman's arms flew high and wide. He looked like he had been crucified. Sunlight glinting through the trees sparked dazzling reflections of Harley chrome as the bike wobbled. Sherman slumped forward. I saw his brake light flash and stomped my own brakes before I ran into him. The bike swerved toward the ditch, veered away, crossed the road, skidded on the far shoulder and slammed on its side.

I pulled past, stopped the car in the road with flashers blinking and headlights on to block on coming traffic, and ran to him, bracing for gore.

He never wore a helmet, of course. Connecticut motor vehicle law still permits such nonsense, and topping the list of things Sherman believed that a real man did not do was wear a helmet on a motorcycle. Even though it is a medical fact that when most people fall on pavement their head lands first. Even though any emergency room doctor will tell you that they enjoy a happier success rate with broken legs and shattered arms than spattered brains.

There was so much blood I had no idea where his brains were. His face was covered in red as was his tee shirt. Possessing no brain surgery skills I decided to tackle the problem of getting the crushing weight of the bike off him. I crouched down and lifted with all my strength. Seven hundred pounds of steel would not budge. Spots flashed in front of my eyes as I concentrated everything I had and tried again. I heard a roaring in my head, the spots merge into lightning bolts. Suddenly the bike began to tilt upward. I thought I must be having one of those adrenalin experiences where your body does things it can't ordinarily. Then I heard a grunt next to me.

"*Pussy.*"

Sherman was helping push.

We got it up onto its wheels, and I dragged him away from it before it fell on him again.

"You okay, Sherman?"

"What are you, whack?"

"I'll call an ambulance."

"You want to get this blood out of my eyes?"

I called in 911 and then I took my jacket off and laid it over him to keep him warm and went looking for a stream. A car stopped. It was driven by an old woman who came running with a blanket and we covered him with that, too. She sat down on the ground and held Sherman's hand. I said, "Ambulance is coming. I'll find some water. Be right back," and hurried up the road toward a culvert that I hoped carried a stream that the summer hadn't dried up. It was still flowing. I took my shirt off and soaked it and was just up standing when I heard rustling in the brush less than ten feet away. I saw the gleam of a rifle and the glint of a scope.

Chapter Fourteen

I dove head first at it before the muzzle could swing at me.

A boy, no older than pre-teen, with the dark, pinched features I associated with the abysmally inbred, intently villainous Jervis clan glared from the bush. I grabbed the barrel and tried to twist away from the business end. The kid tugged on the stock. His little arms and legs were stick thin, and I had almost got it away from him when he yelled, "Finders keepers!"

I was so surprised I actually let go of what I saw was a shiny new .22 woodchuck rifle—which was all the time the kid needed to crash off into the woods with it.

"The cops need that for evidence," I shouted after him.

"Screw them," he hurled over his shoulder, confirming his Jervis credentials, and disappeared, iterating a now-exultant, "Finders keepers!"

It was clear what had happened. The gunman gunning for Sherman had been spotted, as any stranger would be, by a Jervis kid out trapping muskrat or digging up rare wild flowers to sell to unscrupulous collectors, or hoping to steal a truck when the driver stopped to pee in the woods. The gunman took his shot and with every reason to believe that Sherman was thoroughly dead, tossed the evidence, bought cheap at Wal-Mart, and split. The kid saw a free weapon that would elevate him from trapper/digger to deer poacher. Such a small caliber weapon required a highly accurate head shot to kill a deer, and he would practice hard as soon as he convinced an adult to steal him some ammunition.

I poked around for confirmation of my theory. There were footprints in the stream bed other than mine and some scrapes in the moss where the shooter had steadied the gun on the culvert.

Then I went back to Sherman who was sprawled on the shoulder with his hand being held by the old lady who had stopped.

"How you doing?"

"Legs hurt like a sonofabitch—excuse me, Ma'am."

I wiped the blood off his face and out of his eyes with my wet shirt and had a close look at his scalp, which had a shallow furrow in it—not gouged by falling on his head, but by .22 slug that had come within a quarter inch of relieving the Department of Corrections of further responsibility for Sherman's rehabilitation. The lady who had stopped went to her car to call her daughter who was expecting her, and I took the moment of privacy to say to Sherman, "The guy knew you were coming."

"What guy?"

"The guy who shot you, you idiot. What are you into Sherman? He set you up. Told you to meet him at the Hitching Post and almost blew you away. Why?"

"I don't know what you're talking about, Ben."

"I just found the .22 he shot you with."

"Oh shit! Ben, you got to hide it."

"Consider it disappeared."

"Thanks, pal. You're the best."

"So we agree that you were shot?"

"Something hammered me in the head."

"He had a scope. You're lucky he missed."

"I turned my head to spit," Sherman said, with wonder warming his voice. "Kind of thing could almost make you believe in God," he marveled. We heard sirens, an ambulance howl and Trooper Moody's whoopers clearing the way.

"Don't say nothing to Ollie."

"Who did you see at the mausoleum?"

"What?"

"You heard me. Who did you see at the mausoleum?"

"Latino guy."

"What Latino guy? The picture I showed you?"

"Not him."

"Not Charlie Cubrero? Who?"

"I don't know," he lied, but by then Betty Butler and Trooper Moody had arrived. Betty had an assistant and a stretcher. Ollie had handcuffs which he snapped around Sherman's bony wrists and told him he was under arrest.

"What for?" Sherman and I chorused, Sherman indignant, me wondering if the State Police could prove he had shot Brian Grose.

"Credit card fraud."

"*Credit card fraud?*" Where in hell did that come from, I wondered, until I looked at Sherman who did not appear surprised.

Betty worked on him for a while. Then they loaded him into the ambulance. "Hey Ben," Sherman called. "Do me a favor, pal. Tell my Mom I'm okay."

I drove back to Newbury, picked up Aunt Helen and drove her to the hospital to let her see for herself. Turned out he wasn't exactly that okay. They had him in surgery for a long while, inserting steel pins in leg bones, and the doctor said he would be in intensive care until Sunday morning. The elderly officer the cops stationed at the door to keep Sherman, who was well known for such shenanigans, from clumping off on crutches would double as protection. Which relieved a grateful me of having to introduce dicey subjects like Sherman's possible witnessing of Brian Grose's murderer, and the rifle taken by the scavenging Jervis kid. Nobody, including me, spoke to the police about the Jervis clan, who made my Chevalley cousins look like life members of the Men's Literary and Social Club of Newbury Street (Founded in 1894). Though with me it was also personal as Gwen Jervis, the red-haired daughter of Old Herman, Gangster Boss Emeritus, had been my friend since Eighth Grade.

I drove Aunt Helen home with a promise of bringing her back in the morning—less out of cousinly kindness than a desire for a close family connection to a patient whose visiting privileges would be curtailed.

Then I cancelled Sunday's house showing appointment with the not unattractive New York lawyer, shaved, showered, and got to Aunt Connie's in time to fill an ice bucket and greet our first guests.

Chapter Fifteen

Grace Botsford was first. Early, in fact. Connie was still upstairs. I offered her a martini. She said, "I felt last night's this morning. I'll have a glass of white wine, please."

Connie had a fine old Prohibition bar, the kind that closed up to look like an ordinary cabinet until the teetotalers went home. I poured Grace a glass of wine and one for myself.

"I've always admired this house."

"Connie said you used to come here as a little girl."

"It was the first 'mansion' I had ever been in. That grand staircase and the magic of a second staircase off the kitchen. It was quite magnificent to a child." She took a second sip and looked around, as if confirming we were alone, though of course we were as no one else had come yet. Lowering her voice, she said, "Part of its charm was that I thought I might live here—before your aunt turned my father down."

"What do you mean?"

"When he asked her to marry him—you knew that, didn't you. Oh, good Lord, I'm so sorry Ben, I just assumed you knew."

"No, but I'm fascinated. When was that?"

"Oh, Lord. I was a small child. I mean my mother died when I was four and Dad was raising a little girl by himself, and I'd hear relatives whispering the way they do as if children were deaf: 'Gerard should marry.' Back then it was still frowned upon for a man to raise children alone. I began to fantasize about a new mother. Then we started coming here, often. I was dazzled. She was so beautiful."

"Why did Connie turn him down?"

"Dad told me, years later, that Connie told him to wait until he grew up."

"How old was he?"

"Thirty-five."

"Grew up? He had already taken over the Cemetery Association. He was a man of substance. What did she mean?"

"All I know is that when he was in his seventies Dad said, 'Connie Abbott was right. Saved us both a lot of trouble'—here she is. Hello, Constance, how are you?"

Connie was coming down the steps a little unsteadily and I went to help her, but Grace mounted the stairs and shook her hand briskly, while smoothly offering support.

Connie said, "Hello, Dear—Benjamin, I overheard that. For your information, I turned Gerard Botsford down because he was very full of himself. We remained great chums anyway. No harm done, except poor Grace didn't get me for a new mother, which was probably just as well, as I was quite full of myself, too, and together we would have driven the child nuts."

The door bells chimed. I greeted Rick and Georgia Bowland. Rick was wearing a coat and tie. Georgia was wearing her trust fund in the form of a beautiful Asiatica jacket made of antique Japanese kimono cloth; she seemed happy, not at all fragile tonight. Both looked pleased by an occasion to dress up on a Saturday. I shook Rick's hand and kissed Georgia's pale cheek. "Loved your Notables. A portrait painter and a shopkeeper—quite a range."

"We exposed our deepest fantasies," Georgia said, in her low, compelling voice.

I poured wine for them. Rick started to ask about the case, but the bells rang again. I excused myself and found Dan and Priscilla Adams and Wes and Cynthia Little bunched on the front steps, faces so bright that I assumed that one couple had stopped at the other's for a couple of quick ones before they came.

Priscilla, whose proudly glossy, perfectly straight, lustrously golden hair announced, Mayflower Daughter, said, "This is so great. Thank you for inviting us."

I said, "Connie's idea. I'm just the bartender."

Cynthia Little said, "I'm glad your aunt still feels up to a party."

Cynthia was quite pretty, tonight, wearing some sort of goldish shadow that made her hazel eyes glow. "Connie is looking forward to meeting you," I told her. "Come on in." I took Priscilla's shapely arm, which was summerly bare, and led them to the living room.

The guys, who would not be wearing jackets if they weren't visiting Connie, were wearing them over polo shirts. Neither of the couples had been in Connie's house before. Priscilla had grown up in comfort. But Cynthia appeared somewhat overwhelmed. I heard her whisper to Wes, "It's like a museum."

Wes, easy going as always, said, "That's why she's leaving it to the Historical Society."

"What about Ben?"

"He'll have to buy a ticket like the rest of us."

I let go of Priscilla to say, "Admission will be free." Wes grinned and hit me on the arm, pulling his punch as he had when we were kids.

Everyone said hello to everyone and I asked, "What would you like to drink?"

Beer for the guys. White wine for the ladies. Connie took all four women out to the garden. The guys surrounded me and I didn't even have to prompt Rick Bowland to ask, "Any progress?"

"Brian," I answered, having resolved to repeat his name repeatedly, "was shot, in my opinion, by one of three people who were inside his mausoleum Sunday morning."

"Which one?" asked Dan.

"Precisely which one of them shot Brian, I cannot tell you at this point. But I can tell you that it was not the Ecuadorian the cops are after."

"Jesus, Ben," said Wes. "That's incredible."

"That's what you're paying me for," I answered grandly, basking in their sudden awe until Rick Bowland said, "But if the cops arrest Charlie Cubrero, we're right back where we started with an 'employee' of the Cemetery Association charged with murder on Cemetery Association property."

"Which reminds me," I interrupted with a change of subject. "If I'm still authorized to 'buy' Charlie from the bounty hunter, I'm going to need it quick and in cash."

Wes said, "Give me five minutes heads up and the money'll be waiting for you on my desk."

"What if it's after banking hours?"

"Call me, and I'll meet you at the side door."

"Good. In the meantime, Brian Grose is the direction I am turning my attention—while of course still attempting to get Charlie to turn himself in—to discover whatever Brian was involved in that would have annoyed the killer enough to shoot him."

"How many hours have you run up?" Wes asked. "What's this costing?"

"I've been working flat out since you hired me."

"That was Tuesday night, late. So: Wednesday, Thursday, Friday—did you work today?"

"Oh yes," I said. "Today was quite a day."

"It's getting expensive."

"Do any of you want me to stop investigating Brian Grose?" I looked sternly at Rick Bowland; Rick looked away. I looked sternly at Wes; Wes shrugged. I looked sternly at Dan Adams; Dan said, "Investigating Brian could take weeks. What could you possibly find that the cops can't?"

"If I have to answer that, I'm back on the clock—Hey, come on, it's a party. Why don't we join the ladies?"

I stepped through the French doors into Connie's garden. They followed. Across the lawn I saw Connie holding forth among her daylilies. Her white dress glowed in the evening shade. Grace, Priscilla, Cynthia, and Georgia were listening with smiles on their faces. The flowers were bright, the grass green as a jewel, the air in perfect balance between afternoon heat and evening chill, and I felt suddenly so glad to be alive. Connie greeted me with the smallest of winks and said, "We were just discussing poor Mr. Grose."

"*You* were discussing him," said Grace Botsford. "I for one have nothing good to say and will therefore say nothing."

"Oh, he wasn't so bad," said Cynthia. "I don't think."

"I only met him twice," said Georgia. "But I do not like a man to come on to me when my husband is standing eight feet away."

"But quite all right when Rick's out of the room?" Connie asked with a smile.

Georgia smiled back, easily. Like me and like Grace, Georgia had grown up with older parents. She wagged a mock finger and said, "Connie, I knew you would say that. I gave that one to you."

Connie said, "Priscilla, did he 'make advances' toward you, too?"

Priscilla did not smile. "I noticed what Georgia noticed. I just didn't take him seriously. I mean, there are guys who just can't help themselves. It's like they have to get a return look so they think they've won points. Do you know what I mean?"

"You should have told me," said Dan. "I would helped him."

"Which is why I didn't tell you. It wasn't serious. But you would have thought it was serious. And threatened to punch him in the nose, which certainly wouldn't help business."

"Were you doing business with Brian?" I asked Dan.

"Of course I was doing business with him. I work for a bank, don't I?"

"I thought he was retired."

"Well, he still needed a checking account."

Wes Little said, "Come on, Dan. You haven't done checking accounts since you came home from college."

Dan said, "The checking account is the foot in the door."

"Brian's foot in the door, too," I said.

"What do you mean?"

"Well you guys and Grace let him into the Association. Which surprised a lot of people. Maybe it started with the checking account."

Wes Little laughed. "Got you there, Dan. You're the one who brought him in."

"I did not."

"First time I met Brian, you introduced us. Remember, you had a cookout. Just Cyn and me and you and Priscilla and him. Hey, Cyn, was he on you too, that night?"

Cynthia drilled him with a cold stare. "Not that I noticed." Connie, too, was looking a little chilly as Wes's "on you" was moving outside her bounds of party talk. But she rose to the occasion, saying, "And how did you meet Brian, Georgia?"

"I'm trying to remember. I think Rick and I were having dinner at the club. And, Priscilla, you brought him over, didn't you?"

"Cynthia and I brought him over. We were waiting for these two," she indicated Wes and Dan, "who were working late as usual, and we ran into him at the bar."

"Well," said Connie. "A checking account goes a long way, these days. Dan, if you would allow me your strong arm, we could go inside and fill our glasses." She took Dan's arm and got two steps before she said, "Grace? Where did you meet poor Mr. Grose?"

"Dad wrote the policy for his house. Next thing I knew he had invited himself to supper."

⟨⟩⟨⟩⟨⟩

After they all went home, Connie went upstairs to get ready for bed. I made her tea and brought it up when she was settled in. "What do you think?" I asked her.

"It seems Mr. Grose was very clever at getting to know people."

"And wives?"

"I have no idea. Beyond the obvious fact that little Cynthia has a roving eye."

"Sounded to me like Dan was his wedge."

"Certainly no love lost between Grace and Mr. Grose."

"Grace told me that Brian used her father. Took advantage."

Connie said, "You must be aware that for Grace everything comes back to her father. They were such companions. She must miss him so."

"Is that why she never married?"

"Who knows such things? You might as much as ask me why I never married."

"Did Gerard Botsford really ask you to marry him?"

"Of course."

"Of course?"

"Well why wouldn't he? He was a widower. I was single, wealthy and, if I could believe half the men who called on me, beautiful enough. Gerard and I had known each other for years, and his father had known my father, and his grandfather had worked for my grandfather."

"Why did you turn him down? He was full of himself?"

"I didn't love him."

"Oh."

"Well why else would I turn him down, for pity sakes? Gerard was available, prospering, and handsome. And what a piano player! Oh my lord, I could listen to him play for hours."

"Any regrets?"

"No more than for any of the others I turned down," she said with a smile. Then she turned serious. "Would I change my life?" she asked, and answered, "No. I was probably meant to be alone. I have a wide circle of friends and acquaintances—had, they've mostly died....As has Gerard. So at this moment I would be a widow instead of a spinster." Then she was smiling again, her face alight; and she said to me, "But I do not believe you were meant to be alone."

"The evidence suggests otherwise."

"The evidence suggests you are dodging involvement. That is different than wanting to be alone. You are alone by mistake. Or confusion."

I went home and was still lying awake thinking about being single, like most of my Chevalley cousins and dead Brian Grose when Father Bobby telephoned. The priest did not apologize for the late hour, but accused in a hard voice that would have made an Inquisition subject's blood run cold, "We had a deal."

"That's right. I agreed not to mention you to anybody, which I didn't. You agreed to talk to Charlie and call me, which you didn't."

"You broke your word, Ben."

"I did not."

"Then who sent the fat guy after me."

"The only fat guy I know is a bail bondsman who calls himself Big Al Vetere, and I did not send him after you."

"Somebody did. Why's he nosing around Bridgeport?"

"He's a sad sack who feels more comfortable in a city. That doesn't mean he's on to Charlie. Or you. Though, just as a point of fact, Father, he told me he met a priest who sent him on a wild goose chase up here. Anyone you know?"

"He told you that? God in heaven."

"Did you?"

"I said the first thing I could think of to get rid of him."

"Well it worked. He's lucky he didn't get shot by the Feds. But speaking of finding, how are we doing with Charlie? Have you talked to him?"

"Not yet."

"What are you waiting for, Father? The Feds are all over the place. Lame as they are, there are so many of them one might actually stumble into him."

"Sorry to telephone so late," Father Bobby said, and hung up. I snared his number from my Caller ID and wrote it on a scrap of paper, thinking it could be handy to have before he got around to changing cell phones.

Now I was wide awake. I started thinking about Brian again. The familiar-sounding phrase "sense of urgency" from his meaning-of-life-statement in Lorraine's death movie, began running through my head. Over and over, like a song you began to wish you had never heard. But I had heard it before, just as I had heard a whole bunch of things he had prattled on about. I stopped pretending to sleep, went downstairs, poured a glass of wine, kicked my computer off Standby and Googled "sense of urgency."

"Sense of urgency" turned out to be a very popular phrase in the self-help world. Google claimed one point two million results to do with managing goals, projects, and employees. It was equally popular in the news; interviews with politicians found them either promising a sense of urgency, demanding one from their rivals, or threatening to investigate bureaucrats lacking it.

What else, I wondered, had struck a memory chord in Brian's speech to the camera? A neat one, "Don't plan too far ahead." I had liked that one and was sure I had heard it before. So I Googled, "sense of urgency don't plan too far ahead."

First result came a web page for another <u>White House Briefing</u>, with the text excerpt reading, "...My displeasure with the President."

"No."

"<u>Press Briefing</u>."

"No."

"<u>Another Press Briefing</u>."

"No."

<u>Marketplace from American Public Media</u>, said the next title, "Fourth is you never should be satisfied. Fifth is **don't plan too far ahead. Sixth was have a sense of urgency.** Seventh is work like hell...." read the except.

I nearly broke a finger clicking <u>Marketplace from American Public Media</u>, which I listened to on NPR whenever I was near a radio at 6:30. Up came a transcript of a "Conversations From the Corner Office" interview I had heard with Joe Gallo, president and CEO of E.& J. Gallo winery. It had stuck in my head because the vintner, an Exxon Mobil of bulk wine, had complained to Marketplace that customers had too many choices in the liquor store. Before I could drop the radio in the garbage, he had spoken from the heart about what he had learned from his father, and I had listened attentively.

"Brian, you self-important Grose, you died a plagiarist. What else were you lying about?"

> > >

"Thank God," said Sherman's mother when she saw the sturdy handcuffs that attached Sherman to his hospital bed. She tugged her kerchief tighter to her hair, crossed herself, and said, "They wouldn't cuff him if he couldn't run."

Sherman, who was wrapped in a head bandage of Sikh turban proportions and had both legs in casts above the knee, opened murky eyes and whispered, "Thanks for coming, Ma. I gotta talk to Ben a minute."

Aunt Helen took off her kerchief, ran a comb through her white hair and a lipstick across her lips, and went out the door with a pretty smile for the elderly security guard standing guard for the cops.

Sherman whispered, "You tell about the rifle?"

"Not yet. Did you tell the doctor how you got the bullet crease?"

"Shuddup, I got enough trouble already." He looked around and lowered his whisper. "They think I banged my head on the road."

"Sherman, what in hell is going on? Did you really steal Brian Grose's credit card?"

"Not in the way you mean steal."

"In what way did it end up in your possession?"

"The yuppie didn't need it. He was dead."

"Oh," I said. "I am beginning to get the picture."

"I ain't talkin' about it."

The last thing I wanted was to be hauled into court to testify about his confession. So I whispered, "Just shake your head if anything I whisper is wrong, okay? Or blink," I added, realizing that shaking his head would hurt like hell.

"Okay."

"After you set up the gas engine Sunday morning at the Notables, you wandered over to the mausoleum to see if by any chance it was open and you might find something inside not cemented to the floor. To your surprise and delight it was open. But inside, instead of moveables, you found Brian Grose shot dead. I'm guessing he had just been shot because you left no bloody footprints and he hadn't bled much yet. And by the time I saw the body he'd bled a river."

Sherman blinked. "There was plenty. I was careful not to step in it."

"But he was sure as hell dead with all those bullet holes in him. So you figured since you couldn't help him, you might as well help yourself. You took most, but not all, of whatever cash he had in his wallet. And then you got really, really smart and lifted only two or three credit cards, so it wouldn't look like he was robbed."

Sherman blinked and mouthed, "One."

"I underestimate you. You snuck out with *one* credit card and went back to the stationary engine and pretended nothing happened. And you stayed smart. You waited nearly a week before you tried the credit card at a gas station to see if it has been reported. You left the motor running and dipped it at the pump nearest the road. Comes up clean. Now you're in business. You gas up a truck, go to Home Depot and—"

Sherman blinked.

"No?"

"Lowes," he whispered. "Not Home Depot. You know the new one down in Danbury?"

"Sorry—Lowes, where you charge a huge mess of 2 x 10s you can sell to a contractor who pays cash for a hot deal on hot lumber. But then for some reason you got really, really stupid and bought something that was traced to you when it was delivered. I'm presuming it's something online."

Sherman shook his head violently, winced, moaned, and blinked rapidly.

"You didn't buy something online?"

"Just a little something for my girl."

"Didn't know you had one."

"There's a lot you didn't know."

"So you did something really stupid like having what you charged online delivered to your girl. The cops, who obviously have been watching to see if anyone, the murderer, for instance, uses the dead man's credit card, lean on your girl and she says, "Sherman Chevalley."

"No way," said Sherman. "I'm not an idiot." Then, forgetting we were in a hospital room with an elderly security guard outside, and for all we knew a state police stenographer under the bed, he explained how to buy something online with a stolen credit card and not get caught.

"You borrow somebody's computer with wireless and take it to a hot spot, download the software you bought onto a CD."

"Software?"

Anyone who can build his own bulldozer with parts from his junk pile (augmented by parts from the town garage—occasioning his most recent incarceration) is a can-do guy, but I hadn't realized he had made the leap to computers.

"Wait a minute. Who gives a girl software?"

"I do. After Effects Ultra. Fifteen hundred bucks. I got it for her free."

"What is After Effects—Ultra?"

"For faking video location. Makes it seem like you're on location where you're really shooting your movie in front of a green screen and keying in the virtual set."

The penny dropped like an anvil. "*Lorraine?* Lorraine Renner?"

"What's it to you?"

"That was kind of fast."

"Yeah, well sometimes you get lucky. I been hoping a long time to meet somebody like her. She makes this movie about me and the engine and puts it in a contest, and all of a sudden we're getting it on."

"You want me to bring her here?"

"I didn't want her seeing me like this." He rattled the chain of the handcuff.

"Should I get you a lawyer?"

"Lorraine got me Ira Roth."

"You can't afford Ira Roth."

"She's making a movie about his horses. He says I'll get bail. The case sucks. All I got to do is keep saying I found the card in the grass. Ira says they won't even bother charging me with the murder."

"What about your parole?"

"We're working on it."

Well, Sherman had moved up. And if Sherman could get lucky, surely there was hope for every man still alone in the world.

"You know what Lorraine told me the other night?"

"No," I answered, thinking, Please God, spare me Sherman's pillow talk.

"Told me that the yuppie had something bent going on the side."

"What side?" I wondered why she had never mentioned that when we talked about Brian. "He didn't have a side. He wasn't married. He didn't even have a girlfriend anyone knew about." Unless you count the lovelies he was romancing to get his mausoleum, but Sherman knew nothing about them, which was not much less than I did.

"Lorraine thinks he was scamming somebody—Hey, you know what?"

"What?"

"I can help her. I can be her grip. You know what a grip is?"

"A guy who carries stuff for a filmmaker."

"Yeah, I could do that while she makes her new movie."

"Which new movie?"

"Lorraine's thinking she could make a documentary movie about a murder victim."

"She already did one."

"No, no, no. Not the snuff flick. That was for the mausoleum. She means use all that extra video for like background. Cool idea, right? She said there'd be clues in the film about who blew him away. That's really cool, isn't it? I never knew anybody who made stuff up like that."

"You've been making up stuff your whole life, Sherman."

"I'm gonna help her."

"Excellent idea. Now could we go back to this guy who's trying to kill you?"

"What guy?"

"Who dropped the woodchuck gun I saw in the woods. The gun I know *exactly* where to find if I have to."

"Oh."

"Does the guy trying to kill you have to do with the credit card you acquired?"

"I don't think so," said Sherman.

"Then it had to do with who you saw go inside Brian Grose's mausoleum?"

"Maybe."

"So who did you see, Sherman? Goddammit!"

"Latino guy. I told you."

"But not this Latino guy?" I showed him Charlie's photograph, yet again.

"Told you no, Ben. That's not the guy."

"The guy you saw walked in the same unlocked door you walked in?"

"I saw him walking out."

"Before or after you went in?"

"Before. Yuppie was dead by the time I got there."

"Aha," I said, walked to window, and looked down at the crowded cemetery across the street. The hospital stood on a high hill. Across a valley of hundred year old frame houses and old factories and busy roads I could see the gold domed cupola atop Danbury's City Hall. "How did you find him, Sherman?"

"What do you mean find him?"

"In order to blackmail the Latino guy—in order to threaten to tell the cops that you saw him coming out of the murder scene immediately after the murder—you had to know where to find him."

"I'd seen him around."

I sat back down by his bed. "Where?"

"A joint down in Waterbury, once. And up at the River End when he was delivering something."

The River End Bar, a Jervis-owned establishment, was a fine place to take delivery of "something" not stocked at Lowes, Mike's Hardware, or your corner pharmacy. Though you ran the risk of someone taking it away from you in the parking lot.

"What's his name?"

"Angel."

"*Angel?* The guns guy?" That did not make any sense at all. I knew Angel of Waterbury as a standup gentleman who dealt in contraband arms. And, it was rumored, explosives, which I doubted, though I knew him only slightly. Wide Greg had introduced us, and I owed the bar owner big for it. Angel was not a man to kill unless he was actually surrounded by people already shooting at him.

"Not *that* Angel," said Sherman. "Another one. There's a lot of Latino Angels, in case you didn't know."

"What does your Angel look like?"

"Like they all look. Short."

"So you're blackmailing him?"

"Kind of wish I wasn't," said Sherman. "He took it the wrong way."

I stood up for another gander at the cemetery across the street and found myself wondering if the surgeons' lounge overlooked it. "Any chance of you introducing me to this Angel?"

"What are you nuts? The dude's a stone killer."

"Well, I'm working on who killed Brian Grose, so there's a kind of symmetry."

"Angel didn't kill him."

"You just said he's a stone killer."

"Yeah. But Angel didn't shoot the yuppie."

"How do you know?"

"He said he didn't."

"Why do you believe him?"

"Because when I bumped into him when he was coming out the door, he wasn't carrying."

"How you know he hadn't stuffed the gun in his pants?"

"Because he was wearing tight bicycle shorts and a muscle shirt."

"I have never seen an Ecuadorian in bicycle shorts."

"If I were Ecuadorian that's what I'd wear so I didn't look like the rest of them."

"You're sure he wasn't carrying?"

"Nowhere he could have hid anything as big as blew that humongous hole in the yuppie. Cops never found weapons that I heard of, and I didn't see any when I went inside right after Angel left."

"If Angel didn't kill Brian, how are you blackmailing him?"

"It don't matter he didn't do it. That's the beauty of the plan. I knew the cops would blame him, anyhow. Being a wetback and all."

The calculated callous bigotry shocked me, and the disgust must have showed on my face because Sherman got indignant. "Hey, *he* started it."

"Started what? You blackmailed a guy because he was an illegal who couldn't go to the cops."

Sherman tried to sit up straighter in bed. "I didn't blackmail him, first," he said staunchly. "He threatened *me*. Said he'd kill me if I said I saw him. You expect a man to abide that attitude?"

"He threatened you first?"

"Yeah. Had nothing to do with being illegal. He threatened me. So I threatened him back."

"With blackmail."

"What's wrong with making a couple of bucks while I protect myself?"

"It might explain why he kept trying to kill you." In fact I was immensely relieved to discover that my cousin was not a vicious bigot, and not one bit worse than the conniving thief and weasel I had always believed him to be.

I suggested to Sherman that he pass a message to Angel that he was not going to blackmail him anymore, and stay in the hospital as long as he could. Sherman said he was planning on borrowing a shotgun, sawing off the barrels, and going down to Waterbury.

"On crutches?"

"I'll be on a cane before you know it."

"Why not just call it a draw? I mean, come on, you got lucky with a nice girl. She found you a hotshot lawyer. Why not move on?"

Sherman admitted that he had also been thinking along those lines, because serving hard time for murdering Angel while he knew a girl like Lorraine on the outside would be a real pain.

I drove Sherman's mother home. She said, "Sherman met somebody."

I said, "Nice girl."

Sherman's mother said, "Are you sure?"

I said, "She's an interesting person." We rode the rest of the way in silence, an uncharacteristically glum Aunt Helen thinking God knew what, while I wondered if attempting to locate Angel would be counterproductive. It would gobble up a lot of time on the doubtful premise that he knew anything more about Brian's murder than Sherman did. I was curious, of course, what an illegal immigrant from Waterbury had been doing in Brian's mausoleum. It was unlikely he came to Newbury's burying ground to steal; that sort of activity was best left to locals who wouldn't be noticed, like Sherman. Although, as Sherman had noted, bicycle shorts on a summer weekend looked local. Pedaling a bike, wearing helmet and sunglasses he would look to cursory glancers like just another "desirable inhabitant."

Maybe Angel had known Brian Grose. Dealings with Brian Grose could have ranged from rewiring his Eternal surround sound system to delivering recreational drugs. Or—if he really was the stone killer Sherman claimed—carrying out a hit only to discover that someone had beat him to it. But with what weapon? Bare hands?

Soon as I dropped Sherman's mom at her trailer, I gave Marian Boyce a ring. I hadn't seen her around town since Friday evening at the flagpole. That she rang right back told me nothing. Only the mobile service could have pinpointed whether she was in the General Store or on the moon.

I said, "Thanks for calling back. Sorry to bother you on a Sunday, but this is business. Are you still on the Brian Grose case?"

"None of your business."

"I only ask because I haven't seen you around. I wondered if you and Arnie had been 'ICEed' by the Feds. So to speak."

Marian, who knew the power of silence, remained silent.

I said, "Do you know any Angels in Waterbury?"

"I know one whom I intend to nail some day for converting semi-automatic rifles into assault weapons. And I believe you do, too."

"I've heard of him. No, this one shoots. And hacksaws Harley brake cables."

"Is this about your jailbird cousin cracking up his bike?"

"That had nothing to do with brake cables."

"Then why are you asking?"

"Trying to save time."

"At tax payers expense. "

"I'll pay you back. If you're still on the case."

"How?"

"By telling you that I am reasonably sure that two different people entered Brian's mausoleum *after* he was shot."

"You claimed that the door was locked when you found the blood and called 911. Trooper Moody confirmed that it was locked when he got to the graveyard and secured the scene. It remained locked, despite the worst efforts of three of your cousins, until the treasurer of the Village Cemetery Association arrived with a key."

"The door was locked *after* the two different people left the mausoleum."

"Which one locked it, Sherlock? Last one out?"

"Neither."

Marian was satisfyingly silent for a full second. Then she nailed me right between the eyes. "Which one was Cousin Sherman?"

"What do you mean?"

"Of the two different people you imagine entering Brian's mausoleum, do you imagine your cousin was the last one out?"

I countered with a less satisfying, "You've had your payback, but you haven't told me a damned thing."

Marian laughed. Then she said, "Okay, okay. We've heard about an Angel. Haven't had the pleasure of meeting him, yet."

"Is he a suspect?" I asked. Sharp as Sherman was, maybe he missed spotting Angel's gun. Maybe a hungry raccoon failed to notice a plate of raw liver.

"Some people think he is," she said, reminding me that her brain was working a different track than that of her temporary colleagues from Immigration and Customs Enforcement.

"Does Angel happen to have a hot rep as a driver?"

Marian actually sounded impressed when she said, "As a matter of fact yes." She even added an admiring, "My, my, you've been busy."

So Al Vetere was not a complete fool.

"How the hell big was that gun?" I asked casually, trading on my new-won respect.

"Goodbye."

"Wait. Wait."

"For what?"

"You know as well as I, neither of those immigrants killed Brian Grose."

"I know nothing."

"The real killer, who locked the door after Sherman and Angel came and went, is laughing at us."

"I sincerely doubt that," she said, so soberly that I wondered if she had the same feeling I did about this murder.

"It's about tears, isn't?" I asked.

"Ben?"

"What?"

"This Angel? If it's the same Angel? Don't mess with him, Lone Ranger. He's as bad as they get."

"I'll be very careful, thank you."

"Goddammit, don't you listen? I'm warning you to stay away from the man—what, Arnie?"

I heard Arnie Bender say, "Gimme the phone—Jailbird, you there? Listen to what your friend is telling you. Her and me we get in trouble with this Angel, we call for back up. Another major crime unit. SWAT team. A thousand road cops. The Connecticut National Guard. Okay? You get Angel trouble, who you gonna call? Your ninety year old grandmother?"

"She's my great-Aunt, but I get your point, Arnie. Thank you for caring."

As soon as they hung up on me, I dialed the number I had snared for Father Bobby. A wary "Hello" told he hadn't had time to swap cells.

"It's Ben Abbott in Newbury."

"Why are you calling me? I told you I would call when I had something."

"I'm looking for a bad guy named Angel. Know any?"

After a long pause, Father Bobby asked, "Does he sell guns in Waterbury?"

"Not that one. I know that one. This one has a rep as a driver."

"It is not an uncommon name."

"Acquaintances refer to him as a stone killer. Does that ring any bells?"

"I am not a gangster, Mr. Abbott. I'm a priest. The only way I would know a man like that would be if he confessed, in which case I would not be free to confide in you. Please don't call me again."

"Any word on Charlie Cubrero?"

"Not yet. I have put feelers out. I've received nothing back."

"Father, talking to you is like asking the cable company what's wrong with my internet connection."

"Perhaps you should convert to DSL," said Father Bobby and I was hung up on again for the second time in a row.

Chapter Sixteen

I walked as fast as I could up Main Street and knocked on Lorraine Renner's door. "In here," she called through the screen. She was in the birth/editing room. "Hey, it's you. How you doing?"

"I saw Sherman in the hospital. He's in pretty good shape, all things considered."

"Yeah, we talked on the phone. What's up?"

"Sherman said that you said that you wondered if Brian was 'gaming' something—working a scam."

"Sherman has a big mouth."

"Sherman is so pumped about meeting you that he couldn't help bragging a little."

Lorraine smiled. "Yeah, yeah, yeah. I know. He's pumped. So am I. Boy, I gotta tell you, Ben. The things you don't plan for. A twenty-year-older-than-me felon. Barely house broken. He smiles, and I completely lose it."

I nodded encouragingly, although leer would best describe a Sherman smile. "I found it interesting that he didn't seem to be lying. Or exaggerating."

"Did he happen to mention the documentary?"

"It came up."

"He's the first person I've told anything about it."

"Yeah, I wondered why it didn't come up when we talked."

"It's a very complicated 'rights' situation. I've got all this footage about Brian. In theory it's the mausoleum company's, but only in theory—they haven't seen it. They don't know it exists and couldn't care less, I'm sure. But I do. I mean I'm really intrigued. It's a unique situation, to have all this tape on somebody who suddenly got murdered."

"Sherman said something about clues?"

Lorraine shook her head. "I don't know if we should be talking about this."

"I'm not a cop. I'm only trying to find out who killed him. I don't see how that would hurt your film."

"I don't know."

"I mean it wouldn't hurt to find out who did it, would it?"

"That's what I mean," she said, suddenly eager to explain. "The clues would lead us to the murder. Right? Don't you think?"

Everyone wanted to be a detective. I said, "It would probably help the film. Give you an ending. So what are the clues?"

"He got a telephone call when I had him wired with a radio mike." He said, 'I told you never to call me here,' and hung up."

I said, "If the first phrase ever spoken on the telephone was Alexander Graham Bell calling to his assistant inventor, 'Watson, I need you,' the second must have been a cheating spouse saying, 'I told you never to call me here.'"

"No, this wasn't like cheating. He was talking to a guy."

"How do you know it was a guy? Did you hear a man's voice?"

"It wasn't like he was talking to a woman. Wasn't like he was screwing her—or him—it was business. But not business, business. Not an investor. Like somebody you shouldn't be talking to. Here, you listen, you decide. I got it on tape."

She played it for me, and I agreed that Grose sounded pissed-off and maybe, slightly scared. It did not sound like sex, love, or ordinary business.

"Interesting," I said, "What other clues?"

She popped another tape in the machine. "Look at this."

The camera swooped in on an open drawer.

"The hell is that?"

"A drawer in his kitchen desk."

I said, "Remind me never to let you in my house with a camera."

Lorraine laughed. "First rule of shooting a documentary film: hose down *everything* on the assumption you can't come back to shoot what you missed. Do you see what's in the drawer?"

"It looks like about a hundred credit cards."

"That's right," said Lorraine.

"And what clue is this?"

"All I know is when I get a freebie credit card offer in the mail I take it because I can use a new one to pay the last one. But I'm not living in a gazillion-dollar house. Why would a rich guy have so much plastic?"

I said, "Good question." In fact, gaming credit card offers matched Banker Dan's hint about financial difficulties. "What else?"

"His library was off limits. He never let me shoot in the library."

"When you shoot that walking baby home movie, do the parents let you in every room in their apartment?"

"Yeah, but Brian kept it locked all the time. Major lock. Here. I shot it." Lorraine's camera lingered on an ASSA high security lock cylinder for a mortise deadbolt. It looked too expensive for even Mike's Hardware to stock, and of a heavy duty grade I'd expect on the front door instead of the library—if not an Iraqi arsenal.

"What do you think it means?" she asked.

"Beats me," I said. When I asked about any other clues, I was not surprised to hear that "Don't call me here," a drawer of credit cards, and a locked library were the extent of it.

Nonetheless, after dark I put on my wood-chopping boots and a long-sleeve shirt, and tucked my pant legs into thick socks which I sprayed with Off! to discourage deer ticks. (It was late in the summer for Lyme disease—the little bastards are most dangerous in June—but tonight I was taking enough chances already.) Then I grabbed a backpack with a few things in it and went for a drive.

The streets were Sunday evening quiet. No traffic to speak of, a lot of people off on vacation, others early to bed to get a jump on Monday morning. No ICE agents. No Major Crime Squad investigators. And Ollie's cruiser was parked outside the little cottage the town supplied for his residence.

Coast clear, I drove out of town and up Mount Pleasant Road, past the twisted black lines of Tom Mealy's skid marks, which still showed in the headlights. Up and over the top of the hill, I stashed my Pinkerton rental on the service road just inside a stretch of Forest Association land. I waited ten full minutes for my eyes to adjust to starlight, slung my pack over my shoulder, and walked along the edge of the woods until I got to the stump-pocked open section that Brian Grose had been clearing surreptitiously, until the Forestry Association threatened to sue him into oblivion. I worked my way through the trees quick action had spared and emerged on his side lawn.

The house was dark.

I stood there for a while, scoping out the swimming pool and the tennis court, not moving, except to slowly, quietly swat mosquitoes. Satisfied that I was alone, and not particularly surprised, I walked quickly across the grass, aiming for a sunroom that had a trellis. The house was quite new, of course, but some landscape architect had billed Grose to uproot another client's ancient wisteria vine and secured it to the trellis; and it had settled in nicely, as wisteria will. I assumed that the landscape designer or gardener did not know much about wisteria; or didn't particularly care that, left to its own devices, the wisteria would soon pull down the trellis and much of the sunroom with it. To me, it offered a stairway to the roof, if not the stars.

I changed out of boots into grippy-soled running soles, and put on pig-skin driving gloves, climbed onto the sunroom roof and from it onto the steeply pitched main roof where I crept precariously around for awhile looking for a skylight not wired to the burglar alarm.

The first two I found were the type that opened and they were wired. The fact that I knew how to circumvent a house alarm did not mean that I was good at it. It's a skill best honed by regular practice, but as a trustworthy Realtor with keys to many houses, it is very rare that I find myself breaking and entering in the illegal sense. Very rare. Which was why I was prowling the unpleasantly-steep roof for a fixed-glass skylight, the kind that didn't open for venting. I found two and chose the one that a toilet vent pipe suggested it lit a bathroom.

The pipe gave me something to brace against while I drilled holes in the plastic dome with a battery-powered Makita, inserted a Japanese key hole saw any Samurai would have been proud to own, and sawed four cuts that allowed me to remove the dome and duct-tape it to the shingles so it wouldn't slide down the roof into the patio. Under it, of course, was double-pane insulated glass. I taped it, scored its edges with a glass cutter, bashed it with the butt end of the Makita and pulled the top layer of glass away with the tape and secured it to the roof. Now came the part that could wake anyone sleeping in the house if I weren't careful, though I had no reason to believe that anyone was.

Again I taped glass. Again I scored the edges. In theory I could bash it open, but it would fall to the floor with an ungodly crash. There was a ninety-nine percent chance no one was around to hear. But just in case, I intended to keep as quiet as I had kept things so far. I drilled a hole through the tape, in the middle, then took a length of twine from my pack that I had pre-tied around the middle of a 10 penny finishing nail. I inserted the nail through the hole. When I pulled the string the nail spanned the hole, giving me a grip on the glass. I looped the twine around the vent pipe, and rapped the score lines with the Makita. The whole piece broke loose, quite suddenly, and hung from the twine.

I felt cool air rise from the room, grabbed the dangling taped glass, turned it diagonally and drew it up through the hole. Now, for the first time I turned on a light, a little Mag Lite, and shielding the narrow beam with my hands, discovered that I had managed to cut a hole in the roof over a hot tub.

It had a cover on it. God knew how strong it was, or if there was water in the tub. There had to be water in the tub. Brian hadn't planned to be shot in his mausoleum. He hadn't closed up his house. He had gone to the graveyard the Sunday before last to tour the Notables like the rest of Newbury and, unlike the rest of them, hadn't come back. So there had to be water in the damned thing.

On the other hand, everyone knows we live in an increasingly litigious society where the lawyers make the rules. Surely, hot tub covers, like swimming pool covers, had to be strong enough to hold an elephant. Disinclined to cell phone Grace Botsford at this late hour for an insurance agent's opinion, I swung my feet through the opening and grabbed the roof with my gloves, and took a chance. It was not a long drop so I wouldn't accelerate that much. I took additional comfort in the fact that while I'm not a lightweight, I'm not of Dennis or Albert Chevalley proportions, either.

I let go and immediately discovered that the cover would not withstand a lawsuit by the owner of an elephant; and that, while Brian Grose did not plan to get shot to death the Sunday before last, he had apparently not planned a warm soak later in the day, either, because the hot tub was anything but. It felt like I had fallen through the Ram Pasture skating pond in the dead of winter. God it was cold. I squished out, soaked from running shoes to waist band. The air conditioning which hadn't felt much cooler than the night breeze when I was dry, now felt like a Cape Horn gale.

I pulled off my shoes and socks and pants and wet underwear, grabbed a wonderfully thick towel from the rack and dried off. My shirt tails and the bottom of my sweatshirt clung in a chilly, wet way. I spotted a creamy white Turkish bathrobe, thick as the towel, pulled off the rest of my things, wrapped myself in the robe, and found a long hallway and padded down the stairs. If anyone asked, I was a privileged householder repairing to his library.

Which reminded me, I had left my backpack beside the hot tub. Halfway down the grand staircase I went back for the tools I would need to enter the library. Lock picking, like home alarm circumventing, was something I had been taught years and years ago, courtesy of the United States Navy, Office of Naval Intelligence. About all I remember of it was that lock picking is lot more difficult than rewiring an alarm, which was why I padded in robe and bare feet and pigskin driving gloves to the library door with little hope of opening it without a saw, though I vowed to at least try rather than wreck a perfectly fine door.

But it was not locked. The door was closed, as Lorraine had said. And the lock was the ASSA I had seen in her video. But when I tried the knob, it swung on quiet hinges. I stepped inside, cupped my Mag Lite to contain the beam and worked my way to the windows, where I found a switch that caused the drapes to slide almost soundlessly across the windows. Then I followed my Mag beam to the wall switches by the door, located a dimmer and brought the room lights up just bright enough to see shapes.

Like many modern libraries, it had no books. I exaggerate. Two narrow cases of uniformly bound leather volumes acted as a frame for a huge HDTV screen. It did house a handsome set of library steps and some beautiful library lamps and an antique library card catalog, and some library shelves filled with glass knickknacks.

A splendidly long and broad library table with carved legs and ornate, inlaid coaming filled one end of the room. On the table sprawled the reason Brian Grose had not allowed Lorraine Renner's camera in his library.

I felt behind for the wall switch to brighten the lights for a closer look. I felt, instead, something cold touch the back of my head.

Chapter Seventeen

The only good news I could think in the first millisecond I felt the gun touch the back of my head was that if thieves who had broken in ahead of me wanted to kill me they could have done it already. In the next millisecond I thought of bad news: to thieves I must look like the homeowner in my bare feet and bathrobe. At least until they noticed I was wearing driving gloves.

I could think of no more good news. Thieves surprised by the homeowner in the middle of committing a felony would be very bad news, if getting rid of the homeowner would seem the simplest way of getting rid of the problem. In the next millisecond, which seemed to drag on like a fair portion of eternity, the person pressing the gun to the back of my head finally spoke in a voice as hard and cold as her weapon.

"Stop. Don't move. Police."

I said, "Hi, Marian."

She and her partner Arnie Bender spun me around, stared in angry disbelief and said, "What the hell are you doing here?"

"I understand the house is going on the market."

The first time I met Detective-Sergeant Arnie Bender, I had barged in on him while he was executing a warrant to search my house. He had had a rookie partner with him who hit me in the face, so I hit him back. Arnie had done the right thing: he helped the young fool stand up and told him it was wrong to abuse the subject of an investigation; then he told me that next time I hit a Connecticut State Trooper they would send me to the hospital. He had clear standards, and I didn't expect him to slug me, even though he looked like he wanted to. Nor did I expect my old friend Marian to slug me, even though she looked like she wanted to, too. Boy was I wrong about that.

She didn't knock me off my feet, only because the wall I bounced into kept me upright. Of course, I didn't hit her back—not because of Arnie's threat, I hasten to add.

"Goddamnit," she said, "I'm sorry I did that."

"Did what?" asked Arnie.

I said, "I didn't see anything, either."

My head was spinning. Not only had she hit me hard, she knew how to hit.

Marian said, "I'm not really sorry."

I let myself sort of lean on the wall for a moment while I scoped them out. "You two look terrible."

They did. Arnie hadn't shaved in days. Fried food crumbs stuck to his stubble. Marian's normally short, sleek hair cut was stringy as Sherman Chevalley's. She had bags under her eyes and the pallor of indigestion.

I said, "It's a stakeout."

"It was," said Arnie. "It just turned into a solid arrest for B & E. You want to frisk him, Marian, or shall I?"

"Only with a cattle prod."

"Hands against the wall." said Arnie, gesturing for me to spread arms and legs to be frisked.

I said, "Come on, I'm wearing a bathrobe."

"We want to know what's under it. At least I do. Spread 'em!"

Neither of them were cracking anything near a smile. Which said I had problem. Stakeouts may be boring, but they're done with a purpose, and it looked like I had screwed it up. We went through the ritual that established that the police ruled. It reminded me too much of prison to accept it with a philosophical smile, and I had to put serious effort into containing the impulse to lever off the wall and kick him in the head. After it was over Arnie said, "All right. Straighten up. Turn around—close the robe first for crissakes."

"Who?" I asked.

"Who what?"

"Were you staking out?"

"Ben, we just caught a fucking burglar."

"I'm not a burglar and you know it."

"You are not a burglar until we find evidence that you broke into this house. Then you are a burglar. Want to show it to us, or are you going to make us hunt for it?"

I began to realize I was really in a jam.

"Okay, we'll cuff you to that table and hunt around until we find a jimmied window somewhere."

"Skylight, second floor. In the hot tub room."

"Now save us more trouble. Tell us why—by the way, should we be reading you your rights?"

"I know my rights, thank you. And it is a privilege to assist you in your inquires."

"Start by telling us why you broke in and entered this house."

I could get out of the jam, temporarily, by demanding a lawyer—which I would get after they cuffed me, drove me across the county to their barracks in Plainfield, and locked me in a cell overnight while I waited for my lawyer to wake up so they could ask me why I had cut a hole in a murdered man's roof. I would eventually at some expense and waste of time get the charges dropped or at least reduced, but at the additional cost that neither high-ranking State Police Major Crime Squad detective would ever speak to me again, much less trade information.

"I will confess," I said, "that I'm clutching at straws. But I learned that Brian Grose kept that door locked all the time and would not let anyone see what was in this room. I am trying to figure out who might have killed him, other than that poor illegal whom I am sure didn't. I have a strong suspicion you don't either and your bosses aren't happy about it."

"Forget 'little guy against the bosses,'" Arnie growled. "We're not on your team."

"Who told you the library was locked?" asked Marian.

"The source had nothing to do with this."

"But the source knew the library was locked. So maybe the source was around the house. And maybe we would like to talk to someone who was around the murdered man's house."

"One of those little professional tricks you pick up in this business," Arnie added.

I said, "I'm not ratting out a source."

"Then we can't help you," said Marian.

And Arnie said, "Hey, Marian, let's just call it a night. Run Ben into the barracks, go home and catch some sleep."

I said, "I can help you with something else."

"Doubt that. But what?"

"That." I pointed at the long, broad library table. "You know what that is?"

"It's a table."

"What's on it!"

"A model of a bunch of houses."

"Doll houses," I said

"What?"

"Doll houses are props in the dog and pony show developers play for potential investors. Once you're selling units, you move them onto the sales office. And, of course, you shoot a three-sixty video pan of it for your website. If you look closely, Detective Boyce, you'll see that in this case it's not houses, but condominiums. It's a huge project and it's why he kept the library locked."

Marian and Arnie looked at each other, looked at Grose's doll house which depicted about a thousand densely packed condo townhouses and looked at me. "What are you talking about?"

"I heard that Brian Grose was not as retired from the real estate business as he claimed. This proves it."

"Proves what?"

"That he was still in business, big time."

They exchanged looks that said, Ben's losing it. "So what?"

"Which means Grose very likely needed money. Which means he could have been having problems keeping the deal afloat. Which means he could have been butting heads with all sorts of types other than a penniless immigrant."

They looked at the project model again, looked at each other. Arnie said to Marian, "The real estate genius did say he was clutching at straws."

"Which turned him into a cat burglar," said Marian.

"And therefore cut a hole in the victim's roof."

They walked to the table and motioned me to follow. We three stared at it for awhile. What was equivalent to an entire new town would carpet a hill from top to bottom. The higher end units were situated higher up for the views and status, and away from the traffic the project would create. At the bottom was a so-called Main Street with shops and a club house.

"Where was he building it?"

"California?" I shrugged. "Arizona? New Mexico? You could plunk this down anywhere in the Southwest."

"Why Southwest? "

"I'm guessing from the tile roofs and the stucco. What do they call it? Mission style or Tuscan or some damned thing. Besides that's where they do really big projects like this."

"Wait a minute," said Arnie.

And Marian said, "Why lock it up?"

I answered, "Same reason there's no name on the doll houses, yet—when you're good to go you'd put the name here, real big, 'La Hacienda at wherever.' He wasn't ready yet, so there's nothing to start rumors about what he's doing in case somebody sees it."

"What are you talking about?"

"You don't build a project this size without buying a heap of land and you don't buy a heap of land without keeping it secret or you'll pay ten times the asking price…. So as soon as you two let me go, I am going to follow the money. Find out who his New York investment partners are. And see if he's still doing business with his old friends in California."

I watched them mull. Before they could mull too deeply, I asked, "Can I ask a question?"'

"What?" said Arnie, while Marian lifted the roof off one of the units and peered inside.

"Who are you staking out for?"

"Come here, Ben."

I had a sinking feeling that I was about to be driven to the county seat in a bathrobe. I padded after them to the kitchen, a money pot of yellow granite and black granite, and down a hall. I assumed we were heading to the garage where they had hidden their car. Before we got to the garage, we turned down a shorter hall to a door that opened on a staff suite, which was situated so that the servant would enter the kitchen and laundry or exit the house to shop for groceries without violating the master's privacy.

"What do you see?" Marian asked.

It was a semi-spartan room, with a double bed and large TV. On the bedspread I counted twelve cell phones, four walkie-talkies, a police scanner, laptop computers, wigs, sunglasses, and a nylon gym bag.

"Man on the run."

"No shit."

"What's in the bag?"

"Bunch of credit cards. Couple of thou in cash. Three cheap pistols."

"Of the type that popped Mr. Grose?"

"Not likely," said Arnie. "What do you think he was doing here?"

"Got real smart and figured nobody'll look in the dead man's house after the cops make their one visit."

"*You* might pull a stunt like that. But the last day the computer was turned on or any of the phones used was the day Mr. Grose was shot."

"You want another guess?" I asked, determined not to give him my best guess.

"Go ahead. You're not usually as stupid as you've been tonight."

"Okay, the guy worked for Grose. And you've been sitting here for days waiting for him to come back."

"Until you scared him cutting a hole in the roof."

"Did you hear me cut a hole in the roof? Would you even know I was here if you hadn't been cooping in the library?"

"What are we going to do with him?" Arnie asked Marian.

"What time does the hardware store open?"

"I don't know. Seven? Ben, what time does the hardware store open?"

"Eight."

"Okay, so we lock him in one of the closets down in the cellar. At eight we buy a sack of cement and some cinder block and we build a wall around the closet. Who would ever miss him?"

"Let me make two suggestions to help us all get on the same page."

"Why would we want to be on the same page with you?" Marian was looking weary.

Arnie said, "Let's hear it."

"Number one, I suggest that the man on the run is a fellow we've been calling Angel."

"Yeah?"

"Want to hear the next suggestion?"

They said nothing.

I said, "Your ICEy colleagues have somehow mixed up Angel with Charlie Cubrero. And why not? They are both illegal Ecuadorians. Couldn't be more than ten thousand in the state."

"Stop telling us what we know about ICE, already. What's your third fucking suggestion?"

"Allow me to exit the way I came in. I'll put the dome back over the skylight, keep the rain out. And hide the debris and by the time anybody notices, you'll have arrested the perp."

They let me go, which didn't surprise me, for the simple reason that they were working overtime—on their own time—staking out Grose's house, pulling an end run around their bosses and ICE and Homeland Security and the rest of the stupid apparatus that was keeping them from doing their job. As we passed the library, I said, "Could I see the doll houses again?"

We three looked them over, again.

"This is some big project," I said. "His partners must be heartbroken."

Arnie took the bait. "Or glad there's one less guy to share once it gets rolling."

With a little luck Marian and Arnie would shift serious energy into tracking Grose's partners in a project that looked like it belonged in the Southwestern United States. It was an easy mistake to make. For one thing, the best detective team in the State Police had neither the time nor the inclination to dwell on architectural niceties. Nor could they know that Brian Grose had hustled women linked to trustees of the Village Cemetery which owned a beautiful, elm-shaded hill smack in the middle of Newbury, Connecticut.

And there was something else they did not seem to know. The name or names of his Newbury partners.

Chapter Eighteen

"Scooter, I'll buy you a cup of coffee at the General Store. I gotta pick your brain."

"I'm in a rush."

"So am I."

I had at best two days before it dawned on Detectives Marian and Arnie that Brian Grose was the sort of developer who would not think twice about using California building materials, like stucco and roof tile, in New England. Just as somewhere in some lawyer's vault there were very likely documents naming the project "La Hacienda at Newbury."

Scooter asked, "Is this about Scupper?"

"Nothing new on Scupper, yet. I need your help on the Brian killing. Sooner I get it wrapped up I can get back to your brother. Give me twenty minutes."

Having worked since he was six years old at a newspaper founded by his great grandfather, Scooter McKay is a walking Wikipedia of Newbury present and past. I'd begun turning to him for facts I would have gone to Connie for before her memory started failing. Though today I had a secondary motive: I needed some private time with his computer.

"Is Aunt Connie still mad at me?" Scooter boomed as he sat down. He never modulates his big voice, so I had already carried our coffee to an outdoor table in front. Talking indoors with him makes my ears ache.

"What makes you think Connie was mad?"

"She called my grandmother a pig farmer in front of the whole town."

"Scooter, you surprise me. I've always assumed that the richest man on Main Street stands aloof from public humiliation."

"Wealthy people don't have feelings?" Scooter boomed, aggrievedly.

"Let me soften the blow. Connie called your *great*-grandmother a pig farmer. Which she was."

"Granny Em had two pigs in the backyard. That's not being a pig farmer."

"But Connie's *mother,* who was Emily's neighbor, did not keep pigs in her backyard, and as pigs tend to be loud and smell bad and dig under fences to root up neighbors' gardens, it is not surprising that your family was considered to be pig farmers. At least in the eyes, ears, and nostrils of Connie's family."

"What are you picking my brain about?"

"The Village Cemetery."

"You know they're shopping for a new president?"

"Which will be a short-term job if they lose control."

"Unless they choose one of the new crowd," said Scooter.

"Why would they choose one of their enemies?"

"They may not know he's an enemy."

"I knew you knew something. Who's switching sides?"

"My lips are sealed."

"Oh, come on."

"*Sealed.* What else do you want to know?"

"Where'd the Association get all their land?"

"The town laid it out in 1709."

"No, that's just two or three acres in the lower portion. Where we are."

"What you mean, 'we' White Man?"

"Abbotts and Adams and Littles and Barretts, Fisks, Hopkinses and Carters, Botsfords, etcetera. Sorry, no Johnny-come-lately McKays in our section. They were still in Scotland inventing golf."

"The steam engine," said Scooter, who had paid a genealogist to discover a nano-thin strand of James Watt in the family DNA.

"Where'd the Cemetery Association get the rest of their land?"

"Glommed onto the Ram Pasture when the Town Flock expired."

Until the early 20th Century, Scooter reminded me, sheep from several flocks were combined, with their ears notched to distinguish the owners who hired a shepherd to move them from pasture to pasture to mow and fertilize.

"Then Aunt Connie gave them a batch—you should ask her."

"I know that part. Connie inherited chunks of the Ram Pasture that her relatives had bought up. But where did they get the big woods behind the place?"

"Castle Hill?"

"Right. Castle Hill."

An immense private home used to stand on top of that hill on the edge of the Borough. People had called it "The Castle." Really old people, like our great-grandparents had called it "Morrison's Castle." It had burned down years before we were born.

"How'd they get that hundred acres?"

"More like a hundred and fifty," said Scooter. "Old Man Morrison deeded it over in his will."

"That was some generous gift."

Scooter smiled. "According to my grandfather, Gerard Botsford snookered him out of it."

I said, "Of course, a hundred fifty acres wasn't worth what it is now."

Scooter laughed at me as only the very well off can laugh at the feckless. "Gerard knew what it was worth. And what it could become worth. Smack in the middle of town?"

"Wonder how he talked him out of it."

"Why don't you ask Grace?"

"What is that weird smile about?"

"My lips are sealed."

"Come on!"

"I'm serious. I've heard a story, but I'm not repeating it."

"When did Old Man Morrison die?"

"Thirty years ago. At least. Thirty-five. I could look it up."

"Let's."

We carried our coffee containers down Church Hill to the *Clarion* office. Scooter poked his computer and brought it up a lot faster than the *Clarion*'s official website's "Archive Search," which was the lamest I'd ever searched. "Thirty-eight years ago. Time flies."

I was standing next to Scooter's chair. He was still staring at the screen, and I watched his face as I asked, "Was it anything to do with Dan Adams?"

"Dan was two years old."

"Or Dan's father?"

Scooter looked up at me and boomed, "Shrewd guess! But wrong—listen, I gotta get down to the press room. You know the way out."

"Could I check my email?"

"Can't you wait til you get home?"

"My computer's down."

"Again?"

"Cat hair."

"By my guest."

He went downstairs to the press.

I sat in his chair and logged on using the Newbury Clarion website email address instead of mine. Sneaky, I know, but it wasn't like I was buying software on his account. I was merely dashing off a quick email under the screen name "editor@newburyclarion.com."

When I finished writing, I perched the cursor over Send.

Then, using my cell phone, for the benefit of Dan Adams' Caller ID, I rang his office at the new bank.

"Hey, it's Ben. Got a minute?"

"Not if it involves privacy issues."

"Relax. I'm not asking, I'm reporting. You keep bugging me how it's going; I had a second free, so I wanted to fill you in where I'm at the moment." Slowly, attempting to make it boring, I told him essentially what I had told Grace Botsford last Friday regarding the hunt for Charlie, minus Father Bobby, who so far had been a real disappointment calling only once and then only to complain. I added that I was looking more deeply into Brian Grose's background.

"Why?"

"Standard operating procedure." I blathered on. "You know—what did Brian do that pissed somebody off enough to shoot him? Are there other incidents like the lawn kid rip-off the cops are talking about? Did Brian really retire from California real estate? Did he retire at all?"

I hit Send.

Chapter Nineteen

In ten seconds I heard Dan's computer tell him he had mail. I blathered on until I heard Dan suck in his breath and blurt, "Oh shit!"

That answered a very big question. I knew now who had been Brian Grose's local partner. I shouldn't have been too surprised. He went to the right bank. And, sadly, to the right man.

"You okay, Dan?"

"Later, Ben. Got to go."

Quickly I went to Scooter's Mail You've Sent and deleted "Condo Rumor?" which had read:

"Dear Dan,

"Can you give me a hand running down these crazy rumors about the Castle Hill Condo proposal? Is it true you guys are underwriting it? How many units? Age restricted or school kids? Any idea what P & Z will say? And, last but not least, is it as mega-huge as they say? Or is the whole think a crock?"

Thanks,
Scooter

PS: The reason I copied Ben, BTW, is that he's working for the Association, which of course owns all that land. I figure what you don't know, he might."

I raced home, jumped in my anonymous Pink rental and parked down Church Hill from the new bank's cookie cutter office. A tap on Dan's telephone might let me listen in on frantic calls to God knew whom. But I had no tap, of course. Nor did I believe he would trust the telephone. Seconds later, Dan's red Jeep Grand Cherokee came screeching out of the parking lot. I followed, hoping for a glimpse of his partners.

He drove straight to the Village Cemetery, and parked by the gate. I circled the Ram Pasture, and watched from the other side, wondering who would show. I doubted Rick Bowland, only because he would be at work at IBM a full hour away. Wes Little? Maybe. Or some other trustee of the association I hadn't even considered.

Dan got out of the Jeep and started pacing. He stopped pacing when a silver Prius came along.

"Now what is going on?" I muttered to myself. I recognized the Prius, of course. Between their two vehicles, the Adams' were famously averaging twenty-two miles to a gallon.

The hybrid pulled alongside the guzzler. Dan opened its door, extended his hand and out stepped Priscilla. Priscilla kissed him firmly on the mouth and hugged him. Then Dan took his lovely wife's hand and led her through the gates into the cemetery. They walked slowly, along a path, on and off the grass, circling headstones, holding hands, heads bowed, clearly troubled.

They stayed in the old section. Their wanderings never took them near Brian's mausoleum. Several times Priscilla slung a comforting arm around his waist. Finally, in the shade of an elm, they stopped and leaned against the trunk, heads still low, still talking. If Norman Rockwell had been alive to paint the scene he would have titled it, "Talking It Out." Or "For Better, for Worse."

I titled it, "All The Confirmation I Needed." Dan Adams had partnered with Brian Grose to take over the Village Cemetery Association and grab its reserve land to build a development that would change the town for worse and forever.

The fact that my sneaky email had sent him directly to Priscilla suggested that Dan had no other partners. Although he could have made a quick phone call, now, he was just turning to his wife to say: Not only has the deal fallen through, and not only are we not going to be as rich as we thought, but when it all comes out I'm going to get blamed for betraying the town, and our friends and neighbors anyway.

My problem was, so what? Underhanded as the scheme might seem, it still did not explain why Brian was murdered. Or by whom.

I left the rental parked by the Ram Pasture and walked to Grace Botsford's office and reported what I knew.

Grace said, "They never would have dared if Dad had lived."

"But he must have started it while your father was still alive."

"Well, Dad would have finished it dead in its tracks. But it is such a frightening reminder of how institutions are inherently fragile. Volunteer institutions all the more so. Look at the regional theaters that fold, look at the colleges that disappear because their trustees either failed to raise money, conserve assets, or groom a new generation to lead them. That is why this association needs a strong, young new president, Ben."

I said, "When the association hired me to investigate this, you reminded me that I went to prison."

"I'm sorry about that. That was out of line."

"Now I'm reminded how I got there."

"What do you mean?"

"I mean that I have been a fool for love. I know what it's like to be used. When you first find out, you feel robbed and stupid. More stupid than robbed. It's impossible to change the fact of what happened. You can't go back. And it's also impossible to undo the memory. But like most bad memories it doesn't actually fade away, but eventually it gets shoved aside by the weight of new ones, bad and good."

"I don't know what you are talking about."

"I'm talking about a love affair with Brian Grose."

"Well, I don't see that it's any of your business."

"It's not. Unless it's why you didn't want to me investigate for the Association."

Grace looked me in the face. "No offense, Ben, but I didn't believe that your investigatory talents would uncover something that personal in my life."

"Have the police asked you about it?"

She practically flinched.

"How'd they find out?" I asked.

"Cell phone records."

"Was it over?"

"Good God, yes. Yes, it was over." Suddenly she laughed. "I under-rated myself. I always thought he did it to get his mauso-leum. I should have known he wormed his way in for the land. If anyone should have known he used me for the land, it was me."

"Why?"

"Did you ever wonder how I became treasurer of the Village Cemetery Association at the tender age of twenty-one?"

"I figured your father wanted you and few objected."

"Oh, they objected, all right. Dan's father fought Dad tooth and nail. Of course, the Adams were against everything. Still are. Sourest family. Dad used to call them the Acrid Adams—when he wasn't calling them something worse. But truth be told I *was* very young and just out of school."

I didn't know why she was telling me this, but I thought I should encourage her, so I asked, "Were you an accounting major?"

"History. I was going to teach—which meant that Dad was asking the other trustees for quite a leap of faith."

She sat back and gazed up at the painting of her and her father casting thin, knowing smiles on the office.

I said, "They were right, in the end. You turned out fine. I guess you learned on the job. Like you learned insurance on the job."

"I didn't 'turn out fine,' thank you Ben. I began 'fine.'"

"Yes, but like you say, you weren't that qualified. At least looking at it by the numbers. They'd expect a treasurer to know something about numbers. That's why I asked if you were an accounting major."

Grace got color in her cheeks and a proud smile on her face. "Numbers? Here is a number: One-hundred-and-sixty-two point seven-four."

"One-hundred-and-sixty-two point seven-four? What is one-hundred-and-sixty-two point seven-four?"

"That is how many acres I brought into the Village Cemetery Association. Five times the land it held before my contribution."

"I don't understand."

"Where do you think Castle Hill came from, Ben?"

"Old Man Morrison."

"'Old Man' Morrison was younger than my father, dear."

I looked at her. She smiled. "Get it?"

"Ummm."

She continued to smile so frankly, openly, happily that I felt welcome to ask, "So he was the reason you came home? Remember we talked about coming back to Newbury? I came home disgraced and destroyed to the only place that would take me."

"I think you'll find it's much more complicated than that, Ben. It certainly was for me. I came home for many reasons. I missed my father. I missed Newbury. I missed home. I was a twenty-year-old very-old soul. I couldn't connect at college. I never did. Kids my age were marching in the streets for Civil Rights and against the war. I knew I should, too. I was too strait laced, too old—old soul. My first lover was a fifty year old professor. My second was a graduate student only five years older than me and he was a terrible disappointment. But I wanted to do something important, something to help, like the kids marching were. I was home for Christmas in my junior year and Dad sent me up to talk to Andrew."

"Andrew?"

"Andrew Morrison. He lived in the gardener's cottage since the "Castle" burned down. He had become a painter after he lost his money. He was somewhat reclusive. Not entirely. He had clients in New York. He did this painting of Dad and me."

"Gorgeous work."

"Oh yes, he was very talented, very skilled. I was dazzled. I've always admired skills. Dad at the piano. Your cousin Renny with automobiles. I enjoyed watching you cook the other night—Anyway, I called him Mr. Morrison. And then I called him Andrew. And then I called him Andy. When Dad asked was I falling love with Andy, I told him that I was falling in love with winter afternoons in front of the fire—Biter bit, Ben."

"What do you mean?"

"Brian Grose used me to get to Dad the way I got to Andy Morrison and dropped me as soon as he did. But it never struck me until you walked in with news of his condo project that it wasn't about that stupid mausoleum. He wanted the land. Thank God he didn't live to make it real."

"They just couldn't take the land."

"Who would stop them? With Dad out of the picture and me losing control to small town wannabe deal makers like Dan Adams? Whoever controls the association ultimately controls its assets. Cash, machinery, contracts, and land. Unscrupulous trustees could assert, that for the good of the Association, reserve land should be sold to keep the cemetery solvent. There's nothing written in stone that says our land is not an 'asset.' In truth it is not an asset. It's a reserve. We'll need that land for graves, one day. Perhaps not in my life time, or yours, but someday. Unfortunately, that is not written in stone. They can do anything. They'll play the public-good cards. You know: that asset belongs to everyone in town, not just the Association. Or, the town needs affordable housing; or, it would generate more income, create jobs, lower school taxes. They'll throw up all the developer excuses until one sticks." She looked at me, sternly. "Which is why the Association needs real leadership."

I said, "Let's ask Dan to meet with us."

"Why?"

"To find out if the condo scheme is on or off."

Without hesitating, Grace telephoned the bank. She was told Dan was away from his desk. "Would you ask him to call Grace Botsford at his earlier convenience?"

They must have beeped him, because he called back within a minute. Ten minutes later he walked into Grace's office. Before he could speak, Grace said, "Let's not beat about the bush. Are you going to push this condo thing, or drop it?"

He looked at me. "You saw Scooter's email?"

"I saw the doll house."

Dan looked like I had hit him in the face. "What did you do? Break into a dead man's home?"

"You hired me to investigate who killed Brian. What did you expect me to do, Google it?"

He turned to Grace. "I hope you're not taking this the wrong way."

"Who are your partners?"

"My only partner is dead."

"Is it over?"

"Yeah, until someone else tries to take over the board. A hundred and sixty unused acres of open space in northwestern Connecticut is an asset that won't go away."

"One-hundred-and-sixty-two point seven-four," said Grace. "And it is not 'unused.' It is waiting. Would you please resign or will the board have to force you out?"

"Will you keep it quiet?"

"Of course. I have no desire to air our laundry in public."

"Then I resign."

He turned around and started to walk out. Grace said, "I would like that in writing." She shoved a pen and a sheet of letterhead across her desk and watched Dan write. When he was done and out the door, she said, "Well that's that. Thank you for your help, Ben. Send us your bill."

"Let me hold off until I see if I can buy Charlie. I've given my word to a bounty hunter."

"Let's hope he escapes safely home to Ecuador. It'll save us a fortune." She rubbed her eyes. "Dan is right. The wolves will keep on circling. Which is why the Association needs fresh blood in leadership."

Wondering, pondering, I drove out to my mother's farm in Frenchtown. She was surprised to see me. I'd been more than usually remiss about visiting, lately. She made a pot of excellent coffee and insisted I eat some toast. Her enormous dark eyes bored accusingly into me as she reported that Aunt Helen said Sherman had a wonderful new lawyer. I knew that she feared that I was somehow involved in Sherman's legal troubles. I assured her that I was not: I just happened to be driving behind him when he crashed his bike; and no one was more surprised than I that the cops had arrested him as he exited intensive care.

"How can Sherman afford Ira Roth?"

"Lorraine Renner is horse trading a movie for him."

"Lorraine?" She smiled as the meaning of that sunk in. "Helen didn't mention Lorraine."

"Aunt Helen gave me the impression that she doesn't like the idea of competing for the privilege of feeding Sherman free meals. On the other hand, I doubt the Renners will rate Sherman as a prime addition to the family, either."

My mother laughed. "What do they see in each other?"

"Mutual perversity is my guess. Want to go for a walk? I'd like to see the plot."

She was, like most Chevalleys, happiest out of doors; and we had a pleasant stroll the length of the property, across the swamp, up barren fields, and through the woods to the Chevalley Cemetery.

There were nine lonely headstones in the family plot, tilted by frost and enclosed by a tumbled wall overgrown with brush. They bore dates from the early 19th Century, when the Chevalleys finally got the money together to buy land no one in his right mind would try to farm. The most recent date on a headstone was 1920, after which the long climb up Church Hill to Newbury's Village Cemetery did not daunt the generation that grew up with cars and trucks.

"They've been stealing rocks from the wall," said my mother.

The tail end of a new subdivision was just visible through the trees. I saw a wheelbarrow track where someone had been trundling stone. I thought about tracking the thief down and threatening to realign his grill. Except he was just a homeowner who was willing to work hard for some rocks to build his own wall.

"Do you still want to be buried here?"

"Yes."

"I'll be right back." I knew she didn't want to come with me. She was too shy. But I had to do something before they got the idea that a headstone would look authentic in their family room.

I followed the track into a backyard of a new house and knocked on the door. Dogs barked. A woman answered. I introduced myself and explained that my family's burying ground was in the woods, and would they please stop taking stone. She was very embarrassed. They didn't realize anyone lived there. She promised to tell her husband. I gave her my card, said he was welcome to call me, went back into the woods, and walked my mother home.

Chapter Twenty

Early the next morning, I phoned the Botsford Insurance Agency. Grace was already at her desk.

"Okay," I said. "You win."

"I hope you are going to say what I think you are going to say."

"If you think you can bamboozle the board into it, I'll be president of the Village Cemetery Association."

"Consider them bamboozled. Thank you, Ben. May I ask what changed your mind?"

"Funnily enough, something Dan Adams said last week: 'Changes I hate, kids will take for granted; but we owe protection to the people already in the burying ground.'"

"We'll make our last stand in the cemetery?"

"That's what I told Dan—kidding, I thought."

"Thank you very much, Ben."

"Gotta go. I'm getting another call. Talk to you later."

It was Al Vetere. Whispering.

"Say again, Al."

"I been calling and calling."

"I was in the woods with my mother. What's up?…A little louder?"

"I'm on stakeout," he whispered. "In Bridgeport. I don't want 'em to hear me."

I pictured a garbage can in an Ecuadorian neighborhood, partially concealing a two-hundred-and-eighty-pound white guy crouched behind it hissing English into his cell phone.

"I got him. Bring the dough."

"Charlie?"

"I'm watching the house. You got the cash?"

"I can get there in two hours, maybe less. Tell me exactly where you are."

I telephoned Wes at home and told him to get over to Newbury Savings. I Google-Mapped the address Al had whispered. I looked out the window to see what surprise vehicle was waiting for me in the driveway. It was a bicycle. I telephoned Pink. "Very funny. I need wheels and I need them now. I gotta get to Bridgeport."

"Look in your barn."

I ran down to the barn.

"All right!"

Yesterday's blue silliness had been replaced by a low-slung, lemon-yellow Mini Cooper. I fired it up, whipped out of the drive, stopped at Newbury Savings, ran in and ran out a minute later like a cartoon bandit with a canvas bag of cash.

What a car! The first hour of the trip passed in forty-five minutes. I hadn't gone so fast on country roads since a lady lent me her front-wheel drive Passat. It accelerated nearly as fast as my old Olds and bonded to curves like an Olympic bobsled. The color troubled me. The cops could see it coming for miles. Hyper alert, I spotted a state trooper coming the other way on the Black Rock Turnpike in time to slow her down to legal.

But a second after we passed in opposite directions, he stomped his brakes, pulled a tire-smoking one-eighty and came after me with his light bar blazing. I hoped he wouldn't delay my getting to Al Vetere, but I wasn't worried. I was doing forty-five in a forty zone. I hadn't had a drink since yesterday. I had not drifted across the yellow line in the middle or the white line on the verge of the shoulder. And I certainly wasn't exhibiting road rage, as I had had the road to myself until the trooper came along.

I pulled my license from my money clip and the Cooper's registration from the glove compartment where Pink always left the rentals' paperwork. The trooper walked a slow circle around the car.

I opened the window. How often can any of us ever ask in complete innocence, "What's the trouble, Officer?"

"You're driving my wife's car."

‹ › › ›

The list of plausible explanations was short and not at all sweet. That I had stolen his wife's car might play marginally better than I had borrowed the car from his wife, who trusted me because we were lovers. I floated one from in between, and hoped it would work fast.

"I am test driving your wife's car for her automotive maintenance center. If indeed you are—"I had seen the name on the registration— "Trooper Clark."

"I am Trooper Clark," came the cold reply. "And you—" He shot a look at my license—"Mr. Abbott, are fifty miles from the repair shop."

He was exaggerating, but not by a lot. I said, "We are nothing if not thorough at Chevalley Enterprises."

"For an oil change? Get out of the car."

I got out keeping both hands in view.

"You work for Chevalley?"

"Betty Chevalley is my cousin Renny's widow," I said, intending to deflect the problem from Pink, whose name was more likely featured in police computers than Betty's.

"I remember Renny Chevalley," said the trooper. "He was the pilot who got shot on a dope run."

I stopped being polite. "Your memory is long, but way off. Renny was a good man. He never did anything wrong in his life." (True.) In case the trooper might have talked to Betty on the telephone, I added, "He was a good husband to Betty," (Not entirely true, if you counted an incendiary love affair with Gwen Jervis, which Betty didn't know about or didn't want to.)

The trooper with the long memory started looking me over. "Abbott. Abbott. I know the name."

"Are you stationed at the Plainfield barracks?"

"What if I am?"

Why did his wife have her car serviced to hell and gone in Frenchtown?

One answer was that they were living apart. That he knew the car was in for an oil change meant he still saw her regularly, which could mean they were trading kids. I said something that I would not say if I weren't trying to protect Betty and Pink, as I never played the Marian card. "I used to date an officer in the Plainfield barracks. We're still friends."

He snapped his fingers. "Detective-Lieutenant Boyce."

"She was Trooper Boyce, then, and then Sergeant Boyce. It wasn't that long ago, actually. She went up the ladder fast."

"That's for sure. You're the bird who did time, aren't you?"

"Full time. No parole. No probation. Debt paid. Home free. Which means you get to treat me as kindly as any other citizen."

He looked at his wife's car. He looked at my license. But he wasn't seeing either. "What do you mean you and Detective-Lieutenant Boyce are still friends?"

For a vulnerable moment, he was not a hard-ass road cop with a long memory. Just a man who missed his wife.

"Marian and I had lunch last week. Nice thing is, if you stay friends you don't lose as much."

"How'd you pull it off?"

"Carefully. Very, very carefully."

He almost smiled. "Where you taking my wife's car?"

"Straight back to the garage."

"You're headed south. It's north."

"I was about to stop and ask for directions."

"That way." He handed back my papers and pointed north. He watched me turn around. He watched me pull away.

Bridgeport receded behind me, as did any chance of getting there until I dumped the Mini back in Newbury and found other wheels. I phoned Al to tell him the bad news. I got his voice mail.

Back in Newbury I gave Pink his Mini and demanded another car.

"How'd you do in Bridgeport?"

"Never got there and now I'm late. Is that Trans Am running?" I'd noticed it sitting in a corner of the shop for a few days, a faded-red, second generation hopped up Firebird from the 1970s that would give Charlie and Father Bobby's Integra a run for its money when Pink's mechanics got done with in.

"Can't have it. Just sold it to Miss Botsford."

"Grace? What does she want with a thirty-year old muscle car?"

"Hell do I know," said Pink. "Bald guys buy Corvettes, maybe old ladies buy Trans Ams."

"She's not that old."

Pink shrugged. "Funny car for an insurance agent. It don't even have air bags—Excellent brakes, though. Front disc, rear drum."

"I gotta get to Bridgeport, Pink."

"Mind me asking if it has to do with the sniper?"

"What sniper?"

"Scanner just picked it up." He jerked his thumb at the scanner that trolled the police channels they monitored for the wrecker calls. "Some bail bondsman got blown away."

"Sniper?"

It suddenly seemed like a good idea to steady my hands by pressing them on the warm hood of the lemon-yellow Mini, which also helped me not fall to the floor when my knees turned to water. If I were a sniper on a roof drawing a bead on two fools I had lured to Bridgeport, I'd shoot the smaller one first and take out the bigger, slower man second.

Chapter Twenty-one

I beeped Marian four times. Finally she called me back.

"What?"

"Was that Angel in Bridgeport?"

"None of your fucking business," Marian said, and hung up; which I took as confirmation that poor, dumb Al had blundered into him while tracking Charlie Cubrero. I beeped her again.

"What?"

"He may have been gunning for me, too."

"Why?"

"Maybe for the same reason he shot Sherman Chevalley."

"What? When?"

"Maybe the motorcycle accident wasn't an accident."

"Jesus Christ, Ben. What are you into?"

"Over my head, maybe."

"Sounds that way," she said, carefully.

"I think we better talk, and not on the phone—why don't you bring Arnie to my place?"

"No," she said. "We don't want to be seen with you. Make it the picnic rock."

I drove up along the river and, after it veered away, turned onto a dirt road that re-joined it. The water was low. The picnic rock was a flat piece of ledge exposed in the middle of the river, twenty feet from the bank. Marian and I used to cavort on it. Once, to the amusement of the Newbury Riding Club, which trotted by on their carriages in period costume. Stepping stones offered a dry route across the water. Marian and Arnie were already there, sprawled in the sun like wolves on a coffee break. I step-stoned out to them.

"You two clean up well." They'd caught sleep since I'd seen them staking out Brian Grose's library—showered, shaved, washed hair, found fresh clothing and improved their diet. But despite the pleasant surroundings, which included a lot more sunshine than they had enjoyed skulking indoors for days, neither appeared in a pleasant mood. Arnie said, "What is going on?"

"When I met him in Danbury, the bail bondsman was trying to make a buck playing bounty hunter on the side. I convinced him that my clients would pay better than the Feds so they could get the credit for turning him in."

"Why?"

"My clients are in a court action trying to retain control of the Village Cemetery Association. It's small town politics. But it is very real to them."

"Jesus Christ."

"You will go home when this over. They live right here in Newbury. Okay?"

"What's the Sherman connection?"

"What I'm going to tell you is confidential."

"We're the police, Ben," Marian reminded me, and Arnie said, "In case you forgot."

"You can't use this against Sherman."

"We can and will use any illegality against Sherman."

"I'm not ratting him out. You give me your word, or this conversation is over. Come on, you know as well as I do that Sherman will be back inside for some damned thing or another soon enough."

"No way, Ben. You come to us with some make-or-break deal, we'll knock a few miles off a speeding ticket. But we are not authorized to plea bargain. You want that, you talk to the prosecutor." I declined to remind them that their prosecutor would offer what they recommended and tried to move along by saying, "If Sherman shot Brian Grose, of course you can have him. I'll hand him to you myself. But he didn't and you know it."

"Stop presuming what we know," said Arnie.

"What's the Sherman connection?" asked Marian.

I watched the sun dance on a rock-strewn stretch of rapid water. "Okay, I'll give it to you as hearsay. You want hearsay?"

"What hearsay? What are you talking about?"

"I'm talking about hearsay—something I can not testify to in court because I overheard some guy saying it in a bar. It was too dark to see who the guy talking was. Here's what the guy I couldn't see in the dark said to another guy I couldn't see in the dark either: he said that Sherman recognized a guy he saw coming out of Grose's mausoleum right after Grose was shot. Sherman had seen him around and thought he was called Angel."

"How did Sherman know that Grose was shot?"

"I heard that he went in to see what he could steal and saw the corpse, saw the bullet holes, and put two and two together."

"Then what happened?"

"He knew that Angel had seen him see him. Sherman thought quick and decided to blackmail Angel—threatening to tell you what he saw if Angel didn't pay him off. In his defense, in Sherman's mind, blackmail was sort of preemptive self-defense."

"Huh?"

"He figured that since Angel would come after him anyhow, he might as well scare him off and make a buck."

"Good thinking," said Arnie. "Now Angel had two reasons to shoot him."

"Only after sabotaging Sherman's bike didn't kill him."

"Who told you all this?"

"Sherman told the guy I couldn't see in the bar who told the other guy I couldn't see. I just heard hearsay. Keep in mind, Sherman won't repeat it to you in a million years. Besides, it has nothing to do with anything. Because I don't think Angel shot him, either."

"Sure about that?"

"Not a hundred percent," I admitted.

"If Angel didn't kill him, why is Angel running? Not to mention murdering the bail bondsman?"

"I don't know. I mean, beyond running from ICE 'cause he's illegal."

"Illegals don't ordinarily assassinate bail bondsmen and low-life swamp life like your cousin," said Arnie. "No offense intended to your family. Answer us one thing. Why did you drag us out here to tell us what you don't know?"

"You are the only cops in this investigation who won't be satisfied arresting the wrong guy."

"You're going to swell our heads, Ben."

"It's not saying much. ICE makes their bones deporting illegals, the more the merrier. Homeland Security turns attempts to get driver licenses and work permits into "identity theft" so it can appear to be actually doing something to justify its existence. And your bosses are paid by the Feds to go along, and are harassed if they don't. We're not talking about a high standard here."

"Why are we sitting on this fucking rock?"

"I think the sniper maneuvered Al Vetere into luring me down there."

"Are you asking for police protection, Mr. P.I.?"

"No. But it's sobering enough to make me offer to pool resources to nail the bastard before he tries again. I've told you what I know. What can you tell me?"

Arnie stood up. "Here's my advice. I heard it from a guy in a bar I couldn't see in the dark: Go online to Travelocity and book an open-ended ticket to Europe. We'll call you when it's safe to come home. You coming, Marian?"

Marian said, "Oh yes," stood up and followed him back across the stepping stones.

I called, "How come a perfect crime shooter panicked and ran away without his cell phones, dough, wigs, and weapons?"

Marian stopped so quickly she slipped on a wet rock and started to fall backwards into the water. Arnie caught her hand, gracefully and saved her. I felt a blaze of jealousy. I knew they weren't lovers—didn't even really like each other—but their interplay was so intimate I wanted to kill him.

"What do you mean 'perfect crime?'" she called across the water.

"Gloves," I called. "No prints in the crypts." Then I took a not so wild guess and said, "No hairs, no fibers."

They re-crossed the water faster than competing messiahs.

I said, "You must be asking yourselves the same thing. The shooter killed him like a pro. Boom in the back. Guarantee shots in the head. *Then* he panicked? Left all his stuff? Can't be the same person."

"He split," said Arnie. "Mission accomplished. Outta here."

"Only if he came the same way. Like a real pro. Parachute in. Scope out the situation. Kill the target and split. Didn't happen that way."

"How do we know?"

"The room full of man-on-the-run gear. Which means, by the way, since Grose had the guy in his house he knew he was on the run."

"Why did Grose have him in the house, Ben?"

I almost blurted, *Because Grose gave a stone killer a job.*

But I could tell by their suddenly smug faces they had figured that out long ago and that I was way, way behind. They quickly unsmugged and tried to change the subject by demanding what made me think they found no hairs and fibers in the crypt.

"Logical guess."

They also wanted to know how I knew there were no prints in the crypts, either. Two guesses was too much to expect them to swallow so I said, "I saw nothing about fingerprints in the newspaper." They accepted that because they had bigger fish to fry.

I headed back to town, concerned that I could not remember a time in my life that I had lied so often. I'd been hanging out too much with the cops. And I knew they felt the same way about me. Though I still could not figure out why they were letting me as close as they were. Unless I had something they wanted.

When I drove back inside cell phone coverage I got a beep for a message waiting. I didn't know the number. I dialed it, thinking, Father Bobby. No one answered. When I got to Newbury I went to the cemetery,

They still had yellow tape around the mausoleum. But this time I did not invade the space. I just stood there and tried to walk through Brian's last morning on the planet. It was all over before ten when first Angel and then Sherman found him dead.

Angel goes to Grose's mausoleum. Why? To meet him or confront him. He knows he's there. He's living at Grose's house. Grose says see you later, I'm going to the mausoleum. Angel does not know that Grose is going to be shot. He goes to meet Grose or confront him. Why not at home? Why in the mausoleum? Because he was going kill him in the mausoleum, and the shooter beat him to it. Kill him with what? Sherman saw no gun in his tight bicycle shorts. Why is Angel wearing bicycle shorts? Because that way he doesn't look like an Ecuadorian laborer. He's got a helmet on and sunglasses; and he looks like a guy on a bike, an ordinary "desirable inhabitant" of Newbury, riding his bicycle on a weekend instead of mowing his lawn.

My cell rang. "Hello, Ben, it's Father Bobby. Sorry I missed you before. Sorry about the other night."

"Have you spoken with Charlie?"

"That's why I'm calling. I think he'll take you up on your offer."

"When?" I asked, fed up with vagueness.

"I'll still talking him into it."

"How long is that going to take?"

"It's close. He's getting tired, Ben. It's hard to run."

"I'll meet you anywhere you want."

"Will you bring the lawyer?"

"That depends on when and where. Obviously I can't bring him if he's in court. So you might want to consider bringing him to some safe spot, like my house, some place we can stash him until we get the lawyer to walk him into the cops."

"You're saying, 'we.' I don't want to be there."

"You don't have to be. All Charlie needs is the lawyer. I'll go along to put him at ease."

"I'll get back to you."

"Do me a favor?"

"What?"

"Hang on to that cell so I can get a hold of you."

He hesitated. "All right. I'll take a chance the cops don't trace my calls."

"I'm not asking you to take a chance. Get another phone for your other business. Just keep this one for me and Charlie. Okay?"

"You think I'm paranoid, don't you?"

"I'm not saying you don't have reason to be. But I wish you had more of a sense of urgency. If you're going help this kid, you gotta do it fast."

He said he understood.

I said, "Good bye," with little hope.

There was only one place I could think to go, and that was Steve's Liquor Locker.

Steve had long since sold the store to Dave who did so well with it that he was going to buy a second store and, demonstrating faith in the power of Twelve Steps that few liquor store owners would, installed Tom Mealy as manager of the first, which was still called Steve's, it being bad luck, apparently, to rename a booze shop. The place was empty when I walked in. Tom was down on the floor, stocking shelves.

He grabbed my hand in both of his huge paws. "Ben, I gotta thank you for standing up for me the other night."

"I just had a feeling that Ollie wasn't bullish on redemption."

"You can say that again. That man will see me as a drunk until the day I die."

"How's the leg?"

"Not bad. Didn't break the skin. Wrenched the heck out of it."

"How's Alison?"

His face clouded just a little. "I don't know, Ben. Some of her little friends are showing up dressed like hookers. I don't know how I'd handle it if she did."

"You've got my sympathy," I said, thinking better thee than me. When she and her mother lived in the barn I used to worry what I would do when the first date appeared on a motorcycle.

"Janet says she's so busy with the horse and music and computers and her lessons she won't have time for that shit, but I don't know man. What can I get you?"

"I want to ask you something, Tom. The night you rolled over? You got cut off?"

"Son of a bitch cut me off."

"Deliberately?"

"No, no, no, just some damned fool drunk comes passing me down the hill on the curve, weaving like a snake. The lights came up so fast behind me I thought it was Ollie—you know how cops charge up behind you—but then I saw him cross the double yellow to pass and I thought, Oh shit, the man's drunk as a skunk. He whips across my nose, and if I hadn't slammed on the brakes and turned away he'd a nailed me. So he keeps going and now I'm in deep shit, car's all over the place, skidding, sliding. I'm standing on the brake, I'm spinning the steering wheel; and just when I think I'm okay, I hit the curbing—that hump they put alongside to keep the water from washing out the road?— and over she goes, bang, bang, bang. Slams into a rock and slides on the roof back into the road. First thing I thought was: hope no nine-yard cement truck runs into me. Thank God it was too late at night for that. Thank God I was wearing my belt. Thank God for air bags. My nose still hurts from them. They popped when I hit the rock."

I said, "Wow."

Tom shrugged. "Funny thing is when I used to drink, never wore a seat belt. Cracked up so many cars, never got hurt, much. But you're so loose—God looks out for drunks, right?"

"Sounds to me like that night He was looking out for the sober."

"You can say that again."

"So it was the curb that got you?"

"Skidding's okay as long as you don't hit a tree or another vehicle. But when those wheels stop sliding all of a sudden against the curb you've got nowhere to go but over. Especially in a truck or a SUV. I'm buying a little car when I get the insurance. Something that won't turn over."

I drove down to Frenchtown to Chevalley Enterprises. Pink, Betty informed me, had gone out to 'clear his head.' I found him in the White Birch, which was busy with the late afternoon crowd. That long-haired, heavy-set patrons had left two stools empty on either side of him indicated that my cousin was judged to be in a testy mood.

"Remember when Gerard Botsford got killed?"

"Poor old bastard. That was a bitch."

"You brought the wreck in?"

"Who else?"

"What did it look like?"

"What would you look like if you rolled over three or four times down hill at forty?" The gentleman nearest to Pink's left got off his stool and carried his beer to a distant corner.

"Cops inspect it?"

"Looked it over."

"Quickie because he was old?"

"No, the troopers looked it over pretty careful."

"What did they find?"

"Found a car that rolled over three times."

"What was it? Something tall? Land Rover?"

"You kidding? Those rich old Yankees don't waste money on cars. Just a Chevy Blazer."

"Did they find any sign of another vehicle?"

"Found a little green paint on the fender from something that hit him. Miss Botsford said it was news to her. But he'd been out all day. They figured he got dinged in a parking lot."

I called to Wide Greg who was recommending his parking lot to two fellows who had begun shouting at each other. "Couple of more, Greg?" The weather had been so beautiful for so long that it had reached the point it was kind of nice to sit in a loud, dark bar.

"Pink, can I ask you something?"

"What have you been doing so far?"

"I don't want to screw up your contract with the cops." Chevalley Enterprises held an exclusive towing contract for recovering wrecks, partly because they got there fast and did a good job, partly because competing bidders tended to have terrible things happen to their tires. "Okay? Don't answer if you don't want to."

"I never do anything I don't want to. What are you asking?"

"Did anybody else ask you about Old Man Botsford's Blazer? Recently? Maybe asked, and told you to keep it under your hat?"

Pink ruminated for a while. Then he tugged his greasy Chevalley Enterprises cap off his head, turned it over, and peered inside. "I'll be damned."

"What?"

"You know how when you stick your ear in a seashell you hear the ocean?"

"Yeah?"

"Well when you look inside this hat you see a lady with a fine butt."

I never liked the word butt. Or ass for that matter. Call me old-fashioned. Call me prissy. But just this once, it didn't seem right to tell Pink to leave my friend's anatomy out of it. So all I said was, "Thank you."

We clinked bottles and my cell rang. I put it to one ear and a finger in the other.

"This is Father Bobby. Charlie Cubrero is ready to turn himself in."

"Fantastic! Great! Thank you. I'll take him to my lawyer's office and we'll proceed from there. Where is he?"

"We'll meet you in Newbury."

"Perfect. My lawyer's office is above the General Store. There's a stair on the outside, but I'll be waiting right out front."

"Hold on," said Father Bobby.

I heard rapid Spanish. "No, Ben. He's afraid to do that. There's a trooper stationed in Newbury."

"Resident state trooper Moody, the one you talked out of the speeding ticket." I saw Pink's eyebrows rise. *Nobody* talked Ollie out of a speeding ticket.

"Charlie's afraid if he sees him he'll arrest him before you get upstairs to the lawyer—he's scared, Ben."

"Do you want to come to my house? You can pull in the drive and come in the kitchen door."

The priest hesitated. "Hold on." I listened to more Spanish.

"Okay, here's where he wants to meet. There's a cemetery where he used to work? You know this place?"

"I know it."

"He says there's a mausoleum in it? Oh, of course, where the white man was shot,"

"I know it."

"Charlie wants to meet there. By the mausoleum."

"You won't be able to drive in," I said. "The gates are locked at seven."

Father Bobby said, "Why don't we just meet at the gates?"

"Fine."

"Hold on."

I held on.

"No. He says the cops will spot us at the gates."

"Yeah, well the cops could spot you climbing the fence, too," I said.

"Charlie knows a safe place to climb—One more thing, Ben. Remember what I said, I'm going to hand him to you and split. Once you have him you are on your own."

"I'll do it anyway you want, Father. But I gotta tell you, you should take the credit for talking him in, make some friends with cops who could help you next time you need friends."

"Absolutely not. Under no circumstances do I want to talk to the cops."

He hung up. I looked at the phone and said, "Later, Pink. Gotta meet a guy. Thanks for everything."

"Hey, want me to ride along?" asked Pink.

"Why?"

"You look a little worried."

"No, no, no. Just thinking." I was thinking the obvious. If Gerard Botsford, who controlled a hundred and sixty-two acres of open land, was deliberately run off the road, then Brian Grose, who wanted to get rich developing those acres, was the man with the motive. It would certainly explain why he kept a stone killer around the house, which made Grose the real villain, and wheelman Angel his instrument. How they had hooked up, God knew. Could have started with Angel mowing his lawn, or a recreational pharmaceuticals purchase. Had they had a falling out? Grose had a consistent record of those. Had Angel extended his stone killerism to Grose. Had he killed him or had he found him dead? I didn't know. But I knew one thing for sure: Now the instrument is running around loose, scared, angry, murderous. And in deep, deep trouble—until Charlie Cubrero was arrested.

Just as Sherman Chevalley assumed the cops would blame illegal immigrant Angel, Angel could assume that the cops would blame illegal immigrant Charlie Cubrero if he could make poor Charlie his fall guy. Charlie caught meant end of case. I wondered if it was Angel who sent poor fat Al to the Kantor farm, hoping he'd get shot in the ICE raid he'd somehow caught wind of.

I had to sympathize with Father Bobby. Paranoia was catching. Had Angel somehow snookered the priest into setting up Charlie?

"I may take you up on that later, Pink."

"On what?"

"Riding along with me."

First things first.

First get Charlie safely booked with a lawyer.

Then go Angel hunting.

Chapter Twenty-two

I couldn't find Tim to come with me to hand Charlie over to the cops. I called Vicky. She said he was over in Hartford at a Connecticut Bar Association meeting. "Actually, I'm on my own for dinner."

"I'd love to," I said. "I can't."

"Heavy date?"

"No, just wrapping up a job—when you talk to him, tell him we're ready to make our move. He'll know what I mean. In fact, Vicky, do me favor? When you talk to Tim, ask him if he'd call Ira Roth to cover, if he can't get here in two hours."

I got to the cemetery before Donny Butler locked the gate.

"Did a priest go in?"

"Nope." Donny looked away. Stand-offishness was emanating from him like a Klingon force field.

"You got a problem, Donny?"

"I hear you're my new boss. Mr. President."

"Donny, for crissakes you've known me since I was born."

"Planning any changes?"

"Yes, I'm trying to get the trustees to up your salary to half a million dollars a year. If they don't go along I'm hoping you'll stay on anyhow. Did you see a priest?"

"No I didn't, Ben. No one's in there. I gotta lock up, now. Need anything?"

"No, fine, thanks."

"You know the way out."

I nodded toward the low stone wall at the wooded end of the old section.

I walked down there through the long shadows of evening light and stopped a moment at my father's grave. Under his name and the dates of his life it said, "First Selectman." Under that, his friends had persuaded my mother to allow them to have chiseled, "He Served His Town." In a rare instance of voicing a complaint out loud my mother had remarked while he served the town: she had served warmed-over supper most nights of the week.

He had died, suddenly, when I came home from prison, and we had left most of a lifetime undiscussed. So it was with intense pleasure that I was able to say, "The president hopes you're pleased." Then I walked up the slope to the new area and sat on the damp grass in front of Brian Grose's mausoleum and watched the low wall that lovers climbed on warm summer nights.

An older Honda Civic came along the dirt road that passed beyond the wall, trailing dust. The black-clad priest jumped out, ran around the car, opened the passenger door, and helped Charlie out. Charlie was limping. He was clutching a gym bag and seemed quite unsteady. The priest helped him over the wall and hurried up the hill.

I ran down and met them part way. "Charlie, you okay?"

"I had to give him a Valium," said Father Bobby. "He's so scared."

"A whole bottle?" I said, and then to Charlie, "You're okay, now Charlie. Everything's going to be fine. Thank you, Father Bobby. You can split. I'll take him from here."

But the priest didn't hear me.

"You brought the cops?"

"No, I didn't."

He was staring at the road beyond the wall, and I saw Arnie and Marian pull up in their unmarked unit.

"*You brought the cops!*"

My cell phone rang. I looked at it with a sinking heart. "They tracked my phone." I answered. Sure enough it was Marian, climbing over the wall with her phone pressed to her face. "Don't do anything else stupid. We'll be right there."

"You fool," said Father Bobby. "You stupid fool"

Actually, I felt a little stab of pride that two stars like them could think I could get close enough to the killer to make it worth tracking me.

"All right," said Father Bobby. "Stay with Charlie. I'll deal with them."

Good, I thought. A priest was almost as good as a lawyer when it came to giving up.

"Hang on to Charlie." He spoke Spanish to Charlie. Charlie returned a dazed smile.

"What did you tell him?"

"I told him to wait here with you. Let me see what I can do with the cops."

I said, "There's nothing left to do with the cops. Tell them you're turning Charlie in. A priest is almost as good as a lawyer. Tell them my lawyer will meet us at the barracks."

Father Bobby took the gym bag from Charlie's hand and hurried down the slope toward Arnie and Marian.

"Hey, wait," I said, "I thought you don't want to talk to the cops."

He quickened his pace, and waved to Marian and Arnie. It was part hello, part benediction. "Charlie, what's in your bag?"

The snap in my voice penetrated and he said, "No my bag."

I ran after Father Bobby.

Twenty feet from Marian and Arnie, he reached into the bag.

"Gun!" I yelled. "Not a priest. Not a priest. That's Angel."

Angel had not snookered the priest into setting up Charlie Cubrero. Angel was the priest. And the priest wasn't a priest, but a stone killer named Angel.

"Gun!"

Marian and Arnie flared apart, Marian reaching for her shoulder holster, Arnie for the pistol on his hip, both shouting, "Stop. Police."

But he was way too fast for them. God he was fast. He fired three times in a heartbeat. Three heavy caliber *booms* echoed like cannon fire. All three hit. Arnie pinwheeled backwards. Marian went down, clutching her body. Angel was on top of her before I could reach them, jerking her gun out of her hand and leveling both weapons to fire again at Arnie who was trying to stand. Marian flopped back on the grass arms and legs spread wide, thighs flashing white. She pulled her backup gun from her leg holster. But she had been hit too hard to be quick, and before I could get between them, Angel kicked it out of her hand.

She convulsed into a tight ball, rolled toward Arnie with a cry of pain and clutched at the back of her neck. I dove for Angel. He fired at Arnie, then turned both guns on me.

"Angel!" Marian shouted.

He whipped fiery eyes at her. She flicked her arm forward, pointing like a snake tongue . *She's hidden a second backup derringer in her sleeve*, I thought, filling with crazy hope. But her arms were bare and dead silence told me she had no gun.

Something flashed through the failing light. Angel jerked back with a cry, dropped Marian's gun, and clawed at his cheek. A five-inch throwing knife jutted from it at the odd angle of a boar's tusk.

"Bitch," he screamed, spraying blood. He ripped the blade out of his face and swung his own heavy weapon at Marian.

I got my hand around his wrist.

He was strong and his wrist was slippery with blood. But Marian's knife had sent him into shock and I was motivated.

Chapter Twenty-three

Arnie told the troopers I was a hero.

They allowed it when Marian insisted I ride with her in the ambulance. She told the paramedic and the nurse that she was scared. The two worked on her the whole time. I crouched out of the way, holding her hand. They gave her something for pain but she stayed alert and kept asking, "How's Arnie?"

I kept saying, "He'll make it." Arnie, in fact, was the less injured of the two, his bullet proof vest having stopped the slugs, which were so heavy the impact had shattered his ribs. The slug that hit Marian, however, had skidded across the fabric and inside of the vest where it had puckered open under her armpit.

"I can't believe she could throw a knife," the paramedic muttered to the nurse, to which Marian croaked, "It wasn't like I had a choice."

"Almost there," said the nurse. "You'll be fine."

Marian whispered me closer. "I don't want Bruce to see you at the hospital."

"I'll split. Don't worry."

"Come here."

I put my mouth to her ear. The ambulance hit a bump and her lips touched me. "You know," she said.

"Know what?"

"Don't fuck with me," she whispered and I realized she was not one bit scared, but raging, and that it was a ploy to get me alone. "Who shot Brian Grose?"

"Angel did it." I said.

"No he didn't."

I said, "Angel did it."

"*No he didn't!*"

"ICE says Angel did it."

"He didn't, you bastard. Tell me."

I said, "Homeland Security says Angel did it, now that they've figured out he's their missing gang leader. Your bosses say he did it. And the State's Attorney already has a list of Angel murders from here to Ecuador."

Marian raked me with a look of cold hatred. Then she closed her eyes and turned away.

I waited in the hospital parking lot, avoiding her boy friend. The Major Crime Squad caught up with me there, and we had a long talk about how it went down in the cemetery, and when it was over they shook my hand.

I waited until I learned she was safely out of surgery. Then, suddenly very, very tired, I phoned Pink. "I need a ride."

"Already here," said Pink. He'd figured out where I would end up without wheels and was just rolling into the parking lot on his Harley. I rode on back, helmetless and glad of the warm night wind, knowing I had to figure out what was right and what was wrong before I could decide between them.

Chapter Twenty-four

Next day, I waited until it was after business hours to stop by the Botsford Insurance Agency. Jeannie had gone home. Grace's beautiful wooden office was quiet and peaceful. A regulator clock ticked on the wall and it was a comfortable sound.

I got right to it. Still on my feet, I said, "You and I have caution in common, Grace. We know too much not to. I learned caution in prison. You learned yours selling insurance all these years. You've probably seen every insurance scam known to man."

"And woman."

"How people set fires. Fake deaths. Stage car wrecks."

"Most clients don't," said Grace.

"Oh I'm sure it's a very small part of the business. But as in any business, the small part represents profit or loss. Miss too many fraudulent claims and there goes your living. Breaking even never pays the bills."

"Insurance spreads risk, Ben. That's all there is to it."

"But insurance companies profit by minimizing risk. That's where the money is. That's why they give seminars to their agents on how to recognize fraud, forestall it. Don't they?"

"Actually, you learn as much from experience. Dad used to say, 'I've been doing this so long I would not trust my own mother.'"

"Or daughter?"

"He did not worry about his daughter. He was on top of everything until the day he was killed. I could not have pulled any wool over his eyes."

"But you had learned from a master."

"What are you driving at, Ben?—Sit down, Ben. Sit down. Take that chair."

She indicated the customer's chair and I sat.

"Somebody set a timer on Brian Grose's mausoleum audio system so loud music would alert everyone at the Notables that there was a dead man inside. Why do you suppose he did that?"

"So that his body would receive a proper Christian burial and not rot alone."

"Why do you suppose they shot him in the head? Twice."

"So that he would not suffer a slow death from the wound in his chest."

"That would be the kind Christian thing to do, but I wonder if they wanted to make absolutely certain that Brian was not alive to tell who shot him in the chest."

"Minimizing risk?" she asked.

"Your phrase, not mine."

"No, Ben, minimizing risk was your phrase. I said spread risk."

"You are very precise, Grace. What we've been calling the chest wound was actually an exit wound. He was shot in the back."

"I know."

"I spent a lot of time thinking about that. A shot in the back doesn't jibe with a—I don't know, what would you call it?"

"Call what?"

"Crime of passion? For want of a better phrase. But the crimes of passion I'm familiar with involve face to face confrontation. You're mad at somebody for doing you wrong—breaking your heart—you shoot them in front, face to face. Maybe the guy turns and runs, and you shoot him in the back, but there was nowhere to run in the mausoleum. As oversize as it looked compared to ordinary headstones, it was basically just a closet, inside. There really wasn't enough room inside to run from somebody with a gun. Was there?"

She looked back at me with the same quizzical stare as she did from her portrait of her and her father. In fact, had there been a gold frame around her desk, I would have thought I was observing another painting by Andrew Morrison.

"But," I said, "There is another kind of crime of passion. Not the kind that comes from a broken heart. But the kind that stems from revenge. Revenge in the old legal sense of an eye for an eye. Revenge isn't even the right word."

"Retribution?"

"Yes. Someone kills a member of your family. You kill them. Until the modern state demands the sole right to retribution, we are mired in feuding and tribalism. But state retribution can't always satisfy the desire for retribution. The state introduces subtleties. The state—the court—entertains the possibility of nuances. The state might say: You think that person contributed to the death of your father by making his life hell, but making another person's life hell is not punishable by death according to our laws."

She started to speak.

I said, "Please, Grace, don't. Don't tell me anything. Just listen to me....Okay?"

She waited, still as stone, for awhile before she nodded.

I said, "But a person who didn't agree to those laws and demanded her own retribution would be a person who commits a crime of passion—like the heartbroken lover—by shooting the son of a bitch, excuse my language, face to face. Which did not happen in Brian's mausoleum....So why was he shot in the back if it was a crime of passion, and there was no room to run?"

I stood up, stood in front of the portrait of her and her father. "Don't speak. Trust me, please.

"Two part answer: one reason he got shot in the back, it was retribution—real retribution for a real crime. But far more important is reason two. Not only was there not enough room to run, there was not enough room for the person holding the gun to protect the gun." I went back to the chair, sat down, and looked at her hands folded on the desk. They were still.

"I'm terrible with handguns myself, but I was taught the basic rule—the safe and cautious basic rule is *the lunge line*—the imaginary line you draw in the air between you and person you are confronting. If they step inside it—if they cross it—you *must* shoot before they can take the weapon away from you. But in Mr. Grose's mausoleum, there was no room for a lunge line."

I looked at her. She was still composed, although there was color in her cheek that had not been there before. I found myself wondering if she kept a gun in the desk, and dismissed that thought as beneath us both.

"So with no room to protect the gun the instant he saw it, and with a clear, cool sense of doing the right thing by taking retribution, the only place to shoot him was to wait until he turned around—maybe to put on music—and shoot him in the back. Or, if the shooter had hidden in one of the casket drawers and popped out gun in hand, shoot him in the back before he could reach the door."

Again, she started to speak. Again, I said, "Please don't tell me anything."

"I won't. But I do have a question. How did the person justify her right to retribution?"

"Well, that goes back to the insurance business. You minimize risk by minimizing fraud. You learn the tricks of arsonists, fakers of death, stagers of automobile crashes. Along the way you learn a lot about fires. Disappearances. And car wrecks. Criminals get away with fraud when we accept general premises. Such as: rickety wooden structures burn down; people who disappear on cruise ships fall overboard; ninety-five year old gentlemen fall asleep at the wheel, veer onto the curbing, spin out, hit the curbing again, roll over, and are killed."

Grace said, calmly, coldly, "The driver who ran my father off the road was not the murderer. He was a monster for hire. The man who hired him was the murderer."

"I will ask you only one question, Grace. Are you sure that Brian Grose hired that man?"

"Beyond any doubt. Dad stood in the way of taking over the association."

"You told me that until I told you about the condos, you thought it was about that stupid mausoleum. But you really knew he wanted the land, didn't you?"

"Brian was a simple, ruthless, disappointed man. It was a long time before I understood how disappointed, and by then it was too late. His dream was to become important and wealthy. His idea of importance was to live in a six-thousand-square-foot apartment in Beverly Hills, or on Fifth Avenue in New York City. His idea of wealth was to never have to work. He had had his eye on a Fifth Avenue apartment, but by the time he made his pile and cashed out prices had gone through the roof. The new hedge fund money had inflated two million dollar properties into twenty million properties. He couldn't keep up with men younger than he who were earning hedge fund money. Priced out of New York, priced out of Beverly Hills, he concocted a scheme he thought would work in a small town. My father stood in his way."

"I am so sorry, Grace. And I don't know what to do."

"Do nothing," she said. "It will all work out."

Chapter Twenty-five

It was the first time Scooter had put my picture on the front page of the *Newbury Clarion* since I rescued the Meeting House Cat from an elm tree. Aunt Connie was not entirely pleased. "It used to be that this sort of news was reported inside the paper, quietly, with dignity, and there was no need for photographs."

"Scooter's got to fill space."

"Well, I suppose that's true. Anyhow, it's a handsome picture. And Grace looks lovely, too." Connie had spread the *Clarion* on her tea table. The article was below the fold, under a picture of Grace Botsford handing me the gavel with which her father had brought Village Cemetery Association meetings to order since the 1950s.

"And I must tell you again that I am so pleased that you took the position. I'm sure it will be a constant bother, but there are certain obligations a young man of the town should honor. What's your first order of business, Mr. President?"

"I'm going to use that gavel on a couple of trustees. They demand to vote on whether or not Brian Grose can be buried in his mausoleum."

"Well of course he can!" Connie practically snorted. "He's dead and he owns his plot—I presume his dues were paid?"

I nodded. "Dues are paid and they are not disputing that he is dead. It's the ugliness factor."

"In a hundred years," said Connie, "no one will notice."

‹›‹›‹›

The meeting was like herding cats, but I came up with a compromise. No one liked it, of course, but they went along when Grace Botsford said essentially what Connie had said: The man was dead and his dues were paid up. Brian could stay, we agreed, but absolutely no more McTombs would ever be allowed in Newbury's village cemetery. Which, when it became time to bury him, turned out to be an even better idea than we thought, because the Bastion Mausoleum company, which had arranged the funeral as the final act of its full service for rainmakers, had, like England's Victorians, hired actors to be mourners. The actors were dressed in black, but were so happy to have the work that it was hard to believe their expressions of grief, much less their sighs, as they slow-marched behind the casket. One very pretty young woman was a convincingly-copious weeper until she was heard to whisper to a colleague, "This is so cool."

I watched from nearby. Grace stood with me briefly, before she wandered off to her father's grave. I waited until they slid the casket in and locked the thing up. Then I went up to a middle-aged gentleman who wore his shirt buttoned to the neck. Earlier, I had seen him park his pickup down on the road. I offered my hand. "Chance Grose? I'm Ben Abbott. May I extend my condolences?"

"Thank you, sir. And I thank you for the welcome your town gave my little brother. I'm sure he was mighty happy here."

What could I say but, "I recognized you from the film they made about Brian."

"Yes, sure, that nice young lady was a-shootin' up a storm."

We passed a couple of pleasantries and I said, "You made a long drive. Do you have a place to stay?"

He said he had towed a camper and parked it at the VFW. Then he threw back his head and fixed his gaze on the mausoleum, which was reflecting the sun like neon.

"I do believe that is the finest looking structure I have ever seen."

"Brian certainly enjoyed it," I said.

"I hate to leave him here, with strangers. He weren't much for mixing with his own family, but he is kin. But how could you separate a man from something he so obviously admired? Excuse me a moment, Mr. Abbott. Just want to get another look around it." He circled the fence, head pitched high, moving backwards and forwards for perspective.

Stealthily, I poked at my cell.

Quietly, I spoke into it.

"Pink? I need Albert and Dennis, a heavy lift crane, and a huge truck....Cost? Damn the cost. Bill the Cemetery Association. Attention: The President."

Having arrived in pieces, the blight came apart as easily as Lego blocks.

Lorraine Renner got a fat contract to film the disassembling and loading. The Bastion Mausoleum Company wished to assure restless consumers that "Built for the Ages" wasn't necessarily etched in stone, and eternal rest should never restrict an American's right to mobility. Lorraine was assisted by Sherman Chevalley who was surprisingly fleet-footed on crutches and was heard by more than one disbelieving on-looker to say, "Yes, dear," more than once.

Brian's casket rode in the back of his brother's pickup.

"Albert," said Pink. "Dennis. Come here."

I nudged Lorraine. "You'll want this."

Sherman, ever sneaky, had mastered eavesdropping with the shotgun mike and would miss not a word as Pink laid a gargantuan arm on each of the brothers and drew them near. "Now, boys," he said. "You will not screw up this important job."

"Sure, Pink."

"Nothing bad will happen to this truck. Nothing bad will happen to the load. You will drop the load in Arkansas, exactly where Mr. Grose wants it."

"Hey, come on, Pink, what do you think we're—"

Pink tightened his grip. Albert and Dennis grew expressions usually seen on an anaconda's dinner.

The mausoleum truck and Chance Grose's pickup truck rumbled out the gates. Pink finished loading tools.

"How's the Trans Am running, Miss Botsford?"

"It's making a clunking noise."

"Yeah, it'll do that," said Pink and left quickly.

Charlie Cubrero came hustling with a bale of salt hay on his shoulder, a rake under his arm, and a sack of grass seed and a pick ax in his hand. Donny Butler kept a close watch on him as Charlie scrabbled the bare ground the mausoleum had occupied with the pick, raked it smooth, scattered the grass seed and mulched it with the hay. It was his day off from the Kantor farm.

Under ordinary circumstances, Charlie would be moldering in an ICE detention center. Federal law enforcement agencies are not famous for admitting wrong, much less apologizing, but the boys at ICE had discovered that getting sued by Fred and Joyce Kantor was an extraordinary experience best ended by fifty lawyers hammering out an agreement to stop suing in exchange for releasing Charlie Cubrero into Kantor custody with a green card. Which made a happy ending for all—with four exceptions. Dan Adams, who was going to have to get used to living on a banker's salary instead of developer dreams. The inaptly named Angel, whose long-term future was being settled in humanity's favor in numerous competing jurisdictions. Me, whose special friend Marian refused all my phone calls, emails and text messages. And Grace Botsford, whose promise, "It will all work out," made me fear that the worst was yet to come.

That night, after we sent Brian Grose and his mausoleum home to Arkansas, I slept in my clothes, next to my fire gear, listening for the Plectron.

Hour after hour I heard the living room clock bong. Hour after hour the fire alarm was silent. I couldn't stand it anymore and went for a walk on the dark streets of the town. If the call came, the volunteers' cars and trucks converging with their blue lights flashing would give me ample warning to race home, jump in my gear, and run to the station in time to board the attack pumper.

Chapter Twenty-six

Here's what happened next.

In the dull light of early dawn, Grace Botsford closed the front door of her saltbox and climbed into her thirty-year old Trans Am and drove up Main Street toward Mount Pleasant. After she passed Trooper Moody's cottage, she unbuckled her seatbelt.

At the top of Mount Pleasant, just past Brian Grose's place, she turned the car around and faced it down the hill and stepped hard on the gas. The old street racer rumbled to life and down it rolled heading for the bend in the road that had done in her father with a lethal assist from Angel.

Suddenly she screamed.

I couldn't blame her. Who wouldn't scream if someone unfolded himself from the narrow slot behind the front seats, and said, "Grace, you have an innocent passenger on board."

She slammed on the brakes, went into a skid, got the car under control and pulled onto the shoulder, screaming, "Get out! Get out!"

"No."

"Ben, I know what I'm doing."

"I know what you're doing, too, and that's why I'm not getting out."

Her eyes were huge. She was breathing hard. Otherwise she was, as always, still as sculpture. The damned-est thing was she did not look crazy. Annoyed was more like it. She glared at me the way you would glare at some dolt blocking a grocery aisle while you were trying to get shopped, get home, and cook dinner.

I said, "The Frenchtown Diner will be open by now. Why don't we drive down and have a cup of coffee and a little breakfast?"

I did not expect her to reach inside her cardigan sweater and pull a pistol from a shoulder holster. But she did. And she pointed it at my face. Her hand was steady, her grip sure. She flicked off the safety without looking down at it. "Get out."

"Grace, what's the gun for?"

"In case I don't die in the wreck I'll blow my brains out before they bring the ambulance. Get out."

"You think of everything, don't you?" Including the snug holster so that even badly injured she could reach the gun to finish the job.

"Leave me to this Ben. I am doing what's right."

"It's not right. If you want to 'atone' for the sin of shooting Brian, atone with good work."

"I have done plenty of 'good work.' Dad and I both. And I know that I am leaving our 'work' in good hands, and for that I thank you, Ben Abbott. It gives me peace. But if you try to stop me from doing what I must, I will shoot you. I will *attempt* to just wound you."

"Okay," I said. I pitched the passenger seat forward, opened the door, and climbed over the seat. Halfway out I tried once more. "Grace."

"Out!"

"If you kill yourself, I will resign from the Association."

"What?"

"I won't be president of the Village Cemetery Association. I won't look after our burying ground for the next fifty years. I'll leave it to 'undesirable inhabitants.'"

"You would never do that."

"I will if you kill yourself."

"Would you give up everything you love in our town in exchange for one miserable life?"

"I will move away. Start over somewhere else. I will leave Newbury to its own devices."

"You can't desert everything you care about."

"Aren't you?" I asked.

She blinked. "Would you rather see me go to prison?"

"I don't see that happening. You were very careful. You'd make a wonderful criminal. No one knows but me, and I don't have any proof."

"Lieutenant Boyce suspects."

"She doesn't have any proof either—I presume this gun in my face is not one that would interest her."

"Of course not. I registered it years ago, while I took shooting lessons. Lieutenant Boyce knew about them, by the way."

"Lots of people learn to shoot. No proof, no case. And one of these days, I'm hoping, Lieutenant Boyce will remember how much she loved her own father. He was her hero. A cop. Shot in Bridgeport."

Grace Botsford blinked, again. She looked like she was going to cry. Instead she engaged the safety, shoved the pistol back in the holster, made sure it was clipped, and buttoned her sweater over it. I climbed back in the car. We buckled up and drove down to Main Street, hung a left at the flagpole and grabbed the last two stools at the Frenchtown Diner.

To receive a free catalog of Poisoned Pen Press titles, please contact us in one of the following ways:

Phone: 1-800-421-3976
Facsimile: 1-480-949-1707
Email: info@poisonedpenpress.com
Website: www.poisonedpenpress.com

Poisoned Pen Press
6962 E. First Ave. Ste. 103
Scottsdale, AZ 85251

Atlanta-Fulton Public Library